TEMPERED FIRE

Pamela S. Thibodeaux

*Train a child up in the way he should go and he shall
not depart from it. Proverbs 22:6*

TEMPERED FIRE
Book Three of the Tempered Series
By: Pamela S. Thibodeaux
Copyright © 2006

Publisher/Distributor:
Temperance Publishing; an imprint of
Pamela S. Thibodeaux Enterprises, LLC
PO Box 324
Iowa, LA 70647

ISBN#: 978-0-9896728-4-9

Cover Design: Delia Latham (Delia's Designs)

Previous publications:
Oct. 2006;
ComStar Media, LLC.
Salem, Oregon, U.S.A.
ISBN: 1-933866-03-9

All rights have reverted to Author

Note:
This is a work of fiction. Names, characters, places, and incidents either are the product of the author's imaginations or are used fictitiously, and any resemblance to actual persons, living or dead, businesses, establishments, events, or locales is entirely coincidental.

Praise for Pamela S. Thibodeaux

"Thibodeaux leads the reader through from the first page to the last without once relinquishing control. She hooks them, holds them, and keeps them enthralled until the last line." ~ Review of **The Visionary** by Delia Latham, author of the "Solomon's Gate" series

*"**In His Sight** caught my attention from the beginning and it made me wonder if I had given all to God as he gave all to me. Thank you, Pamela, for a story that I would readily recommend to anyone who needs that extra encouragement!"* ~ Reviewed by Wendy for Happily Ever After Reviews.

*"**Winter Madness** is a wonderful romance and an excellent example of Spiritual growth."* ~ Reviewed by Dee Daily for The Romance Studio

*"**A Hero for Jessica is** a good, sweet read charged with attraction but an emphasis on true love. I recommend it to women of all ages."* ~ Reviewed by Violet for LASR

*"**Cathy's Angel** is a short tale that is entertaining as well as inspiring. Well done!"* ~ Reviewed by Marlene for Fallen Angel Reviews

*"Pamela S. Thibodeaux's motto is "Inspirational with an Edge!" Her short story **Choices** lives up to those words and is well worth reading."* ~ Reviewed by Gail for Night Owl Romance

*"**The Inheritance** was my first Thibodeaux work; however, it will not be my last! Her approach to writing about everyday life, while struggling to maintain strict Christian standards and values, is a glimpse into reality which we all must face from time to time."* ~ Reviewed by Brenda Talley for The Romance Studio

Dedication and Acknowledgements

Psalm 9:1-3 says: *"I will give thanks to you, oh Lord, with all my heart; I will declare all your wondrous deeds, I will be glad and exult in you; I will sing praises to your name Most High."*

Praise, glory and honor belong to our Lord Jesus Christ for guiding me—yet again—through another story. May He be glorified in the writing and you be blessed in the reading.

I dedicate this book to my dad, Joseph Randall Sonnier, and to father's everywhere; may God bless you and give you the strength to let go and let Him make what He will of your little girls.

Also to my daughters, Karol and Monica, of the heart and of the flesh—May the love of your lives be as sweet and true as that of these characters and may you always give glory to God for the blessings in your life!

Prologue

Since Stanley Morrison arrived in Bandera, Texas a few weeks ago, the Annual Charity Rodeo hosted by the Rockin' H Ranch had been the talk of the town. Anticipation floated in the air, excitement brightened every eye, and enthusiasm animated every conversation. Now that the day had finally arrived, Stanley understood why. He'd watched all day as riders with skill and style equaling professional rodeo cowboys, and girls, performed on animals of the highest quality to turn around and donate all of their winnings to charity. There had been generous donations, considering some of the top prizes ranged up to five hundred dollars, and he was proud to be a part of it, if only as a hired hand. Though he'd gained employment at the Bar S ranch for his ability in working with horses, today Stan filled the capacity of groom, tack-hand and babysitter.

He looked up from his chore of shortening stirrups as the roar of the crowd increased when the last contestant in women's barrel racing shot into the arena. As usual, the first thing he noticed was the magnificent specimen of horseflesh, but his eyes were invariably drawn to the rider. Despite the distance between himself and them, he saw beauty in the young woman. Long legs encased in designer jeans rested comfortably in the saddle. Pulled into a French braid, dark hair hung like a thick rope down her back. Though her brow was tense with concentration, the fine, porcelain-like skin of her face appeared soft and lustrous despite the thin veil of dust hanging in the air. Style and grace lined every fluid movement of horse and rider as they rounded the barrels in the fastest and smoothest exhibition he'd seen in a long time, if ever. A nudge from the boot resting in the stirrup he was supposed to be shortening, reminded him of why he was here.

"A kiss for luck?" The young girl in the saddle leaned down to brush her lips across his cheek.

Surprised, Stanley stepped back and eyed his boss's daughter. She was a pretty young thing, blond-haired, dark-eyed and would turn fourteen just days before entering her freshman year of high school. "You're too young for anyone but your father to be kissing you, for any reason."

Lori Strickland's eyes narrowed into tiny slits of black fire; she grunted in a very unladylike manner. "You sound just like my father." She whirled her horse around and headed for the paddock to take her place in line for the pole-racing event

Stanley shook his head with a sigh and rested his elbows on the fence to watch the winner of the barrel-racing contest return to the arena. His heart stopped then thundered in his chest when her name blared over the intercom. Her horse bowed and she blew a kiss to someone in the crowd before turning the big stallion around in a fancy whirl and exiting. Intrigued, Stanley found himself looking forward to his first and only, year at Bandera High School.

* * * * *

Craig Harris ambled up the stairs to his daughter's room. At sixteen, Amber Nichole, was usually busy helping her mother this time of day. Today she seemed oblivious of that fact. She'd been in her room for the last several hours.

"What!"

A frown marred his forehead at the frustrated tone which bade his entrance. He opened the door, his eyes widening in shock and disbelief at the mess he encountered. Clothes covered every available inch of her bed. Shoes were strewn carelessly around the room.

Amber was having a problem.

"Is 'what' any way to welcome someone coming to your door?" Craig asked. "What in the world is going on?"

A sound of pure frustration escaped his daughter's lips when she drug her hands through the thick mass of black hair, shaking it off her shoulders so that it settled around her waist.

"I can't figure out what to wear tomorrow."

Craig grinned. "Ace doesn't seem to be having a problem. Since when did it matter so much?"

She snorted. "The only thing Ace is worried about is how he can get his new boots dirty before he gets downstairs," she growled, referring to her baby brother, Adam Craig Harris the Fourth, which was shortened to A. C., then evolved into Ace. "It's always mattered. I've just never worried about it before."

"And what good does worrying do? Does worrying add one more hour or day...?" He stopped quoting the scripture and laughed at the frown she bestowed on him.

"Don't come in here spouting Bible scriptures and don't laugh at me."

Craig's eyebrow quirked in concern. Despite the horror stories he'd heard about raising hormonal teenagers, he'd never had a problem gauging his daughter's moods and coaxing her out of them. Though passionate about many things, he'd never imagined his mature, well-rounded, normally composed child would be in a tizzy over what to wear. Nor had he *ever* considered her taking that tone with him.

"The best book I know," he countered.

Amber heard the concern in her father's voice and rubbed her throbbing temples. Taking a deep breath she let the scripture flow through her, bits and pieces reaching through the turmoil in her mind and soothing her frazzled nerves...

Therefore do not worry saying "What shall we eat or what shall we drink or what shall we wear?" for your heavenly Father knows that you need these things... what good does worrying do, does it add one more hour or one more day... Therefore, do not worry about tomorrow; tomorrow will take care of itself...

Everything took on a new perspective. She sighed, smiled. "Okay, I'll just pray about it tonight and the first thing I grab in the morning will have to do."

"That's my girl," her father soothed, stroking her cheek. "Now, about this room...." She looked around. Surprise registered on her face when she realized the mess she'd made.

"Daddy," she purred slipping her arms around him and resting her head against his chest.

Craig tossed back his head with a laugh. "Oh, no you don't. You made the mess, you clean it," he teased, disengaging himself from the arms around his waist.

She pouted prettily but her eyes were sparkling. "Mean old Daddy."

"Dinner's almost ready," he informed her, making his escape, then paused in the doorway. "Amber?"

When she looked up from her chore, he continued. "No matter what you wear tomorrow, you'll be the most beautiful girl there," he assured, love and pride evident in his voice.

She grinned. "Thank you. And your opinion is in no way biased I'm sure," she teased. "I love you too, Daddy."

Nervous and excited about entering her junior year of high-school, hearing her father's wolf whistle pleased Amber when she came downstairs the next morning dressed in a royal blue denim skirt, western blouse, and boots.

"Go change. You look way too good to leave the house without me."

His eyes glistened with pride. Amber laughed and kissed his cheek. "It's the first thing I grabbed," she said, moving out of the way as, dressed in new jeans, cowboy shirt and boots, Ace barreled down the stairs on his way to the table. Nearly nine years younger than she, he was entering the second grade.

Though she had her driving license and the use of a car, Amber respected tradition. Her mother would drive them today and quite possibly the first week or so, however long it took for Ace to get comfortable with his new class and

Tamera to get comfortable with letting him go. As her baby, long awaited and desperately wanted, she was protective of her son. Sometimes too protective, but, considering what she went through to have him, it was allowed. Amber harbored no jealousy, nor did she feel slighted in any way. She and her mother had a very special relationship. Her father, on the other hand, was her life. He was the one she would miss the most today, she thought. Little did she know that very soon things would change drastically between them.

* * * * *

Craig lingered over a second cup of coffee on the clear October morning. The days were getting shorter already and cooler. Another year was nearly over. Amber had just rehearsed the evening's events with them for the hundredth time.

"Amber, we've been through this twice before already," he chided in a gentle, teasing tone. "Relax."

She fidgeted, unable to keep still for the excitement curling in her gut. Being Junior Maid on the Homecoming Court was not all that was causing her heart to flutter and her stomach to clench like a nervous fist. She was used to that, being both Freshman and Sophomore Maid before. But the boy she had noticed, really noticed, for the first time last night had her as nervous and excited as an untrained filly.

"I met the guy I'm going to marry last night," she remarked, raising sparkling eyes to her father's teasing gaze.

Her voice was soft, husky. Craig grinned. "Oh, yeah? Who's that?"

"Stanley Morrison."

She practically sighed over the name, Craig noted, his grin fading into a frown. "You can't date until your twenty-one or marry until you're thirty-five. What makes you think this boy will hang around that long?"

"By the time I'm thirty-five, you will be a grandfather," she assured, rising from her seat. "Several times over," she added her smile smug.

Craig's jaw dropped and eyes widened as much from her remark as the way she looked, all breasts and hips and curves, with incredibly long legs in an extremely short skirt. He couldn't have been more surprised had she sprouted wings or horns. "You can't wear that, it's indecent!"

She laughed, placing a kiss on his cheek. Short skirts and boots were all the rage. "It's the style," she said, wiping the pale mauve lip print off his freshly shaven skin before walking away.

"To hell with style, it's too short! Who determines style anyway?" Craig demanded, and heard her answering laughter.

"Nobody's father that's for sure! Don't have time to change. Come on brat," she called to her brother. "We're going to be late."

Placing a quick kiss on his mother's cheek and slapping his father's hand with a high-five, Ace ran to meet his sister. "I'm not a brat," he countered in the familiar morning banter.

"Yes you are," she argued, placing a kiss on his silky blond head. "You've been a brat since the day you were born," she concluded, her blue eyes dancing into his gray ones as she helped him into his jacket.

The door closed behind them before Craig found his voice. "Why didn't you tell me?" he demanded of his wife, who was nearly doubled over in a fit of giggles.

"Tell you what?" she asked, gasping for breath. "That she's growing up?"

"That she's built like a..." he stuttered, flushing at the description that came to mind, positive it *wasn't* appropriate for his daughter. "And who in the hell is Stanley Morrison?"

Tamera's giggles turned into shouts of laughter. "Oh man, I wish I had a camera, the look on your face is priceless," she remarked, once she'd caught her breath. "Did you expect her to stay five forever?"

Craig didn't think that was funny one iota. His eyes narrowed, jaw muscle twitched. "No, but I didn't expect her to grow up overnight. Do you know anything about this boy?" His wife's blonde hair bounced off her shoulders when she shook her head, her eyes laughed and mocked him.

"I'm glad you think this is funny," he growled, throwing her into another fit of giggles. "Aren't you the least bit curious?"

Tamera wiped tears of hilarity off her cheeks before answering her husband. Like thunderclouds rolling in over an otherwise clear sky, his glittering gray gaze had darkened with emotion. The muscle in his jaw throbbed as it usually did when he was angry or upset. A shiver of pleasure shook her at the pure, male, animal magnetism he exuded. "Not really. I'm sure he's just some new kid at school. We'll find out soon enough."

Craig watched the play of emotions on his wife's face and in her gaze. Sparkling like rare, precious gems those expressive eyes changed from shining sapphire to smoky, midnight blue. Shifting from laughter to soothing to something more basic, more primitive in the span of a heartbeat, she still had the power to capture him with a single look. Pushing back his chair, he walked to where she sat.

"Ride with me today," he urged, pulling her into his arms.

"It's too cold," she argued. "Stay home today," she countered, slipping her arms around his neck while pressing her body against his in blatant invitation.

His daughter's appearance was forgotten. So was the work he had planned for the day.

Chapter One

Craig rode home after an exhausting day of working cattle, pleased to see his daughter hanging around the barn entrance. Except for meals, he rarely saw her anymore. As she had for the past several years, she immersed herself in charity work from the beginning of November through Christmas. Food baskets for the needy, *Coats for Kids*, *Toys for Tots* and area soup kitchens, as well as various school activities, kept her busy during the long winter months. When she was home, she stayed closed up in her room catching up on homework or pursuing her passion of writing. By the time spring arrived and her schedule slowed down, his increased with the lengthening of daylight hours. Though proud of the consideration she showed for those less fortunate and the efforts she made toward changing that, he sometimes wished her extracurricular activities wouldn't take up so much of her time.

Reining his horse to a stop next to her, he swung down from the saddle and greeted her with a kiss on the cheek. "Hi, Sweetheart."

"Hey."

The sulky tone of her voice made him take a closer look. A frown creased her brow. Those sapphire eyes he loved so much were edged with confusion and a hint of pain.

"What's wrong?" he queried, handing her the horse's reins.

Amber shrugged, not exactly sure how to broach this particular subject with her father. She absently stroked the horse's face while he loosened the saddle. Taking a deep breath, she plunged right in to the heart of her dilemma. "How do you know if someone really likes you or not?"

Taking the reins from her, Craig led the way to the stall, his mind racing back to homecoming morning a few months ago. He'd forgotten the shock of that morning. The memory poured through him now with disturbing clarity. "You mean your fiancé?"

A sharp prick of pain stabbed Amber's heart at the harshness in her father's voice. "Never mind," she muttered, turning away.

"Am, wait," Craig insisted, regretting the outburst. "I'm sorry, that came out all wrong. You want to talk to me, tell me what's wrong?" She turned back and the pain and confusion in her eyes clawed at his heart.

"I don't know," she mumbled, blinking back tears while taking a deep, shuddering breath. Her mind worked back to the eve of homecoming when he'd gazed up at her from the crowd of students. Their eyes met, lingered, and she was infinitely grateful the flush, which started in her toes and worked its way into her cheeks, could be attributed to the excitement and not to the heat in his gaze which had caused the blood to singe her veins. She'd wondered why she hadn't noticed before how incredibly handsome he was.

They'd talked some, teased a little, and flirted a lot since then, until a couple of weeks ago. He wasn't the same. His smile didn't quite reach his eyes whenever his gaze happened to meet hers and he didn't make it a point to speak to her. Quite the opposite in fact, he seemed to avoid her at every turn.

"We were getting along just fine until a few weeks ago. Everything's changed and I don't know why."

"Have you asked?"

She shook her head.

"How do you expect to get to the truth if you don't ask?"

Amber sighed, scrubbing the heels of her hands over her face. "I don't know."

Craig lifted her chin with his finger. "I've never known you to be a quitter, Amber. If you like this boy and you think he likes you, don't you owe it to yourself and him to talk to him?" Craig asked, glad he wasn't sixteen again. It didn't cross his mind that her feelings might go deeper than those of any other sixteen-year-old he'd known, and he had no idea why he'd encouraged her relationship with some boy he knew nothing about! Making up his mind to find out more about Stanley Morrison, he walked with his daughter into the house to wash up before dinner while she helped her mother.

When Amber came to breakfast the next morning she seemed calmer, more self-assured, confident.

"Can you bring us this morning and pick Ace up this afternoon?" she asked her mother. "I need to stay after school."

"Why do you need to stay after school?" Tamera wanted to know. Amber glanced at her father who was watching her, his eyebrow arched intently then turned back to her mother. After hours of praying last night, she'd made up her mind to confront the source of her agony right after school. "I need to get a misunderstanding with someone straightened out."

Tamera nodded. "How will you get home?"

"I'll call if I can't get a ride."

A glance passed between her parents that Amber had long since learned was their way of agreeing or disagreeing with her requests. She waited in silence until her mother smiled and nodded her agreement. Thanking them, she rose from the table, picked up her and Ace's dishes and carried them into the kitchen, her heart beating with a mixture of anticipation and trepidation.

When her daughter was out of earshot and Ace had left the table to get his book sack, Tamera arched an eyebrow at her husband. "Do you know what's going on?"

Craig nodded. "Something's wrong between her and Stanley, whoever the hell he is, and she doesn't know what or why. So she's going to try and talk to him."

"And you approve of this?" his wife asked, surprise evident in her tone and expression.

He shrugged. "I don't know. Hell, what was I supposed to say yesterday when she asked me how you could tell if someone really likes you? I could see she was hurting and confused so I told her she owed it to herself and him to at least try and talk."

"I'm surprised you didn't tell me about this last night," Tamera remarked. "And after your reaction the one time she mentioned his name, I'm even more shocked you'd allow her to stay after school, basically stranded, to talk to him."

Craig sighed. The same thoughts had run through his mind, but it all boiled down to one thing. This he spoke aloud. "I trust her. I trust her judgment, and I trust that she's not going to put herself in any danger. Besides, I'm going to do a little investigating myself and find out everything I can about this boy."

Tamera heard the edge to his voice and cringed. "Just be careful not to overstep your boundaries."

He arched an eyebrow at her. "I'm her father; there are no boundaries," he remarked, and then grinned. "Warning heeded though," he said, pushing away from the table.

Walking to where she sat, he leaned down and brushed his lips across her cheek. "And, if you remember correctly we didn't do much talking about anything last night," he whispered, his tone husky.

A pretty flush filled her cheeks. Craig chuckled, kissed her again then, calling goodbye to his children, went out for another day of working cattle.

That afternoon Amber waited outside the building and prayed her courage wouldn't desert her.

Father give me the serenity to accept the things I cannot change; the courage to change those that I can; and the wisdom to know the difference. Please, Lord, she added. *I can't do this without you. I don't even know if I should. Please don't let me appear forward or foolish. It's just that...*

What? she wondered. It's just what? Closing her eyes again, she surrendered her thoughts to God. *Let Your will be done, Father. If this is the man You've meant for me, then guide this meeting. In Jesus' name I pray, Amen.*

Opening her eyes, she saw Stanley walking toward his truck. Stepping out of the protective shadows, she called his name to halt his journey. He turned, his eyes flared, then narrowed when she took the few steps necessary to close the distance between them.

"What?"

He practically growled the word. "Uh..." Amber stuttered, blushed, and then plunged into the conversation before she could chicken out. "Is something wrong?"

Stanley Morrison had never felt so frustrated in all his life. *She sure has a lot of nerve,* he thought, angry that the mere sight of her still sent longing racing through his system. She'd snagged his attention at the rodeo, his heart homecoming eve.

"I'd say so. I don't like being lied to, stood up, or made a fool of, and that just about covers it," he hissed, ticking off the accusations with his fingers.

Amber's heart fluttered into her throat, heat rose in her veins at his tone. She took a deep breath and forced her voice to be calm. "Neither do I. Which exactly are you accusing me of?"

"Don't play with me, Amber," he barked, grabbing her by the arm. "I'm not some simpering dolt you can manipulate."

A hint of temper slipped through her calm. Amber hissed, jerking free from his grasp. "And I'm not some helpless female you can brush off with the silent treatment and a cold shoulder. I want to know what's wrong between us! I thought we were friends." Her voice softened. "Or beginning to be."

The flare of temper in her eyes set fire to his blood. She was even more beautiful when angry, like a goddess hell-bent on wrath. The thought speared through him like a shaft of ice. Stan ground his teeth in frustration. "I'm talking about the note Amber. You know, the card with the note telling me to meet you after school. Where were you? I waited for over an hour at the hamburger stand. You never showed up. I missed two hours of work by the time I gave up and went home."

The glimmer of hope Amber felt that there was some kind of misunderstanding between them which could be straightened out was quickly drowned by anger.

Someone was playing games with them.

"I never gave you a card, Stanley. I would never do such a thing as you're suggesting."

Soft eyes, sincere tone, she had it down good, Stanley thought, fury clouding his judgment. Her unwavering gaze had him doubting himself. In the months since he lost his heart to her, he'd watched, and listened, and learned a lot about Amber Nichole Harris.

The only daughter of a wealthy rancher, she was liked by many, envied by most. She had a generous heart, often instigating fundraisers and donation drives for the homeless and the hungry. It was also known of the many gifts she'd given to the less fortunate in her school even though she refused to accept recognition for the deeds. Her complete lack of selfishness endeared her to all of the teachers and staff at Bandera High. The overall consensus was that God had His finger on her heart from the moment she was conceived.

The students were a different story. Guys fantasized, girls gossiped. Some liked her, many chided her generosity as showing off, and others outright despised her. Regardless, she never seemed to have a bad day. Always bright and cheerful she didn't hang with any particular crowd and treated everyone with respect, making no preference between the rich, the poor, and the middle class. Despite her wealth, there wasn't an ounce of snob in that beautiful body. Everyone was unique and special in her sight and she treated them as such.

In light of all this, now that Stanley thought about it with his head and not his heart, it was unlikely she would pull such a stunt. "Then who was it?" he wondered aloud. "And why?"

"I don't know, but it wasn't me," she assured. "I wouldn't hurt anyone that way."

Stan raked his fingers through his hair. "I should've known," he mumbled. "I'm sorry, Amber," he apologized, touching her cheek. She smiled and desire twisted his gut.

"There's nothing to apologize for. It was a misunderstanding," she assured, feeling a flush warm her cheeks.

"It was stupid," he countered, not willing to be let off the hook so easily.

"Please, there's no need to say more," Amber whispered, noticing how sunlight bounced off the gold highlights in his chestnut hair. Her fingers itched to run through it, to feel its texture, and see if it was as soft as it looked. She clenched her hands into fists and forcefully refrained from doing so.

Her eyes had gone soft and warm. Stanley couldn't breathe or speak for the desire clamoring at his throat. He managed to smile, wanting desperately to take her in his arms and taste her lips. "I..."

He tore his gaze away from her, commanding control to his raging senses. "Where's your car?"

"My mom brought me this morning."

Her brilliant sapphire gaze beckoned to his lighter blue one. Stan gazed at her for a long moment. Feeling as though he were drowning in a sea of indigo, he broke eye contact, took a deep breath and forced his thoughts into some semblance of order. "How will you get home?"

"I'll call my dad, I guess."

"Would your dad mind if I brought you home?"

She dared to hope. "You want to bring me home?"

Stan smiled, her innocence a soothing balm to his raging hormones. "I'd be honored."

Amber smiled back, resisting the urge to dance a jig. "I don't think he'll mind since it'll save him a trip into town."

"Let's go then," he took her hand, leading her to his truck only to find Lori Strickland leaning against it. "What's up, Lors?" he asked.

"I missed my bus."

Stanley shook his head. "How'd you manage to do that again today?"

Lori hated it when he used that tone with her, as though he were chiding his baby sister. Her eyes narrowed, chin jerked up. "I had detention."

"Great," he muttered, digging in his pocket for the truck keys. "I'm sure your father will be so pleased to hear that," he remarked, then nodded in Amber's direction.

"You two know each other I presume."

Amber smiled. "Hi, Lori, how are you?"

Lori muttered an ineligible reply.

Stanley arched an eyebrow at her. "Rudeness is unbecoming for a young lady of your stature," he commented, as she pushed her way into the truck the moment he opened the door. He eyed her, waiting for her to move on over so Amber could sit next to him. When she didn't budge he rolled his eyes and forcefully refrained from slamming the door. Taking Amber by the hand, he led her around to the passenger side expecting Lori to have the common courtesy of leaning over and unlocking the door. Again she didn't budge. Furious now, Stanley fumbled with his keys then dropped them, adding a layer of embarrassment to the already tense atmosphere. Muttering a curse, he bent down to pick them up, a hot flush stinging his cheeks.

"Sorry about all this, she can be such a brat sometimes," he mumbled, shaking the dust out of his keys.

Rising, he stuck the key in the door and glanced at Amber. Her tender smile caught him off guard.

"It's okay," she whispered, touching his hand.

The caress shot through him like an electrical shock, her gaze drew him in. Their eyes locked in a heated embrace.

Stanley stood there a moment his tongue tied in knots, breath stuck in his throat, blood pounding in his veins, and wondered what in the world was wrong with him. He'd dated his share of girls but no one had ever captivated him with a single look or rendered him immobile with a simple touch.

"Oh, c'mon, get a room already!" Lori shouted, her rude comment breaking the sensual spell.

Stanley jerked open the door and leaned toward her, his eyes blazing like the hot blue of a flame.

"Y'know, Lori, it's a good thing you're not my little sister cause I'd be sorely tempted to take you over my knee about now." Lori's lip curled in defiance. He turned back to Amber. "I'm more than willing to give you a ride home, but I'd also understand completely if you'd rather not be in the company of such rudeness."

One glance at the two of them convinced Amber it would be better if they weren't left alone just yet. She smiled and climbed in. "I'm more than happy to accept the ride, present company included," she said, pitying Lori the tongue lashing which was bound to come regardless of how much she deserved it.

A tense, wary silence accompanied them on the drive to the Rockin' H ranch as each immersed in their own thoughts, though a couple of times Stanley did manage to glance over Lori's head and offer Amber an apologetic grin. As usual, her answering smile took his breath away. She turned to him when he pulled up to her house.

"There's my father now," she remarked, seeing Craig ride up to the barn. "Would you like to meet him?"

Stan hesitated, no doubt in his mind Craig Harris wouldn't be too impressed with him after he found out who he was and that he was just some lowly hired hand with no money and big dreams. And he'd already had enough frustration for one afternoon.

"I really need to get to work," he said. "And I need to get Miss Manners here home before her father starts to worry about who she's with and what she's doing," he muttered, glaring at Lori as he spoke.

Seeing the uncertainty and frustration in his eyes, Amber swallowed her protests. "Okay, next time," she said, masking her disappointment with a cheerful tone, and waited while he climbed out and hurried around to her side of the truck.

"I'll see you tomorrow, Lori," she remarked, not really expecting a reply, and reached for Stanley's hand when he opened the door.

Stan took her hand and helped her out of the truck. Glancing over his shoulder, he was relieved to see her father busy loosening the saddle on his horse. "Tomorrow," he promised, raising her hand to his mouth and brushing his lips across her knuckles. He saw her blush, felt her tremble and released her hand with a smile.

Amber exited the scene as gracefully as she could manage on legs that wobbled. Turning, she waved once before walking toward the barn to greet her father.

Stan watched a moment, decided he was the biggest chicken in Texas, then left, the drive from the Rockin' H to the Bar S no less tense than the entire afternoon had been. Growing up an only child, he had no idea how to handle Lori or her attitudes.

"Move over," he told her, giving her a slight shove with his elbow when she ignored him. Huffing, she flounced to the passenger side and crossed her arms over her chest. The defiant angle of her chin warned Stanley to watch his step while assuring him any amount of chiding would be a waste of breath. Pulling into the Bar S, he parked his truck, disembarked, and slammed the door shut, leaving her to get out on her own.

* * * * *

Craig glanced at his daughter as she approached, his eyebrow arched in curiosity. "I'm guessing by the dreamy look on your face everything's straightened out?"

Amber smiled. "Yeah, it was all a big misunderstanding."

"Good," her father remarked. "I guess," he muttered, taking the horse's reins and walking toward the stall, expecting her to accompany him as usual. "What do you know about this boy?" he asked, when she fell into step beside him.

"I know he's the one for me," she answered with a sigh, grinning when her father glared at her.

"Besides that," he said, tossing her a brush.

Knowing him so well, Amber couldn't help but tease her father.

"I'm sure you've been snooping around since we talked yesterday," she taunted, brushing the horse while he used the currycomb. "So, you tell me what you know then I'll tell you what I know."

His eyes narrowed into tiny slits of shimmering steel, but his mouth twitched in response to her teasing.

"I can tell you that I don't know near enough to allow him to even set foot around you much less consider you two being alone together. Only heaven knows why I allowed it this afternoon."

Amber giggled. "Well then, you should be relieved to know we weren't alone. Lori had detention so he had to bring her home too. And, you'll be happy to know she parked herself right between us the whole way here."

"Remind me to thank Lori the next time I see her," Craig remarked. "Now your turn, what do you know about him?"

Amber thought a moment, realizing she really knew very little about the man she intended to marry. She knew he was new to the area and that he'd moved there over the summer and was currently working and living at a neighboring ranch. It was his first, and as a senior, last year at school. She knew he liked to sing, and could do it very well. He was often seen in the school courtyard during lunch break strumming his guitar and crooning a song with girls swarming around him like bees around a hive. She heard he was nineteen. Relaying the limited knowledge to her father, she wasn't overly surprised to hear his shocked reply.

"Nineteen! What's a nineteen-year-old still doing in high school? Strike two in my book."

"Strike two? What's strike one?"

"Strike one is that he didn't deem it necessary to get down and introduce himself when he brought you home."

"Daddy," she chided. "If you'd been privy to the stunt Lori pulled this afternoon, the brunt of it actually, you wouldn't feel like meeting anyone's father, either. Especially my father."

Craig frowned. "And what exactly does that mean?"

Amber rolled her eyes. "Oh, please. You know exactly what it means. I'm the daughter of the wealthiest rancher in the county, possibly the wealthiest rancher in Texas. What guy wouldn't be intimidated by that?"

He cocked his head. "One who really cares. I didn't realize you felt this way, that you were ashamed of who you are."

Realizing she'd come across all wrong, Amber sighed then smiled. "I'm not ashamed of who I am, Daddy. In fact, just the opposite, I'm proud of who I am. I'm proud of you. I'm proud of what all you've accomplished, and the wealth you've worked so hard to accumulate," she assured, her voice soft, serious.

"I just don't understand why other people put so much emphasis on it. I want someone who'll love me for who I am, not for what I have," she admitted, taking the currycomb from him and putting it away with the brush.

"And you think this boy is the one who'll do that? Especially in light of how little you know about him?"

"I don't know. There's just something about him. Something special. I felt it from the moment our eyes met homecoming eve."

Craig grunted. "Don't tell me you believe in love at first sight."

"Don't you?"

He shook his head. "It sure wasn't love at first sight between me and your mother."

She giggled. "If I remember the story correctly that's because you were being a jerk."

He couldn't help but chuckle. "Watch your mouth, young lady."

In reply his daughter merely offered him a sweet, innocent smile, slipped her arm through his and walked with him to the house for dinner.

*****

Stanley lay on his bunk that evening his feet crossed, hands propped behind his head, hair damp and curling from his shower. His mind relived the afternoon's events. The frustration and anger with Lori had in no way lessened the excitement of being with Amber. The memory of how she looked, her face flushed, those gorgeous eyes flashing with anger followed by depths of tenderness had need curling through his soul, drowning out the doubts which plagued his mind. He knew he wasn't good enough for her, that she was way out of his league. But all he could think about was how beautiful she was and hope everything he'd learned and observed of her was real and that she wouldn't care that they were miles apart on the social scale.

He was born poor, the only son of a wannabe big shot. His father was spoiled, selfish, and illegitimate. His grandmother had raised him after his parents were killed in an automobile accident when he was nine-years-old. He'd left his hometown of Greenville, Arkansas two days after her death. What little cash he had, he used sparingly, saving the bulk of his inheritance for later use. Common sense and thrifty spending enabled him to get to Bandera and held him over until he found a job

Stan knew the best thing he had going for him was his unshakable faith in God and his God-given ability to communicate with horses. He knew horseflesh better than most men twice his age and had an innate ability to pick, break, and train them to be gentle, loyal, creatures. That too had aided him in obtaining a position at the Bar S Ranch, a position which paid a wage plus room and board. The job was nice, but it was just a beginning. Here, in Bandera, he hoped to fulfill his dream of owning and operating a successful horse ranch.

Chapter Two

"Amber, Daddy said to tell you there's a beat up, black truck coming down the road!"

Ace's voice carried up the stairs and through the door of her room. Amber stopped typing, her fingers frozen in midair above the keyboard. She'd been typing all day, pounding away at the keys as the short story she was writing took on the appearance of a novel in the making. Excitement made her lose her train of thought. Saving the material to disk, she turned off the computer, ran a brush through her hair and bounded down the stairs in time to answer the door before Ace could get to it.

Laughing, she looked up into Stan's blue eyes as her brother rushed out between them. "Hi!" she greeted.

Stan grinned. "Hi. I thought I would run out and wish you a happy birthday since I didn't have your phone number."

"How did you know it was my birthday?"

"A little bird told me," he teased. In truth, he'd heard it announced on the radio. "Why don't I have your phone number?" he asked. Amber laughed, a deep, sensual sound that had him smiling in return and wondering what the joke was. Somehow Stan had the feeling he was part of it.

"I'm sorry," she gasped. "I hoped it would work. I was beginning to doubt the wisdom, but it worked," she admitted, giggling, and then explained when his eyebrow arched in question.

"You never asked so I deliberately didn't give you my number. That way you would have to look it up or come out here if you wanted to talk to me. My mother taught me not to be presumptuous."

Her eyes sparkled with laughter and a hint of mischief. "And I fell for it; hook, line and sinker didn't I, you little fox," Stanley accused, feeling like an idiot. But he couldn't be angry at her when he'd chided himself all day for not asking for her number in the first place.

"Come in," she offered stepping back from the door.

"Where are your parents?"

"I'm not sure, but they must be close by since Daddy is the one who sent Ace in to tell me he saw your truck coming down the road."

"Why don't we sit out here until then," he offered, reaching a hand to her then settling on the porch swing.

Touched by his old-fashioned sensibilities Amber sat beside him. They talked, waiting for her parents' return.

"I tried finding out who put that note in my locker," Stan said.

Amber arched an eyebrow at him. "Any luck?"

"No," he admitted with a sigh. "Seems it just appeared out of thin air, but if I ever do find out, whoever's responsible will never pull that on anyone again."

She smiled at his tone. "Does it really matter?"

Stan eyed her. "What do you mean?"

"Well, it's obvious, to me anyway, the sole purpose of the note was to cause a rift between us. And though it worked for a time, whoever is responsible must know by now they didn't succeed. So, what difference does it make now?"

Stan smiled at her point and lifted her hand to his mouth, brushing his lips across her knuckles. "None I guess," he remarked. Catching a glimpse of riders galloping into the barn out of the corner of his eye he wondered if they were her parents, but didn't voice the question aloud, figuring he'd find out soon enough.

* * * * *

Craig paused at the barn entrance. "I wonder what he wants," he muttered. It hadn't set well with him that the boy didn't introduce himself the day he brought Amber home from school, nor had he made a point to do so since. And it irritated him royally that Amber walked around singing some long-forgotten Carpenter's song about a guy with *gold dust in his hair and golden starlight in his eyes of blue.'* She used to hate that song, always said it was corny.

He hated it now.

"He probably wants the same thing you wanted at his age," Tamera teased, seeing his eyes darken and jaw harden.

"That's not funny, Temper. When I was his age I had a truckload of responsibility on my shoulders. I didn't have time to court a girl without the thought of meeting her parents."

"Court?" Tamera laughed, rolling her eyes. "Is that what you call it?" she shook her head. "I swear, sometimes I think you were born in the wrong century."

Craig couldn't help but grin at her teasing.

Tamera pulled him toward her. "Be nice," she warned, her lips caressing his cheek in a tender gesture.

* * * * *

"There they are," Amber remarked when she saw her parents pause at the barn entrance. "Come on, I'll introduce you," she offered, obviously not the least embarrassed by their display of affection.

Taking her hand, Stan steeled himself for the moment he'd avoided for weeks. Though he'd seen her father talking with Mr. Strickland a time or two, he hadn't wanted to overstep his boundaries as a hired hand and appear brash or foolish by introducing himself, especially when his relationship with Amber was so new and their time together so limited.

As a senior his school day ended before Amber's so when the request came to bring Lori early and pick her up late so she could be tutored in order to pass into the next grade, he'd been more than willing to accept. The duty enabled him to spend at least some time with Amber. The fact that he'd recently turned twenty and she was sixteen had been a deterrent also. But now she was seventeen and the time had come. Head high, he met Craig's gaze straight on, noting the guarded expression on his face as they approached and waited in silence while Amber made introductions.

Gazing in amazement at the three of them together, he noted the similarities between Amber and her parents. Tall like her father, she had hair as dark as his, but looked enough like her mother to pass for sisters and shared the same color eyes.

"Nice to meet you ma'am," he nodded at Tamera. "I see where Amber gets her beauty. You're a very lucky man, Mr. Harris," he said, offering Craig his hand.

Craig noticed admiration shining in the boy's sky-blue eyes as he shook his hand. "You planning on cuttin' in on some of that luck?" he asked, coupling the accusation with a mocking smile.

"Daddy!" Amber's shocked admonition cut off Stanley's reply.

"How's he supposed to answer that?" Tamera interjected, giving Craig a firm, chiding look. Grabbing Stan by the arm, she led the way back to the porch.

"Can I invite him to dinner?" Amber whispered to her father.

They always celebrated birthdays and other special occasions by going out to dinner. It was then gifts were exchanged also.

Craig looked down into the pleading eyes of his daughter, so much like her mother, and frowned. He'd never been able to resist that look no matter which of his females used it on him. He barely got out his answer when Ace ran from the barn.

"Daddy, Sam says Sugar will foal this evening. Can I stay with her?"

Craig put his hand on his son's shoulder to slow him down. "I don't know. You'll have to ask your sister, it's her birthday."

Ace frowned then turned to Amber, his gray eyes serious.

"Would you mind, Sissy?"

Amber smiled. "There's someone I'd like you to meet, Brat," she said, making him wait for his answer. Reaching the porch, she introduced him to Stan.

"This is my brother, Adam Craig Harris the Fourth, better known as Ace or Brat."

Stan gazed down at the boy, again amazed at the science of genetics. Ace looked exactly like his father all the way to the gray eyes, but had his mother's blond hair. He grinned offering Ace a hand. "Nice to meet you, Sport," he said, adding yet another name to Ace's repertoire.

"Are you going to marry my sister?" Ace asked.

Stanley chuckled at the curious light in the gray eyes.

"Uh, isn't there something you wanted to ask me?" Amber cut in, changing the subject before Stan could answer.

Ace brightened. "Yeah, would you mind if I miss your party? Sugar's going to foal tonight and Sam said I could help him."

Unable to resist his pleading, as usual, Amber smiled. "I guess not," she said. "But it'll cost you a hug."

"All right!" he exclaimed, flinging himself at his sister. "Sam said I could name the foal. If it's a filly I'll name her Sissy's Pride, after you," he announced, before rushing back toward the barn.

Amber rolled her eyes. "The ultimate honor for a girl, I'm sure," she remarked, as everyone laughed. "What if it's a colt?" she called to her brother. He turned and grinned, a cocky heart-stopping grin that belied his tender age.

"Then it'll be Ace's Pride."

Later that evening, Amber and her parents were munching on appetizers when Stan showed up at the restaurant. "Sorry I'm late, got caught in traffic," he apologized, handing Amber a tiny package.

She smiled placing it beside the others at the table. "That's okay, we just got here ourselves," she assured, hoping to ease his embarrassment.

Craig watched his daughter closely while they laughed and talked over dinner. He couldn't help but remember her birthday last year and the way he'd teased her. Sweet sixteen and never been kissed. He wondered if that were still true. Though highly unlikely, he couldn't begin to imagine her being anything like some of the girls he'd heard about and seen. He just couldn't picture his sweet, innocent daughter giving her affections lightly. Especially not after the long, intimate talks they'd had about chastity and purity and waiting for the right man. Observing her interaction with Stanley filled him with a sense of awe and wonder he'd never felt.

Bright eyes, glowing complexion and gushing with life, she shimmered like a rare, precious gem. Little girl enthusiasm and big girl conversation all overlaid with a level of maturity which surprised and amazed him. For a brief moment he stepped outside of himself and looked at her, really looked, not as a father but as a man. What he saw scared the daylights out of him. Fear curled in the pit of his stomach. A dull ache throbbed through him, piercing his heart like a bad tooth which had been ignored too long pierced the jaw. Clearing his throat, he took control of the conversation.

Tapping his glass with a spoon to get their attention he suggested Amber open her presents. Her reaction to his gift of a cordless phone was just as he anticipated. She thanked him with a kiss, throwing her arms around his neck after he gave her piece of paper with her phone number on it.

"My own private line!"

He chuckled. "I figured the next Homecoming Queen of Bandera High was old enough to have her own phone line."

Eyes sparkling, she copied the number down and handed it to Stan. Her hands trembled as she opened the package from him. Hanging from a slim gold chain was a tiny rose made of blown glass. She fingered it in a gentle caress, amazed at the beauty of colors swirling in her palm. Removing the necklace her mother had given her the year before, she turned so Stan could fasten his gift around her throat. She trembled as his fingers brushed the tender skin of her neck.

"It's beautiful," she whispered, kissing his cheek. "Thank you," she added, then blushed when her father cleared his throat in an exaggerated manner.

Stan fought the urge to sink his hands in that thick mass of black hair, pull her in his arms and cover her mouth with his. In the weeks since they started spending more time together at school, other than a brush of his lips across her cheek or hand, he had yet to kiss her. At this moment he sorely regretted the fact.

Craig noticed the gleam in Stanley's eyes. Recognizing it for what it was, he fought the urge to make a scene by grabbing the boy by the shirtfront and tossing him out with a boot to his butt. Disturbed by the whole scene of her removing the necklace from her mother, a gift she'd worn for an entire year, and replacing it with one from this boy, gave him the feeling that one day he'd regret the fact he didn't. Grinding his teeth, he bit back the comments burning his tongue. His attention reverted back to his daughter when a little sound of excitement bubbled up from her throat

Amber sighed. "I wish this night could go on forever."

Craig's eyebrow arched with interest. "And what would you have us do the rest of the evening if this night could go on forever?"

She shrugged, reaching for Stan's hand under the table. "I don't know, we could rent some movies to watch, or, I know, go dancing!"

"You're too young to go dancing," Craig argued.

"I'm old enough to go if you take me," she countered.

"You're seventeen, not old enough to go traipsing the bars."

"I'm not a baby, Daddy. I'm growing up."

He grinned. "I know it. And I'm ordering you to stop right now."

She arched an eyebrow at him. "And how do you propose I do that?"

"We'll turn back the calendar. I'll take you to school and have you moved back into the second grade."

She shook her head with a smile. "If you go to the school, they'll probably talk you into moving me up to college."

"Well, we'll home school you then."

She rolled her eyes in an exaggerated manner. "Oh, please. Besides, you promised you would take me dancing when I got old enough."

Craig frowned. It had been a long time since he pacified her with the promise to take her dancing. He remembered it like it was yesterday. He and Tamera were getting ready to go out. Amber would be staying with the housekeeper, dear old Maria who'd passed from this life to the next shortly after Ace was born. Amber had cried and clung to him so he made her the promise.

"You were just a baby when I said that, how do you remember?" Amber's smile was smug.

"I always remember a promise."

Her father sneered.

"Really!" she insisted.

Stan felt a tug of longing at the obvious closeness between Amber and her father. It warmed his heart to watch their teasing. His amused gaze sought Tamera's. "Are they always like this?"

She laughed. "Worse. And what's so bad is you can never tell who is winning."

"I always win," Craig announced. "I'm the father."

"You win because I let you," Amber argued, her eyes laughing into his. "Or because I let you think you've won."

Stumped for an answer, Craig merely grunted and waved for the check then addressed Stan. "You're old enough to get into a bar, aren't you, being nineteen and all?"

Far from naive, Stan heard the real question in Craig's voice. "Yes, Sir, but I'm not big on drinking, though I do love to dance. Besides, I'm twenty."

"Twenty?"

Hearing the surprise and shock in his voice, Stan cringed and strove to cover his slip of tongue. "Well, actually I just turned twenty a few weeks ago."

"I can't believe they let you stay in school at that age."

Encouraged by the fact that Craig hadn't thrown him out by the seat of his pants, yet, Stan smiled, and explained. "It wasn't bad enough my date of birth made me a year older than everyone else, but my parents weren't too conscientious about my attending school. I was held back in the second grade. But one of my grandmother's biggest dreams was for me to graduate with my class, cap and gown and all. Actually, she wanted to see me graduate, but that's not possible now," he said, forcing the lump of grief back down his throat. Taking a deep breath, he continued.

"Anyway, it took a great deal of arguing, but I managed to convince the principal I'm an upstanding kind of guy. And when I explained to him about my grandmother, and promised to keep my age and birthday quiet, as well as guaranteeing him that I wouldn't be caught dating girls much younger than me, he capitulated. I can assure you he kept close tabs on me, though," he admitted with a chuckle.

"He made you promise not to date girls younger than you?" Amber interjected, shocked anyone would put such restrictions on a student.

Stan grinned. "Well, I actually made the promise before he had a chance to grill me on the subject. Besides, I wasn't interested in girls at the moment. I was only interested in finishing school like my grandmother had always dreamed." He squeezed her hand under the table, his voice softening when he continued. "All that changed the minute our eyes met homecoming eve, but I'd given my word and a man's word is his honor so I had to keep it."

Craig felt a tug at his heart at the smile which lit his daughter's face. One glance at his wife forced him to swallow the questions rolling around in his head. He could all but read Tamera's mind and hear her voice reiterating the lecture she'd given him while getting ready to leave the house...

"Remember, it's your daughter's birthday. This is a celebration. There is a time and a place for everything but this is not the night, nor is it an appropriate time or place to

get into any serious discussions with the boy she's interested in."

A collective sigh of relief could be heard when he complimented Stanley instead of grilling him. "Well, I guess you're to be commended for sticking it out. A lot of kids wouldn't."

"Thanks, but," he glanced from his watch to Amber's glowing face and shrugged. "Oh, to heck with it, I guess I can sleep in since tomorrow is Sunday."

"Not going to church with the Strickland's?" Craig asked.

Stan heard the edge to Craig's voice and shook his head. "No, Sir. I don't practice their religion. My grandmother was non-denominational but I haven't found a church I'm comfortable with yet. Any suggestions?" he queried, throwing the ball back in Craig's court.

"Not really, we don't practice any type of formal, structured religion," Craig replied, realizing the boy had turned the tables on him. Strike three, he thought, forcing down the comment even as it burned his tongue.

It was well after midnight before things started winding down. Giddy with excitement Amber gazed into Stan's eyes as he guided her across the dance floor for one last song. "You know, we've been sort of dating for several weeks now and you've yet to kiss me." It was her birthday and a girl only turned seventeen once, she reasoned, mentally justifying herself for asking.

Stan's heart jumped into his throat making it difficult to breathe. Desire curled in him like hot flames. His hands tightened automatically, pulling her into dangerous proximity with his hard frame. Taking a deep breath, he consciously commanded control to his senses and loosened his hold on her. "Oh, yeah?" he queried, trying his best to stop the smile tugging at his mouth.

"I just explained to your parents that I'd promised the principal I wouldn't date girls younger than me, so what makes you think we've been dating? Besides, how do you 'sort of' date?" he asked, his voice tinged with laughter.

She regarded him with wide-eye innocence. "Don't the moments we spend together before and after school count as dating?"

He chuckled, enjoying the exchange. Her childlike sense of humor combined with the womanly allure of her in his arms was heady indeed, giving him a whole new insight to the word *temptation*. Still, he hesitated. The rules of gentlemanly etiquette his grandmother had instilled in him discouraged public displays of affection.

"I don't think your father would appreciate me mauling you in the middle of a dance floor."

She glanced over to where her parents were dancing and noted her father gazing intently into her mother's eyes, his ears tuned in to whatever she was saying. She looked back at Stan and smiled. "I don't think he'd mind one little kiss, if he even noticed."

"I would," he whispered, pressing a tiny kiss to her ear.

She rolled her eyes. "God, did he have to be a complete, total gentleman?" she queried, her voice tinged with laughter. "The last of a dying breed."

His laugh was soft, husky. "Be careful what you ask for Amber, otherwise you might be surprised."

With permission, reluctantly given, Stan drove Amber home, careful to follow closely so her father wouldn't worry. Tamera and Craig had gone inside after checking on Sugar and her newborn colt. He and Amber were sitting on the porch swing. "A colt, too bad," he sighed putting his arm around her. "No namesake this time."

"Yeah," she breathed. "Can't have it all, I guess. Thank you for coming tonight and thank you for the necklace."

"You're welcome," he whispered, craving the kiss she so sweetly asked for earlier. He traced her cheek with his fingertips and breathed her name.

The need in his voice shivered through her. He was going to kiss her and all Amber could do was gaze at him, helpless with longing, and wait. A soft groan escaped him when he pressed his lips to hers. Passion exploded as the kiss deepened for one brief moment. She clung to him, wrapping her arms around his neck.

Stan felt her tremble and hauled her firmly against his chest. Digging deep for self-control, he dragged his lips away from hers. "Happy birthday," he whispered pressing feathery kisses over her face.

Chapter Three

Craig awoke to the sounds of a storm in full swing. Thunder rumbled with the force of a stampede, lightning rent the sky like a sword ripping through silk. Slipping from the bed, he watched from the window as the sky lit up in a wild yet beautiful display of light and color. He held his breath counting the seconds until thunder broke the stillness like a blast of gunshot.

He loved a storm for its beauty as much as he hated it for its destruction. From the sounds of it, he'd have a truckload of debris to clean up, fences to mend, animals to round up and a number of other disasters to clear up after this one. He sighed heavily watching for a moment then returned to the bed as Tamera stirred.

"Something wrong?" she mumbled, as he pulled her into his arms. "It's storming," he whispered, his voice husky, his lips covering hers in a tender caress.

Fully aware of the stormy passion that came to life in him as the elements raged outside, Tamera smiled, sliding sweetly into the warmth of his kiss and the tenderness of his caress.

* * * * *

Amber tossed and turned, moaning in her sleep as a dark, ominous shadow approached. She struggled to wake, but couldn't seem to pull herself out of the black fog filling her mind, the weight of it suffusing her limbs with lethargy. Unseeing eyes stared in horror. A soft whimper of fear stuck in her throat as shifting shapes, the shadow drew nearer then formed itself into a hideous creature upon approaching her window. All of a sudden he was there, scratching and knocking, trying to get in out of the rain.

Trying to get to her.

Paralyzed she could only watch him peer at her, his slanted animal eyes capturing her gaze. His wolf-like growls and half-human screams rent the air when he tried again to get in. She screamed in terror when he lunged, ripped the screen and pounded his fist on the glass. A satisfied snarl escaped him when the window shattered beneath his relentless thumping.

* * * * *

Tamera moaned in protest as Craig lunged from the bed. One moment she was wrapped in his embrace, then suddenly, as if a giant hand jerked him away, she was alone. "What's the matter?"

"Amber," he breathed, rolling from the bed and into a pair of jeans. Jerking the door open, he rushed to his daughter's room with Tamera close on his heels.

"Amber? What's the matter, Sweetheart?" he asked, walking over to the bed. Curled up in a fetal position, her eyes, wide with fright, were trained on the window.

"He's here, Daddy," she whispered. "He's come to get me."

The little girl whimper in her voice struck him as odd. "Who, Amber?"

"The monster."

Her tone, childlike and frightened, convinced him that even though she appeared awake, she was still in the throes of the nightmare. "Where is he?"

"At the window."

Craig walked toward the window.

"Be careful, Daddy," she whined. "He broke it trying to get in."

"There's nothing here, Sweetheart. It's not broken. See?" He walked back to the bed. "Come and look, Sweetheart, its okay. I promise," he urged, taking her in his arms and coaxing her to wake up.

"No!" She wrapped her arms around his neck, burying her face into his shoulder.

Craig cradled her against his chest and looked helplessly at his wife. At least ten years had passed since the last time this happened.

"I'll go make coffee," Tamera offered, knowing it would be a long night as Amber clung to her father and wept.

* * * * *

The storm raged on until after one o'clock in the afternoon. Sam and a couple of other hands rode out when there was a break in the weather, but had to hurry back as thunderstorms continued to roll in, one on top of the other.

Amber stubbornly refused to even try and rest. Not willing to leave her alone, Craig and Tamera took turns keeping her company.

They'd been up for two days.

Time dragged on and Mother Nature continued to vent her fury against the earth. By four o'clock, Craig was about at his wits end. He prowled around the house like an angry beast, restless, cagey. Welcoming the diversion, he answered the phone before it could ring a second time. Stanley's voice came across the line.

"Mr. Harris, is Amber there? I've been trying to reach her and there's no answer on her line."

Craig called Amber to the phone and went into the den to give her some privacy. He looked up as she walked back into the den, her eyes red-rimmed and tired. "Everything all right?"

"Yes. He wanted to know if I was okay. I told him I wasn't feeling well."

"You need to get some rest, Honey," Craig urged.

"I can't!" she cried, stifling a sob. "Every time I close my eyes, he's there, waiting for me."

Craig groaned. "Amber, it's just a nightmare," he soothed, cupping her face in his hands.

"I know!" she insisted, pulling away from him, wondering how to explain what not even she understood.

"My left brain keeps telling me that, but my right brain just won't believe it."

"And I'm supposed to understand that?" her father asked with a frown.

"You should! You're my father you're supposed to understand everything."

Craig ground his teeth and fought the urge to take her over his knee. "Well, I don't, so please explain."

Amber buried her face in her hands and fought back tears. "The left side of your brain is the logical part, and the right, creative. I've tried being logical and rational about this. I've even tried praying! But for some reason every time I close my eyes, I see that creature."

"Maybe we should take you to the hospital."

"For what?" she asked. "Having a nightmare? My word, I'm seventeen years old! They'd probably throw us both out of the place."

Craig knew she was right but no amount of reasoning could erase the worry. "So what can I do for you?" he asked, pulling her in his arms.

Her jaw muscle twitched and tears filled her eyes but she shook her head. "Nothing, I'll be okay," she declared, and then nearly jumped out of her skin when lightning flashed anew and thunder roared.

By eight-thirty that evening there was no change in the weather or in Amber's condition. She still refused to rest, burying herself in reading, writing, or computer games, even coloring with Ace, restlessly changing activities when she felt herself getting sleepy or too relaxed.

Craig and Tamera continued to take turns keeping vigil with her. Though it had been years, they remembered the routine well. She would stay awake as long as she could; fighting valiantly until pure exhaustion took over and her body forced her to rest. Then she'd sleep for as many hours as it took to catch up and feel normal again.

Everyone looked at the other in total surprise when there was a knock on the door. Lightning streaked the sky. The house creaked and moaned from the force of the wind as it howled through the trees. Rain battered the windows like a spray of bullets.

Amber stopped pacing, deathly pale, and stared. *He's come to the door.*

Everyone read her thoughts as though she'd spoken them aloud.

The second knock spurred them all into action. Ace ran to the window, Craig walked toward the door, Amber made a mad dash for the stairs.

Stanley stood on the porch. Craig opened the door for him to enter

"Boy, you must be crazy getting out in this weather."

"I've been telling myself that very same thing all the way over here," Stan greeted, shaking out his coat. "I know it's late and all...man, you look terrible," he remarked, stepping out of the dark, rain-filled night into the well-lit foyer.

"I mean..." he stuttered as Craig emitted a weary chuckle.

"I'm not sure I know you well enough to discern how to take that remark, but you're probably right so I'll let it pass."

Stan's grin was sheepish. "I'm worried about Amber. The last time I talked to her, she sounded about as bad as you look. Is she okay?"

"She's been having a rough few hours," Craig hedged, wanting to spare her any embarrassment.

"Do you think I could see her?"

"I don't know," Craig remarked. Weary and exhausted, he picked up the phone and dialed her number instead of walking up the stairs to Amber's room. When she picked up the receiver, he said, "It's Stan, Honey."

"I told him not to come here," she hissed into the phone.

Craig sighed. "Well, he is here. He came out in all this weather just to check on you. The least you can do is come down and let him know you're okay."

"The least everyone can do is get off my case and leave me alone," she insisted, slamming the receiver down then taking it off the hook.

Craig looked at the receiver in his hand with a mixture of shock and disbelief. Amber *never* talked to him like that, he thought with frustration. Raking his fingers through his hair he suppressed the urge to run upstairs and drag her out of the room.

"You owe the boy a spot of courtesy, Amber!" he yelled. He didn't need to drag her out after all; his frustrated, reproachful tone did it for him. She stormed out in an angry huff.

"I don't owe him anything! Now, see!" she faced Stan, her body rigid with accusation. "I'm a wreck!" she raged. "Are you happy now? Now will everyone please just leave me alone?"

Stan stared in shock at the paleness of her skin and dark circles under her eyes. "What's wrong?"

"Nothing! Everything!" She stormed back into her room, slamming the door shut behind her.

Stan looked at Craig, his eyes burning with questions. Craig held up a hand and shook his head to ward them off. "How about a cup of coffee before you go?"

"I'd love one," Stanley sighed. Turning back to the stairway he yelled, "I'm going, Amber, and I'll leave you alone! If that's what you really want." He waited a moment hoping she'd tell him otherwise and heard her call his name as he walked toward the kitchen with her father.

"It's not what I want," she admitted in a soft voice, running down the stairs. Taking him by the hand, she led him into the den.

"Amber, what's wrong?" he whispered, as she let go of his hand and began to pace the floor.

Scrubbing the heel of her hands across her face, she raked her fingers through her hair and sighed. "You're probably going to think I'm the silliest thing in the world," she said in a voice that trembled.

He took a step toward her. "I'd never think that," he assured, taking her hands in his.

Amber closed her eyes and saw the creature from her nightmare as clearly as though it was standing in front of her. A soft whimper escaped, her lip trembled. Taking a deep, shuddering breath she opened her eyes and faced the worry in his.

"When I was little, I snuck downstairs while Mama and Daddy were watching some movie. Actually, they were more interested in each other than the movie," she admitted, remembering how they had cuddled, a soft whisper of kisses and smiles the only words between them.

"Anyway, this monster, some sort of creature half human, half wolf with claws and fangs and horrible, hideous eyes, hungry eyes, jumped out of darkness onto the screen. Scared me to death," she said with a violent shudder.

"Well, you can imagine my reaction. Ever since then I've had these nightmares. He's always at my window trying to get in. And it's always storming," her voice broke. Visibly getting it under control she continued.

"It's been a long, long time since I had one. I don't know what, if anything brought it on this time. I can only assume the force of the storm."

Stan pulled her in his arms, relieved it wasn't something more serious. Though, by the looks of her, it was pretty serious. To her anyway.

"I'm sorry," he whispered, wishing there were something he could do to ease her fears.

"You haven't slept since have you?"

He felt her shake her head.

"Can I stay with you a while?"

She nodded. "Did you bring your guitar?"

"No," he answered, tightening his arms around her.

"Will you sing for me?"

He sighed. "Don't know if I can without my strings."

"Please."

Her eyes, wide, pleading, and laced with fatigue, convinced him he could. "Let's sit down," he suggested, thinking maybe she would relax.

She tensed, shaking her head, afraid of the same thing. "I'd rather stand, with you holding me."

He sighed. "Okay. What's your favorite song?"

She shrugged. "Anything."

Rubbing her back, he hummed a few bars then began to sing. He heard her sigh, felt her relax, and then tightened his arms as she jerked spasmodically, forcing herself to stay awake.

Stanley's voice was as clear and pure as a mountain stream, and as warm as a summer evening, husky and breathless and velvety rough.

Craig grinned as strains of "Unchained Melody" carried through to the kitchen where he and Tamera were preparing the coffee. "He's singing to her. I can't believe it."

"He's got a good voice."

"Yeah, he does. I'm going to call Scott." Though he now lived in Louisiana, Scott Hensley was still his closest friend and most trusted physician.

"Hey, Buddy, how's it going?" Scott asked.

"About as well as can be expected for someone who's been up for two days," Craig muttered.

"What's wrong?"

"Amber's had that damn nightmare again. It's been over ten years since the last time she had it and no one has any idea what to do. She won't sleep, eats very little, and insists on drinking gallons of coffee. I've had about all I can stand."

"Have any idea what brought it on? Has she watched any horror films or read any books that you know of?"

"No," Craig assured. "She's never been into those. But she gave me some cock-a-mammie story about left brain, right brain," he answered with a snort.

Scott chuckled. "It's not a cock-a-mammie story, Craig. For most people the left side of their brain is the logical part and the right is creative. Amber has a very creative imagination. Chances are it's taken over for some reason, could be internal reasons like hormone changes or chemical imbalance. Or, it could be external triggers like extreme stress. It's your job as her father to figure out which."

"And how am I supposed to do that?"

"Well, think about it. Is anything out of the ordinary going on, any major change in her life? Has something happened to upset her lately?"

"No. The only major change in her life is this boy," Craig admitted, wondering if for some reason her relationship with Stanley was adding undue stress to his daughter's life. That thought rolled quickly into another, more suspicious one. "I'll beat the little S.O.B. if he's pressuring her into something she's not ready for or doesn't want. I'll kill him if he succeeds," he added.

"Whoa, now, don't jump to conclusions," Scott warned. "Like I said, it could be anything. If she doesn't give in soon and get some rest, or if the nightmare keeps occurring over several days, get her to a doctor. In the meantime, the best thing I can suggest is an old-fashioned hot toddy, and no more coffee. Caffeine is a stimulant and is probably doing her more harm than good. Call me back in a couple of days and let me know what's going on," Scott said, before ringing off.

Taking Scott's advice, Craig stirred a tablespoon of honey with equal parts whiskey into a mug of warm milk. Taking the tray, he and Tamera went into the den. Ace joined them for hot chocolate before going up to bed.

Craig put the tray down and offered Stan a cup of coffee. "No more coffee, Amber," he said, grabbing her hand as she reached for a cup. "Drink the milk."

"I don't want milk. I want coffee."

He grunted. "You've had enough coffee to float a ship. The caffeine isn't good for you. Drink the milk."

She turned her nose up at him. "I don't like warm milk."

"You've never drank warm milk," he argued, his patience thinning rapidly. "Drink it or I'll pour it down your throat."

"What's it supposed to do, make me sleep like a baby?" she sneered.

Her eyes were narrow slits of brilliant cobalt. Craig's teeth clenched as tightly as the fists by his side as he fought the urge to jerk her over his knee and tan her hide. "You're pushing, Amber."

Emotionally strung out, Amber missed the warning that flashed in her father's eyes and echoed in her brain. Taking the glass mug, she tossed the milk down with one gulp. "Ugh!" she shuddered. "Are you happy now?" she asked, glaring at her father. In one jerky movement, she slammed the glass down on the table, rattling the tray of cups and saucers, splattering coffee, cream and sugar everywhere.

Craig lunged from his seat with a growl, his hands clenched in suppressed fury as he fought not to touch her, knowing if he did, he'd very likely lose control and beat the living daylights out of his child.

Tamera stared in shocked disbelief at the outburst.

Stanley struggled with the impulse to grab Amber and protect her from her father's wrath.

Bursting into tears of fatigue and humiliation, Amber ran from the room. She barely made it to the stairs before collapsing into a crumpled heap on the bottom step, sobs tearing from her in painful torrents.

"Let her go," Tamera insisted in a soft voice, stopping both Craig and Stanley from following her daughter. When they sank back into their chairs, she got up and went to her child, enfolding Amber in her embrace. "How about a hot bath, now, Sweetheart?"

Unable to speak for the heart wrenching sobs shaking her slender frame, Amber nodded and let her mother help her up to her room.

Tamera ran a tub full of warm water, applying a liberal amount of bubbles beneath the streaming liquid.

Piling Amber's thick, black tresses into a knot on top of her head, she secured it with a huge barrette. Helping her daughter undress and slide into the tub, she sat in silence while Amber cried out her fears and humiliation. Nearly ten minutes passed before her daughter could speak.

"He'll probably never speak to me again," Amber sobbed, wishing she could just slide into the bubbles and disappear forever.

Tamera's voice was soft and reassuring when she answered. "If he cares half as much as he seems to, he'll understand. And forgive."

"You think so," Amber whispered, her eyes wide with hope.

Tamera nodded and helped her step out of the tub. Wrapping a huge bath sheet around her daughter, she assisted Amber in dressing then urged her to sit while she took down and brushed out her hair. "He seems very sweet and special," she remarked, hoping to ease a conversation out of her daughter and maybe find out what was bothering her.

"He is," Amber stated, her voice reflecting the depth of her feelings for Stanley. "He's so different, so real. And he doesn't seem at all impressed or intimidated by our so called social status."

"So you've talked about that?"

"A little."

"Is that what's got you so worried and uptight?" Tamera asked.

"No, Ma'am."

"Do you want to tell me what has?"

Amber knew her mother was only asking out of concern. But to be honest, she had no idea why or even if she was uptight about anything in particular. Only that she had a distinct impression her life was about to change and change drastically. As though she were standing on the precipice of womanhood and not sure if she was ready to take the leap. Unsure of how to explain this, she shrugged. "I'm not really sure, Mom. Just growing pains I guess."

Tamera smiled and hugged her daughter. "Well, if you ever want to talk, you know I'm here."

Relieved her mother understood and wouldn't pry, especially since she really didn't understand herself, Amber squared her shoulders and prepared to face what might possibly be the hardest apology in her life.

Meanwhile downstairs, Ace had crawled up beside his father, burying his face into Craig's shoulder. "Sissy's not feeling any better at all, is she, Daddy?" he asked, surprised and shocked by his sister's outburst.

Born two months premature, Ace was smaller than other boys of eight and very sensitive. Craig wrapped his arms around his young son and hugged him. "No, she's not. But you know she's not mad at any of us," he said, hoping to reassure Ace all would be well.

Ace nodded. "I wish I knew what to do to make her feel better."

Still reeling from shock and anger, Craig sighed and closed his eyes. "Me too, Ace, me too."

Unsure what he should do, Stanley started picking up the empty cups. Gathering everything and placing it on the tray, he turned to Craig and his son. "Hey, Sport, I sure could use some help. Can you get me a damp rag or sponge?"

Ace nodded and rushed to do as he was asked.

Craig looked up, noticing the worried frown on the boy's face. "She's not usually like this," he assured Stanley with a tired smile.

"Does this happen very often?"

"No. In fact it's been several years since she's had the nightmare. It's like all of her childhood fears are manifested in that one creature," he said, dragging his hands over his face with a weary sigh. "The mixed blessing of a creative imagination, I guess. We figured she'd outgrown it."

He eyed the boy with more than a hint of curiosity and concern. "Has she been under any undue stress that you know of lately?"

Stanley shrugged not missing the real question in Craig's voice. "Not any more than usual I guess, with finals and all. I mean, she hasn't said anything to me. You think she'll sleep now?"

Craig sighed again, raking his fingers through his hair in a frustrated gesture. "I don't know, probably not for a while yet. When she was little all I had to do was hold her in my arms, rock her, and wait her out. She wasn't as strong then and couldn't hold out as long. I don't know, but I think the concoction we put in the milk will help her relax some. That, or exhaustion will take over soon. I hope."

"Concoction?"

Craig smiled at the concern in Stanley's voice. "Just an old-fashioned hot toddy, cup of warm milk, spoon of honey and a spoon of whiskey," he assured.

Stan grinned. "Usually works like a charm. My grandmother's given me those a time or two. Mr. Harris, I'd like to stay with Amber a while if you don't mind. You and Mrs. Harris both look like you could use a break."

Craig shook his head. "I'm not sure I know you well enough to entrust my daughter into your hands, or arms, while the rest of the household sleeps, and I doubt I ever will."

Stan's smile was reassuring, slightly mocking. "Maybe not, but what better time to find out if you can trust me than now, when she's so exhausted that I'd have to be a fool or an animal to try anything with her, especially with you and your wife upstairs. Besides, I have enough respect for you, your wife, Amber, and *my hide* to think twice or more often if necessary."

That made him chuckle. "Trying to convince me as you did the school principal you're an upstanding kinda guy?" Craig asked. "I can promise you I won't be so easy to convince."

Stanley didn't doubt that for a moment. "What decent father would?" he countered. "But if Mr. Strickland can trust me around Lori who is much younger and a lot less mature, why can't you trust me with Amber?"

"You've no interest in dating Lori, do you?"

Stanley snorted. "Good Lord, no."

Craig grinned. "I rest my case."

Wondering what he could say to convince Craig that his daughter was safe alone in his company, Stanley looked up when, wrapped in her mother's arm, Amber came back into the room. Emotion clouded her beautiful eyes, a glimmer of shame, a hint of fear. His heart twisted with compassion when she walked over to her father and reached a hand to him.

"I'm really sorry, Daddy."

Stanley watched the exchange noting how worry replaced the shock and anger in Craig's gaze.

Taking her hand in his, Craig kissed it. "I know, Sweetheart. You've got to try and rest, Amber."

She nodded and looked away. Her lips trembled, her gaze sought Stan's. "I want to apologize to you too."

"No sweat," he assured with a wink.

Ace wrapped his arms around his sister's waist. "I love you, Sissy. You can sleep with me if you're too scared to sleep by yourself."

Amber hugged him to her breast. "Thanks, Brat. I love you too. And I just might do that."

An awkward silence filled the air. Hoping to reassert his desire to spend some time with Amber, Stanley turned to Tamera, his eyes wide and sincere. "I've offered to stay with her a while so you and Mr. Harris can rest, but he doesn't seem to trust me just yet."

Tamera smiled. "And what makes you think I trust you anymore than he does?"

A thrill of hope flared in his heart when Stan heard the thread of humor in her voice. His gaze snagged hers. He gave her his most charming smile. "Have I given you any reason not to trust me?"

"No, but neither have you had the opportunity to prove to us you are trustworthy."

"What better time than the present?" Stan asked. "I can assure you that you won't find me any less the gentleman than you expect."

Tamera picked up the tray giving her husband a meaningful glance. "Well, we'll just have to see about that," she remarked, heading to the kitchen with Craig close on her heels.

"I can't believe you'd even insinuate we'd leave him alone with her," Craig said.

"What's wrong with giving them a little time alone? It's not like they're primed and ready for anything. Heaven knows she's exhausted," Tamera replied.

"Do you know how long it takes a boy of his age to be primed and ready?" he demanded.

Tamera's eyebrow lifted in question causing a flush to climb into her husband's cheeks. He muttered a curse. She laughed. "You said you trust her," she reminded him.

"I do trust her; it's him I'm not so sure about. Besides, she's so vulnerable right now."

Tamera's lips pursed into a frown. "From what you know of him, do you honestly think this boy would be so shallow, so immature, to take advantage of her like that?"

"And, what exactly do I know of him?" he queried, wondering if his wife had lost her mind. "He's orphaned, alone, from Arkansas and currently lives and works at the Bar S ranch. Rumor has it that he's somehow related to Old Man Morrison who's been dead for ages. So far, no one knows more than that. If you ask me, that's precious little to trust him alone with my daughter."

"But, Roy Strickland likes him and trusts him with his daughter and his horses," Tamera added. "And from what I know of Roy that says a whole lot about Stanley's character, especially when it comes to Lori, who is wild and unruly and can't be trusted, period. Besides you shouldn't listen to rumor or gossip, much less base your judgment of someone's character on either; even if both are grounded in truth."

Craig rolled his eyes and relented. She was right. Roy didn't trust just anyone with his horses much less his daughter, who was another story altogether. No matter how or what the man tried, the girl was a constant source of agony. "I guess you're right, besides, I'm too tired to argue.

But if anything happens to her...." His words trailed off. Unspoken threat hung in the air.

Tamera brushed her lips over his and smiled. "Even if you don't trust him completely, trust me. Trust my instinct and give him a chance. Nothing's going to happen."

Later, Amber sat at her father's desk while Stan flipped through the channels on the television. Her parents had taken Stanley up on his offer and were resting. Ace had long since gone to bed. Finding a country music video station, Stanley tossed the remote aside.

"What'cha doin'?" he asked.

Amber glanced down at the tablet where she'd been doodling. A soft moan escaped her as she tore the page off, wadded it into a tiny ball, tossed it toward the trashcan and missed. With a soft sob, she folded her arms on the desk and buried her face in them, trying desperately not to bawl like a baby.

Stanley rose from the couch and walked to where the paper lay on the floor. Picking it up he uncurled it, smoothed it out as much as possible and gazed in shock at what he saw.

Drawn with amazing clarity, the ugliest creature he'd ever imagined nearly jumped off the page at him. What appeared to be the body of a man with claws instead of feet and hands, the creature sported a tail, long, shaggy hair, the snout of a wolf, complete with fangs, and hideous, hungry eyes. Like a werewolf only leaner, uglier, definitely the substance of nightmares. His eyes closed in mortification, his heart clenched in his chest. No wonder she wouldn't sleep! *God help me*, he pleaded silently, *tell me what to say*

"If I saw this *thing* every time I closed my eyes, I wouldn't want to sleep either," he muttered, throwing the paper away and walking to where she sat. He pulled her in his arms. "Come here," he whispered. "Let me hold you."

Her smile was tender and slightly teasing, her lips trembled. Tears clung to her thick, black lashes.

"My father tried that already. It didn't work." Stanley grinned, his eyes twinkling merrily.

"But I'm not your father. He doesn't care about you the same way I do," he assured, leading her to the couch and pulling her down beside him.

Amber smiled to herself and snuggled her face into his collar, wondering what he meant by that remark.

Stanley settled her in his arms and held her gently, making sure his hands were visible at all times in case her father decided he couldn't sleep and came downstairs. Brushing the hair off her face, he kissed her cheeks, eyes and lips.

"Relax, Sweetheart. I won't let anything hurt you," he assured, his voice soft and tender, stroking her body in a soothing caress. He had no idea how long they sat, talking quietly until her breathing deepened and she drifted into an exhausted slumber.

Chapter Four

Craig shook his head with a smile as he rode up to the barn after a very long day of working cattle in the summer heat. Stanley was sitting on the porch strumming his guitar. Amber, Ace, and a few of the hands were playing audience. He seemed to be a fine young man and everyone adored him.

That boy is beginning to be a permanent fixture around here.

In the weeks since Amber's nightmare, his opinion of Stanley Morrison started to take shape. It began after he woke up from a desperately needed nap that night to find her sound asleep in the boy's arms. He stood quietly, watching with a mixture of relief and dismay.

Amber lay curled up in Stan's lap, her fingers buried in the golden hair showing in the open collar of his shirt, her head nestled in his shoulder. Stan was snoring lightly, a look of pure contentment on his face. He stirred when Craig lifted his daughter from her cradle.

"How long has she been out?"

Stan shrugged.

Bereavement showed in his eyes. Crag smiled. "What'd you do, sing her to sleep?"

Craig's eyes showed relief and gratitude that his daughter was finally resting. Stan shook his head and clenched his fist as if to say he'd knocked her out.

Craig grunted. "Yeah, if there's one bruise on this body I'll kill you," he warned, his voice reflecting that he didn't believe him at all. "There are blankets and pillows in the hall closet. Make yourself at home. There's no need for you to leave in the middle of the night. It's still raining."

The middle of the night was actually after one in the morning. She'd held out for almost thirty-six hours. Later that morning, while Amber slept, they shared a quiet breakfast before Stan left. The storm had abated but a light rain still fell steadily.

He'd been a constant guest ever since.

Dusting his hat off against his thigh, Craig shook his head. "Hey, Boy, you here again?"

Stan grinned up at him, not missing a note on the strings. "Yes, Sir, I was invited for supper."

"Again? Guess I'm going to have to start charging you for groceries unless you think you're singing for your supper?"

Stan laughed. "Yes, Sir."

The boy was a wonder on the guitar, singing anything from country to pop, old and new, ballads, blues, and gospel. He showed no preference to the race, sex, or creed of the original artists. If it was good, it was music. He loved it and he sang it with enough emotion to make the hardest of hearts melt into tears of laughter or sorrow, whichever the words warranted. Craig looked at the flush on his daughter's cheeks and felt a tug at his heart.

"Well, maybe you know Amber's favorite song?"

"What's that?" Stan asked. *She never said she had a favorite.*

"'Close to You' by the Carpenters," Craig confided.

Amber squealed. "Daddy! I hate that song," she insisted, a blush staining her cheeks.

Craig chuckled. "Really? Then why do you sing it all the time?" he queried, his steely eyes lit with amusement.

Stan grinned. Giving her a wink he sang the chorus, changing guy to girl and gold to coal.

Both men watched as her flush of embarrassment turned bright with pleasure and her eyes lowered demurely. "I do love that song," she sighed, raising sparkling, triumphant eyes to her father's teasing ones.

"Boy, you are hopeless," Craig grunted walking around them to the door. "Both of you are," he added. "Keep singing, Cowboy, and maybe you'll get a second serving at supper, and maybe I won't charge you after all."

His wife met him at the foot of the stairs. "I thought you didn't like him," she teased, her eyes laughing into his.

"I don't want to like him," Craig insisted, and then grinned. "Kinda hard not to though. The boy's manners are beyond reproach. Besides, you and Amber keep shoving him down my throat. Next thing you know we'll be cleaning out a room and letting him move in."

Tamera laughed and swallowed her teasing retort. Unless she was mistaken, they'd only just begun.

Giving her a quick kiss, Craig went upstairs to clean up before supper.

Two weeks later his glowing opinion began to dim considerably. They were having breakfast before getting on the road to Mississippi. Ever since Amber was born they took a couple of weeks in the summer to visit Tamera's childhood home. Two weeks of rest and relaxation where they refused to worry about the activities at home. Ace was chattering like a mocking bird. Tamera was trying her best to listen and answer his excited questions. Amber sat, pushing her food around on her plate, eating very little, her manner quiet, subdued.

"Everyone packed and ready to go?" Craig had been champing at the bit since dawn, anxious to get the drive underway. "Okay, help Mama with the dishes Amber so we can get gone."

She looked up, her expression a mixture of fear and determination. "I said last night that I didn't want to go."

The stubborn jut to her chin grated on Craig's nerves quicker than nails on a chalkboard. "And I told you last night to pack your things. Did you?"

"No, Sir. I don't want to go."

"Not at the table," Tamera cut in hoping to diffuse the confrontation that was bound to occur. The standing rule was resolve it and let it go, but not at the table. Table time was family time, sacred time.

Craig bit back his retort and pushed away from the table. His chair scraped the floor when he stood up and glared down at his daughter. "Well you're not staying home by yourself. Now go pack." He turned and strode away.

Amber ground her teeth, her eyes flashing with emotion. Her chair nearly toppled over when she rose to follow him.

"I'm not a baby anymore, Daddy. I'm old enough to stay by myself for two weeks," she declared, stomping after him into the hall.

"Oh, suddenly you're too old for family vacations?" he demanded. "This is all because of that boy, isn't it?"

"He has nothing to do with it. I want some privacy and time alone to work on this book!" she insisted, but a guilty flush gave her away.

Amber loved to write, creating stories of love and romance out of nothing but the thoughts in her head and dreams in her heart. Their yearly vacation had never interfered before. He wouldn't let anything interfere now. Craig saw the excuse for what it was. Her Christmas present had been a laptop computer.

"Now you've resorted to making up excuses instead of telling the truth?"

Hurt underlined the fury in his voice. Amber hesitated in answering. "No, Daddy," she hedged. "Okay!" she admitted. "What if he is *part* of the reason? What would you say then? Would you let me stay home?"

He grabbed her by the shirtfront. "I'd tell you to pack your bags and be quick about it. You are not staying home by yourself with that boy sniffing around here while we're two states away."

With an angry squeal she jerked away and felt the chain around her neck give way beneath his firm grasp. They both looked down in surprise, neither aware that he'd held it in his grip.

"You broke it!" she cried, hurling up the stairs and slamming her bedroom door.

Craig raked his fingers through his hair. Remorse welled up inside him. He squashed it with angry determination. The necklace was replaceable, family and tradition were not.

Tamera came out from the kitchen. Not wanting him to witness the scene between his father and sister, she'd ushered Ace out to go check on the new colt and say goodbye to his animals. "Is she packing?" she asked her pacing husband.

"She'd better be," he snarled. "If she's not down here in fifteen minutes with her suitcase, I'm going after her. She's going with us even if I have to drag her kicking and screaming all the way."

Tamera fought a smile. He hadn't expressed that arrogant jerk attitude in years. "I'll go help her," she said.

She entered Amber's room to find her daughter carelessly tossing things into a suitcase. Tears streamed down her cheeks, her eyes flashed with undisguised fury. "You need some help, Sweetheart?" she offered, holding out her arms as Amber collapsed into angry sobs.

"I don't care," she muttered. "I don't understand why he won't let me stay. It's like he doesn't trust me, Mama. He knows Stan well enough to know that he wouldn't come into the house if you weren't here. And it's not like I'd be totally alone. There are a dozen of his most trusted men here minding the ranch."

Tamera pulled Amber down on the bed to sit beside her. "Be patient with him, Amber," she soothed, stroking the hair off her daughter's face. "He's not used to the idea of you growing up and he definitely hasn't come to terms with the possibility of sharing you with Stanley."

"He broke my necklace," Amber sobbed, fresh tears rolling down her cheeks.

"I'm sure it was an accident. We'll take it to a jeweler and get it repaired," her mother soothed.

"It won't be the same," she insisted, slightly hysterical, not sure why the thought tore at her heart. "It'll never be the same again."

Remembering her own experience of dealing with her father's difficulty in letting go as she grew up, Tamera doubted Amber understood how true that statement was and in how many ways. Closing her hand over her daughter's and wrapping the necklace securely in Amber's palm, she prayed silently for wisdom and direction. "No, it may never be the same, but it can be stronger," she said in quiet assurance.

Amber's eyes widened when the meaning of her mother's words sank into her heart and mind. She nodded slightly, indicating she understood.

Tamera smiled. "Now, go wash your face and brush your hair and I'll finish packing for you."

Amber gave her a quick hug and did what she was told. Carrying her suitcase downstairs she clasped it firmly as Craig reached for it. Enlightened but still angry, she clung to it in a tiny show of independence. Craig sighed and opened the door. Bringing it to the truck, she set the suitcase on the ground while he made room for it. In a soft, hesitant voice she asked, "Can we stop by the Bar S on the way out?"

Craig swallowed his angry retort. The Bar S wasn't on the way out and they were already getting a late start. Glaring down at his daughter's face, he felt a tug of remorse. Damn those wide, pleading eyes, and double-damn his weakness for them. She was twisting him into knots of confusion, pain, and anger. A curt nod passed for an answer.

"Thank you," she whispered, stepping back from her suitcase. It was a concession and they both knew it. A tenuous cease in a battle which was just beginning. They knew that, too.

The knowledge hurt.

Stan watched them drive up and turned his back on the barn entrance not wanting Amber to see his disappointment. He felt her arms slide around his waist, her head press against his back.

"He won't let me stay," she mumbled in a choked whisper.

"Did you expect him to?" The question was soft, not accusing. Feeling her nod he smiled to himself. Turning, he wrapped his arms around her. Looking down into her face, his heart twisted at what he saw there. Tears shone bright against the dark pain in her eyes.

"You fought with him didn't you, Amber?"

She nodded again.

"Amber," he breathed. "I told you, I don't want you fighting with your father over me."

Her lip trembled. "He broke my necklace."

He shrugged. "It's just a necklace. I'll get you another one." Silently he prayed her relationship with her father was stronger than the tiny, delicate chain.

She shook her head. "Mama said we'd get it fixed. But I feel empty without it," she mumbled, burying her face into his chest.

He ran his hands up her back in a soothing caress. "Maybe this'll help," he offered, taking his graduation ring off and handing it to her. "Think about me, Amber," he insisted, his voice husky with emotion.

Her smile was brilliant when she placed the ring on her finger. Taking her own tiny ring, she put it on his pinkie. "Don't forget me while I'm gone," she whispered.

"Never," he muttered. Succumbing to the need, he buried his hands in her hair and his lips on hers. A soft whimper escaped her when he dragged his lips from hers. Wrapping his arms around her once again, he pulled her against him.

"I'm going to miss you," she wailed, on the verge of tears again.

"Shh," he hushed her with a tender kiss. "I'll be here when you get back," he promised, stroking her cheek. "Come on now, I'll walk you out before your father comes in after you."

She hesitated, standing firmly in place. Locking her gaze with his, she ran her hands up his chest and around his neck, curling her fingers in his hair. Reaching up on tiptoe, she placed her lips against his once more.

Cupping her cheeks in his hands, Stan controlled the kiss and ended it before it got too passionate. His smile tender, he nuzzled her nose then kissed it. Turning toward the door, he put his arm around her waist and walked her out.

Opening the back passenger door on the Suburban, he guided her onto the seat. "Y'all have a safe trip," he remarked, his gaze locking with Craig's in the mirror. He saw anger there, and pain, and accusation.

Afraid of exposing his heart, Stan jerked his gaze away and touched Tamera's shoulder.

Tamera patted his hand and smiled. "We will," she promised. "We'll see you in a couple of weeks. Take care of yourself while we're gone."

Stan nodded. "See you, Sport," he greeted Ace, exchanging a hand-slapping high five.

Caressing her face with his fingers, he kissed Amber's cheek. "Don't look back," he whispered, knowing if she turned around and looked at him with those beautiful eyes full of tears and longing he'd crumble, and quite possibly make a complete fool of himself by running after them until her father had no choice but to take him along or let her stay.

Amber nodded her smile tight.

Stepping back, Stan closed the door, smiling his approval when she buckled her seat belt and locked the door. With a tiny wave he backed away from the truck as Craig started the engine. When he could no longer see the truck for the dust in its wake, he walked back in the barn and went to work. It would be a long two weeks.

They'd barely gotten out of Bandera when Amber asked to drive. Craig nodded and pulled over so they could all change places. He would sit in the front with her while Tamera kept Ace occupied in the back seat. Getting back on the road, he turned to his daughter.

"It's going to be a long two weeks if we're not talking, Amber," he remarked, and watched tears filled her eyes.

She blinked them away and swallowed the lump in her throat. "What do you want me to say, Daddy? That I'm sorry for wanting to stay home, for growing up? I can't do that," she whispered. "But I am sorry we fought."

Remembering her mother's words and how upset Stan was that she'd fought with him, and still feeling the ache in her heart because of it, she smiled over at her father. "We'll be fine, Daddy," she promised.

Chapter Five

Craig sat on the patio talking with Scott. Since he had moved to Louisiana, the first few days of their vacation were spent with him. They'd arrived at "the palace" a little over an hour ago.

Scott owned a large Colonial-style plantation house located on one of the many bayous Louisiana was famous for. They'd teased him dubbing it "the palace." His reply had always been that it wouldn't be so big when he began filling it with children.

Tamera was busy getting Ace cleaned up and ready for bed. Amber too was upstairs. Supper had been deli sandwiches which Scott brought home with him after his shift at the hospital.

The two men sat enjoying a strong cup of coffee and conversation, catching up on each other's lives since their last visit. Though they talked regularly, they enjoyed the visits more each time they were together. This too, became a time-honored tradition. Scott had dominated the conversation, talking about a woman he'd met several months ago.

"So, do we get to meet her before tomorrow?" Craig asked, pleased at the sparkle in his friend's eyes.

Scott shrugged. "I asked her to come by this evening when she got off work, but she never knows when she'll have to work late."

"Katrina, it's a pretty name. What's she like?" Craig asked. Scott's eyes danced.

"She is pretty. She's petite but tough. She's young and sweet and vulnerable and despite all she's been through, incredibly naive. There's a natural strength in her that she's coming to recognize and use. She's been going through some rough times, and a real nasty divorce, but she's holding up. She's got the most beautiful laugh. And her hair," he shook his head at a loss as how to describe it.

"It's thick and silky, and the most unusual color. Not red, not gold, but an intriguing combination of the two, reminds me of a fiery sunset. And she has the most beautiful brown eyes," again he hesitated. "Big and soulful and incredibly, rich, brown. Like dark, liquid chocolate."

Craig chortled. "Liquid chocolate? I've never heard of anyone having eyes like liquid chocolate," he teased. "Looks like you've got it bad."

"She's thirty," Scott added in a chuckling under-breath.

"Thirty! You dirty old man," Craig accused good-naturedly.

Scott grinned. "She reminds me of Tamera."

Craig rolled his eyes. "Oh, Lord. Stay away from her," he warned with a laugh.

Scott shook his head. "No, really, wait until you meet her."

"Don't tell me you've been in love with my wife all this time," Craig teased. Scott hesitated, stroking his mustache, his smile thoughtful. A hint of mockery lit his dark eyes.

Had he been in love with her? Scott wondered. He remembered the first time he saw Tamera, lying on Craig's couch badly broken and incredibly beautiful. He loved her laugh and shining sapphire eyes. He loved her, true, but he loved her for who she was—his best friend's wife. Out of the corner of his eye he saw a frown tug at Craig's lips, when he apparently took too long to answer what should have been an easy question.

He grinned. "Let's just say I've considered you one lucky fool all these years," he answered with a tiny shrug.

Craig tossed back his head with another laugh. They looked up in unison when Amber walked out to join them.

Scott held his hand out to her. "Finish your call?"

"What call?" Craig demanded before she could respond.

She stiffened turning with deliberate caution toward her father. "I called Stanley to let him know we were staying here a couple of days before going on to Mississippi." She looked down at Scott. "You did say we were going to tour some plantations down around White Castle and maybe go to New Orleans didn't you?"

Scott felt the friction between Amber and her father and frowned over at Craig, then nodded in answer to her question.

"Is there a problem, Daddy?" she queried in a soft, accusing voice. They glared at each other for a moment, the tension escalating.

Choosing to ignore the challenge in her voice, Craig answered with a curt shake of his head. Though a truce had been called between them, even the long trip to Scott's house hadn't eased the pain of their fight.

"Thank you," she said softly, taking Scott's hand before plopping down in his lap.

"What's this?" Scott toyed with the ring on her finger. "I thought you were my girl."

She pouted. "Got tired of waiting for you," she teased, kissing his cheek.

Scott chuckled laying his forehead against hers. "Thought I'd wait until you grew up some." Glancing over, he saw Craig frown, watched his eyes narrow at Amber's defiant reply and arched an eyebrow at him. Urging her from his lap, he offered Amber a walk along the bayou. He squeezed Craig's shoulder and felt a tug at his heart for his friend. Their little girl was growing up. And her daddy wasn't happy about it.

Craig watched them walk away. Frustration and jealousy warred in his heart. Not aimed at Scott, but at the boy they'd left behind in Texas. Lunging from his chair, he sought the comfort of his wife.

Tamera was finishing her bath when Craig stalked into the room. Her heart ached at the emotions in his eyes. Smiling, she put her arms around him. "You and Scott have a good visit?" she asked, expertly pulling his thoughts toward more pleasant meanderings.

He chuckled. "Yes. His girlfriend, Katrina, is all he can talk about."

She sighed. "Good. It's about time he gets on with his life."

Craig laughed. "She's thirty," he informed her with a grin.

"Does age have anything to do with their loving each other or them being happy?"

"Of course not," he grunted. Seeing the questioning expression on her face he snorted. "That's different," he hissed. "She's a grown woman. They're just kids."

"Craig, I didn't say anything," she chided.

"But you were thinking it," he accused.

She smiled and shook her head. "What I was thinking, Cowboy is that you'd better not get any ideas," she purred, tugging at his shirtfront, determined that he wouldn't dwell on the situation which seemed uppermost in his mind.

"Ideas about what?"

"Younger women."

He grunted. "Why would I want to train one all over again?"

His gray eyes glistened like dewdrops on sheet metal. Tamera wrinkled her nose at him and rolled her eyes. "Arrogant jerk," she muttered, before his lips covered hers in a thorough kiss.

"Where is Scott now?"

"He and Amber are enjoying a stroll along the bayou. Katrina may stop by a little later."

Tamera smiled. "What's she like?"

Craig grinned. "Let me see if I can get this right: She has hair the color of a fiery sunset, eyes like liquid chocolate and she reminds him of you." He shook his head amazed and pleased to recall the special light in Scott's eyes. "You should see his face when he talks about her."

Tamera wrapped her arms around him and raised her lips to his for another kiss. "I can't wait to meet her," she murmured brushing tiny kisses across his chin, down his throat and over his chest.

Craig moaned when she nipped at his shoulder. It still surprised him that his body would respond to her teasing after all these years. Dragging his fingers through her hair he covered her mouth with his, hungrily, hotly, until she trembled in response. Picking her up, he carried her to the bed, taking advantage of the diversion from his tortured thoughts.

Outside, Scott turned a tender gaze to the young beauty on his arm. "I take it something's bothering your father?" he queried, his tone gentle.

Amber snorted in a very unladylike manner. "Nothing a fence post to the skull won't cure," she remarked, tossing her hair off her shoulder with an angry shake of her head.

"Wow, kind of harsh, don't you think?"

Amber heard the gentle admonition in Scott's voice and flushed. "I guess so, but he's just so frustrating!"

"Want to talk about it?" Scott offered.

She shrugged. "He treats me like a baby. I'm seventeen years old and he still thinks I'm his little girl."

"You'll always be his little girl."

"I know that, Scott, but he doesn't have to treat me like an infant."

"You don't expect him to just let go now that you're seventeen, do you?"

A heavy sigh preceded her answer. "No. But it wouldn't hurt for him to loosen up."

Scott smothered a grin. "Wouldn't have anything to do with this Stanley guy would it?" Though the sun hung low on the horizon there was still enough light for Scott to see the pretty flush which filled her cheeks and the sparkle in her eyes when she told him about the new man in her life.

"Can I have my phone card back now?" she queried, holding out her hand.

He'd taken it from her earlier that evening and refused to give it back when she asked to call Stanley. Adamant as ever, he stood over her a while ago to make sure she didn't call collect or charge it to her own phone.

"If you promise not to use it," he teased, holding it just out of her reach until she promised.

Amber rolled her eyes. "Will I ever be free of chauvinistic men?"

He chuckled hugging her to his side. "Probably not. Be patient with your father, Amber, he's not used to sharing you."

She rolled her eyes again. "Mama said the same thing. I'll try," she promised.

Despite the fact that she worked late in the evening, Katrina showed up early the next morning to accompany them to White Castle and on to New Orleans. Caught in the generation gap between Tamera and Amber, she got on famously with both of them. The two men braced their wide shoulders as the women assaulted them with feminist wise cracks and jokes, harassing them mercilessly over their chauvinistic attitudes. They tolerated the teasing insults until they had no choice but to retaliate.

The fight with Amber forgotten, Craig found himself teasing his daughter about telling Stanley of her distinctive feminist attitude. Amber just smiled and reassured him that she could handle Stanley.

* * * * *

Craig settled in the hammock hanging in the backyard of Tamera's childhood home, his daughter wrapped securely in his arms. They would be going home tomorrow. He smiled remembering the lighthearted arguments regarding his idea of taking an alternate route home, one which took them across the northern part of Louisiana and would take an extra day. His family accused him of trying to prolong their vacation. They were right. Things were changing too quickly for his taste. His children were growing up and would soon have lives of their own. He'd enjoyed this vacation more than any other he could remember. Selfishly, he didn't want it to end.

Their two-week vacation had stretched gloriously into three. Three weeks of roughhousing with his son, making love with his wife and having long walks and intimate, enlightening conversations with his daughter.

A contented sigh escaped him when Amber cuddled closer to him. Warmed by memories, he drifted off.

Amber snuggled closer to her father. He was so strong, so solid. Even in sleep she felt safe and secure in his arms. Her eyes flew open when he pulled her closer and mumbled her mother's name. "Daddy," she whispered, lightly shoving her elbow into his ribs. "Daddy, wake up."

Craig opened his eyes to look into the amused gaze of his daughter. It took a moment for his sleep-fuzzed brain to register what she was saying.

"I'm not Tamera, but if you'll let me go, I'll get her for you," she teased, brushing a lock of hair off his forehead and her lips across his cheek in a tender caress before rolling out of the hammock.

It wasn't until she moved that Craig realized how he'd been holding her. A mortified groan escaped him, but it was the realization that he'd have to stop holding her as he had when she was little that bothered him the most. She was a young woman now, he thought, overwhelmed by a sense of loss. The ache started in his heart, traveling through his body until he hurt all over. His arms ached with emptiness as he remembered all the years he'd held Amber on his chest, wrapped securely in his arms, while she slept. He struggled against tears as truth broke his heart. She wasn't his baby any longer and he knew without a doubt, things would never be the same.

Amber found her mother in the kitchen. "Mama, Daddy needs you out back," she informed her with a pout in her voice and a grin on her face.

Tamera laughed. "Be a big girl about it Amber, you have to share him sometimes," she teased, patting Amber's cheek.

Amber emitted a dreamy sighed. "I hope my husband loves and desires me as much as you two even after nearly twenty years together."

Tamera smiled. "True love is a gift from God, Sweetheart. It may burn as bright and hot as a shooting star or be soft, warm, and intimate like candlelight. But, like everything else, it has to be nurtured to grow and be strong. I'm sure you'll know when it's right."

Amber nodded, wanting to ask more questions but needing to think about what she'd just been told. Her feelings for Stan were both of those things. She smiled at her mother, unaware her thoughts were reflected in her eyes. "Well, you better go nurture," she said watching a sweet flush rush to her mother's cheeks and a light fill her eyes.

Tamera climbed into the hammock beside Craig. Her heart ached at what she'd seen in her daughter's eyes and the pain now reflected in her husband's. "Amber said you needed me," she whispered, pulling him against her.

"Do you remember when I used to hold her on my chest while she slept and you would accuse me of spoiling her beyond repair?"

Tamera smiled, the memory as vivid as though it was yesterday. "Yes. You did, and she is."

"Then, when she got older, you told her that when her feet touched the floor she would be too big to sit on my lap."

Tamera chuckled. "I'd remind her but to no avail. She'd look at me with that smug, cocky grin she inherited from you..."

"And those sassy eyes she inherited from you," he interrupted.

Tamera picked up where she left off. "She'd look me dead in the eye, a defiant lift to her chin, her eyes sparkling with triumph and very slowly, very deliberately drag her knees to her chest then settle more comfortably right where she was. And you would shift around in your chair to make room for her, acting like you didn't know what was going on."

His chuckle ended on a strangled note. "Temper," he moaned in a suffocated voice. "My little girl's growing up."

"Her legs have long since drug the floor," Tamera murmured when he pulled her in his arms and buried his face in her hair. She wrapped her arms around him, holding him in a tender embrace, understanding and sharing the emptiness which threatened to overwhelm.

Chapter Six

Amber pushed the Suburban to the maximum speed limit allowed by law. They would be home in less than three hours and she could hardly wait!

Though she'd talked to Stan regularly while they were away, at her mother's suggestion, she indulged her father by not talking about him too much. For three weeks and three days, she acted as though she didn't miss him, but that was far from the truth. Every day she missed him more than the day before. Sometimes he sounded so lonesome on the other end of the line, she wished she could just hop on a plane and hurry home to his waiting arms.

Now, the desire to see him, to touch him and to feel his arms around her and his lips on hers was almost overwhelming. Warmth surged through her making the cool air in the truck seem like an old blue northern. Goosebumps rose on her flesh, a shiver danced up her spine.

The closer they got to home, the more excited she got and the more evident it became. She laughed and teased her father, nearly giving him a heart attack when she let go of the steering wheel to dance along with the song on the radio.

Craig shot her a glare and grabbed the steering wheel. "Enough Amber, pay attention or get out from behind the wheel."

"Okay," she agreed, acting as though she were going to cross over him while attempting to watch the road, and let him take over the driving.

"Amber!" Her husky laugh when he pushed her back behind the wheel, made Craig sigh. "Have you lost your mind?" Thank God theirs was the only vehicle within sight, he thought. She gasped, her hand moving to her cheek as she glanced over at him, her eyes wide with innocent horror.

"That's what I forgot in Mississippi."

Craig couldn't help but chuckle.

"Wait, no," she exclaimed. "Is my mind in any way connected to my heart? If so," she continued before he could answer, "then it's okay. It's waiting for me at home."

He snorted. "Get off at the next exit. We're going back to Mississippi." Her eyes laughed into his.

"Oh, no, you can go back if you want, but I'm going home even if I have to hitch-hike the rest of the way." She smiled at the frown he gave her.

"Behave then, before I make you pull this vehicle over and beat you," he threatened.

She giggled. "Oh, I'm shaking in my boots," she assured him with a laugh.

Craig eyed the long expanse of leg scantily clad in cutoffs and trim, brightly painted toenails encased in strappy sandals. It's a miracle and a blessing the boys hadn't come running before now. He frowned at the thought, hating the fact that she'd grown from his precious little girl into an attractive young woman practically overnight. "You don't have boots on," he grunted.

She grinned. "And I'm not shaking either," she taunted, smiling in the mirror at her mother, whose chuckle could be heard from the back seat.

Craig turned to his wife. "What, exactly, do you think is so funny?" he asked arching a dark brow at her. Tamera regarded him with wide, innocent eyes, shrugged and grinned but refrained from comment.

* * * * *

Stan lay on his bunk, hands propped behind his head, hair still damp and curling from his recent shower. His heart thudded thickly in his chest. Excitement and need curled in the pit of his stomach. She was coming home. *Finally.* Though it aggravated him to no end, he couldn't blame Craig for wanting to keep her all to himself for ten days longer than they planned. He'd probably do the same thing if she were his daughter. But all the reasoning in the world didn't ease the ache of loneliness he'd suffered these last three and a half weeks. He closed his eyes and for once, wished he had a television or something, anything to occupy his mind.

Stan never cared much for TV. Music was his thing and his collection rivaled the best. But music wasn't soothing him as usual this afternoon because every song reminded him of Amber. He could see her, hear her soft, husky laugh and envision her shining sapphire eyes. The images were driving him crazy and firing his blood to molten lava. He prayed her call would come before he went totally insane.

The phone hadn't finished its first ring before he grabbed the receiver like a drowning man would a life ring. "We're home."

The silky tone of her voice washed over him like the brush of satin on bare skin. "I'm on my way," he assured, and slid trembling feet into his boots.

Lori was waiting for him when he walked out of his room. "Where are you going?" she asked, following him to his truck.

"Amber's, they're back from vacation."

She caught the truck door, preventing him from closing it. For more than three weeks she'd had him all to herself and didn't want that to change. Amber Harris didn't deserve a guy like Stanley. She did. She gazed up at him, grasping for a reason, any reason, to make him stay. "But, I thought you were going to work with me and Sampson today." Sampson was the colt they had been working with to train for barrel racing.

Stanley recognized her ploy, the dark eyes wide, innocent and shimmering with hopeful tears; the pouting lip. He'd seen her use it on her father countless times in the year since he began working and living at the Bar S. He smiled and tucked a curl behind her ear. "Not today, Lors. You're both doing great so give it a break. Go do something fun."

"But..."

He shook his head and gently but firmly pulled his door shut and started the truck. "Later, Lori." He put the truck in gear and eased away.

Watching her in the rearview mirror, he grimaced when Lori plopped down in the dirt and buried her face in her hands. Part two of the ploy used to get the desired results; only her shaking shoulders didn't fool Stanley or affect him the way they did her father. That child was way too used to getting what she wanted, when she wanted, every time she wanted.

A nagging sensation suggested she wanted him, but Stanley pushed it away. She was fourteen years old, a child. Besides, his heart was set on another, someone much more suited to his taste than a spoiled little girl. His heartbeat quickened in anticipation when he pulled in the drive of the Rockin' H ranch.

He barely had time to stop the truck and turn off the engine before Amber was out of the house and in his aching arms at last. Wanting nothing more than to crush her lips to his, he tempered his, and her, response. Pulling her firmly against him, he swung her up in his arms, brushing feathery kisses across her lips, cheeks and eyes. She trembled, a tiny sob escaping her smiling lips.

"Oh! I missed you."

He put her down, caressing her cheeks with shaking hands. "I missed you too." He glanced toward the house. "And if your father wasn't glaring at me through the kitchen window, I'd kiss you like you've never been kissed."

"How's that?"

He grinned, nuzzling her. "All lips and teeth and tongue," he said and felt her tremble.

"What makes you think I've never been kissed like that before?"

"Because, I've never kissed you like that."

"So?"

Her eyes sparkled in blatant challenge, tempting him. "Amber," he managed between a chuckle and a groan.

She waited, moving closer, absorbing the heat emanating from him, curling her fingers in the rich, gold-tipped, chestnut hair.

Willing all of his control, he pacified her, and himself, brushing his lips softly over hers and nibbling at the corners of her mouth. "Lord, I missed you," he assured, his voice husky, and pulled her against him once more.

Craig didn't need to ask what was going on when he heard Amber's excited little cry as she raced down the stairs and outside, the door slamming in her wake. He looked out the window when she flew into the outstretched arms and watched, a worried frown on his face, when Stan hugged her to him, pressing tiny kisses over her face. Her shoulders shook suspiciously. Whether from laughter or tears or both, he didn't know. A low growl sounded in his throat. Turning on his heel, he strode the three paces separating him from the back door one hand reaching for his hat, the other stretching toward the doorknob.

"Where are you going?" Tamera's admonishing voice deterred his mission when she walked into the room.

He hesitated and shot her a glare. "It's about time I had a talk with that boy."

She hurried to where he stood and edged herself between him and the door, placing a firm hand on his arm. "Leave them alone, Craig," she commanded in a soft, steely voice. "Save your 'honor my daughter' talk for later."

"You see what's going on out there? I won't have him pawing at her like that," he snarled.

Tamera moved enough to glance out the window. Stan's hands were completely visible and not at all pawing. She looked back at her husband, an eyebrow arched.

"Pawing? He's not pawing at her. What I see are two kids, crazy in love, greeting each other, rather sweetly I might add, after being separated three-and-a-half weeks for a two-week vacation." He snorted and tried to walk around her.

"Listen to me you arrogant jerk," she demanded, tightening her grip on his arm. "If you go out there right now you're going to embarrass yourself and your daughter. Not to mention me."

His eyes narrowed into dangerous slits of steel and the muscle in his jaw throbbed as it always did when he was angry or upset.

"I never liked it when you used that tone with me. I like it even less now," he insisted. "Besides, twenty is too old for her."

Her chin jerked up a notch. Her eyes flashed fire. She rolled them and stood her ground.

"Well, I never appreciated you acting like a jerk. And I like that even less now. Good Lord, Craig, she's seventeen. How do you figure twenty is too old? You're nearly five years older than I am."

"That's different," he snarled. "Get out of my way, Temper," he ordered. Grabbing her by the arm, he forcefully restrained himself from moving her from his path. "This is getting too thick too fast and I won't let it."

Though his fingers bore into her flesh, Tamera sighed and placed a restraining hand on his chest. She knew his reaction went far deeper than fatherly concern. He was jealous at sharing her, and that was dangerous. If he went storming out there, he would only succeed in angering Amber. And that was even more dangerous. He would end up pushing her right into Stan's arms.

"Listen to me," she urged, her expression changing from anger to pleading. "Let them alone for now. Let them say hello. You can have your talk with him, just not right now. They're kids, Craig," she reminded. "If you assume too much too soon and react accordingly, you're going to regret it," she warned.

Craig swore vilely and all but shoved her against the door. Turning on his heel, he slapped the hat on his head and stormed out of the room. She was right. Damn it. He knew she was right but he didn't have to like it.

Tamera blinked back tears, tucked a trembling lip under her teeth and rubbed her arm. She hadn't seen Craig that angry or upset in years. Walking over to the window, she watched the kids talking, saw the tender way Stanley brushed his knuckles over Amber's cheeks and felt a tug at her heart for the struggles which lay ahead.

Amber emitted a lusty sigh and smiled up at Stan. "Did you bring your guitar?"

"Do I ever not bring my guitar?"

"Good. Sing for me."

He tightened his arms around her. "I don't want to hold a guitar right now," he muttered.

She turned wide, pleading eyes on him. "Please. I've been listening to the radio for more than three weeks now and no one sounds as good as you do."

Looking into those sparkling gems Stan felt his knees weaken. His chuckle was thick, throaty. "Oh, you're good. Don't pull that look on me. It might work on your father but it won't cut here. Flattery will get you nowhere, Darling."

Amber knew defeat when she heard it and she heard it in those weak-hearted words. She savored the taste of victory in silence. She stepped away, tugging at his hand. Her smile was sweet, innocent, inviting. "So does that mean you're going to sing?"

Feeling bereft, he pulled her in his arms again, laughing softly at her insistence. "In a minute."

She giggled, wrapped her arms around his waist and pressed a kiss to the throbbing pulse in his throat. He groaned, running his hands over her back in a restless caress. Taking her hands in his, he pressed them to his lips.

"Know what else I missed while you were gone?"

His voice was soft, his gaze tender, teasing. Amber's breath caught in her throat. "What?" she croaked.

"My ring." He smothered a grin when her expression changed from delight to despair.

"Oh. Well, I guess you'll want it back." She tried not to look as disappointed as she felt and knew she sounded when she took the ring off and handed it to him.

He put it on his finger with an exaggerated sigh. "Now, man, I've been lost without it."

She smiled, flexing her fingers. "Now I feel lost without it."

Tucking his fingers into his pocket, Stanley withdrew a tiny gold band that curled into a single knot at top center. "I thought you would. Maybe this'll help." He would've given all the gold in Texas to capture her expression on camera. Her eyes widened, lips curled into a brilliant smile, a sweet flush covered her cheeks.

"It's beautiful!" she assured, while he placed the ring on her finger.

Lifting her hand to his lips again, he waited until her eyes met his. "Will you promise to be my girl, Amber? Only mine."

"Yes!" Flinging her arms around his neck, she kissed him firmly on the mouth.

He chortled. "Now I feel like singing." Grabbing his guitar with one hand, he held onto hers with the other and they walked to the porch.

Craig walked around the house relieved to find them sitting on the porch swing instead of wrapped in each other's arms. Stanley was strumming his strings as gently as he would a skittish colt and crooning, "Come Monday."

"Daddy!" Amber jumped off the swing. "Look!" She flashed a ring in his face. "Isn't it pretty?"

Craig eyed the tiny gold ring then glared at Stan, whose unwavering gaze stared right back. "It's nice, Sweetheart. Why don't you go show Mama," he ground out between his teeth.

Stan knew what was coming. He'd expected it long before now. Without lowering his gaze, he slid the guitar pick between the strings and put the instrument down.

Too late, Amber felt the tension between them. The glower on her father's face spoke volumes. So did the determined glint in Stanley's eyes and the stubborn jut to his chin. She hesitated, frowned. "But?"

Stan ran his hand along the braid down her back. "Go on, Sweetheart, show your mama."

Fighting a wave of panic, she smiled at Stan, squeezed his hand in a gesture of support then went into the house to find her mother.

"Take a walk, shall we?" Craig motioned for him to follow. It's time they had a talk. Man to boy. Taking a deep breath, he eyed Stanley. *Man to man.*

"Tamera told me to save the 'honor my daughter' talk for later but it looks like there's no use waiting."

"I guess not," Stan agreed. "And I wouldn't dare do otherwise."

Craig leaned against the fence. Resting his arm on the top rail, he looked down into the eyes of his foe. "Look, I know you think you have strong feelings for her..."

"I love her," Stan interrupted.

Craig's eyes narrowed, jaw muscle twitched. "I know you think you have strong feelings for her," he bit out, refusing to consider the boy's declaration. "But don't you think this is moving a little too fast?"

"I love her," Stan repeated.

He said it simply, honestly, unwaveringly. Craig felt a cold lump of fear in the region of his heart. His breath escaped in a hiss. "I could throw you off this ranch and forbid you to see her."

"Yes, Sir." Stan's gaze never faltered. "I'm sure you could"

Craig couldn't help but admire the boy's courage. Or maybe brashness was more like it, or stupidity—considering he could break the boy's neck with one and only one snap of his hands. Whatever, he was taken aback by Stan's firm stance and unyielding gaze. "Wouldn't do a damn bit of good would it?"

Stan risked a smile, a real tiny one. "I'm sure we'd run into each other from time to time. But, I'd respect that restriction. And I'd wait. The day she turned eighteen, I'd be back."

"Cocky little brat, aren't you?" Craig asked. Stan's eyes flared at the insult but he wisely checked his temper.

"No, Sir. Not really. Look, I know you think I'm too young, that we're too young to be in love, but I do know my own heart and mind. And what I want in life."

"And Amber's what you want? How can you tell? You barely know her."

"I knew the minute I laid eyes on her. I've always envisioned the kind of woman I wanted for a wife. Amber's everything I've ever dreamed of. Except..." his voice trailed off at the thought of her...the dark hair like silk between his fingers, the laughing eyes, the husky, sensual voice.

Craig's eyes narrowed while he waited, wondering where his daughter was lacking. *She* was perfect.

Stan's grin was sheepish. "Except she's more beautiful than I ever imagined," he admitted, awestruck.

"Amber still has a year of high school. Then college," Craig insisted.

Stan's smile was mocking. "I haven't asked her to marry me. Yet."

Craig grunted, scowled, not knowing if he should kill the boy or congratulate him for his show of spirit. "I know very little about you; who you are or where you come from. Don't you think it's time I know a more about the person who claims to be in love with my daughter?"

He watched Stanley, noting the boy's discomfort, and waited for an answer.

Chapter Seven

Amber paced the kitchen floor in restless agitation, stopping to look out the window. "You don't think Daddy's killed him do you, and at this very moment is burying his body?"

Tamera chuckled. "Did he have his shotgun with him?"

"No, but they've walked around the barn. There are pitchforks and things in the barn."

Tamera laughed again. "Calm down, Amber."

She sighed. "You're right. Daddy's too smart for that. He'll just think of some other way to scare him off."

"You think he can?" Tamera asked.

Amber's eyes sparkled. "I hope not," she admitted, her voice breathless, a flush on her cheeks. "What do you think is taking them so long, Mama?"

Tamera's smile was tender. "They're just talking, Sweetheart, trying to get to know each other a little better."

Amber snorted; disbelieving that was the only motive behind her father's sudden interest and anger at Stan. "Huh! More like rutting bulls establishing dominance. You should have seen them," she insisted, her emotions tumbling one into another, excitement to fear then anger. "Daddy all tense, grinding his teeth and scowling. Stan rising off the swing his expression just as hard. I swear you'd think they were about to engage in a duel!"

Tamera laughed and patted her cheek. "He's just exercising his parental rights as any father would do when a boy shows an interest in his daughter. I'm assuming that ring means he's interested?"

Amber's expression softened. "He asked me to be his girl, Mama, only his. And I said yes."

Tamera hugged her. "Good for you. But remember, Sweetheart, Daddy is not used to sharing you. Be gentle with him."

"I'll try," she promised then sighed. "I sure wish they'd hurry though."

Outside Craig waited for Stanley's response, concerned at his hesitation and the way Stan avoided his gaze. Noting the quick flash of panic in his eyes, Craig wondered what on earth could be hidden in the twenty-year-old's past that would make him afraid to answer a simple question.

Stanley fidgeted, wondering what to say. The time had come for truth, but how much truth? He sighed. "I'd hoped we could save that talk for later," he hedged, not sure where to begin. Giving a tiny shrug, he turned, standing beside Craig instead of facing him. "Mr. Harris, what do you know of the old Morrison place about five miles east of here?"

Craig searched his memory, recalling details of a scandal which occurred when he was just a kid. "A long time ago, Old man Morrison had a daughter. She got pregnant out of wedlock. He threw her out. She was pretty old too when it happened. Close to thirty I think."

Stan's eyes met his, again unwavering. "His daughter was my grandmother. She raised me after my parents were killed in a car wreck."

"And that shames you?" Craig asked, noticing how emotion darkened Stanley's sky blue eyes.

Stan shook his head in quick denial. "My father may have been illegitimate but I'm not," he said then flushed, wondering if that sounded as dumb to Craig's ears as it did to his own. How much difference would it make whether or not he was the legitimate son of an illegitimate son? Raking his fingers through his hair in an agitated gesture, he continued.

"Shame me? Maybe a little. Infuriates me more than anything else. My grandmother was the kindest, most compassionate woman alive. Her father was a hardhearted old goat." He snorted. "And mine wasn't much different."

Craig felt a momentary pang of unease. "And who was your grandfather, Stanley?"

Stan smiled, knowing where the question came from and why. "It wasn't whom you're thinking," he assured Craig.

"Oh, everyone assumed it was your father, but it wasn't. My grandfather's name was Arthur Stanley. He was a traveling salesman, a *married* traveling salesman. He sold everything from insurance to encyclopedias. And promises. Empty, broken promises. My grandmother forgave him for his deception, but never forgot the pain. Nor did she ever completely get over the shame of having a child out of wedlock for a man married to someone else. Especially when my father turned out to be nothing more than a self-centered fool. She loved him beyond reason but no matter what she tried, he was selfish and self-centered, thinking of what he wanted, the world be damned. 'Stanley,' she used to say. 'God's given me a second chance with you. You'll turn out just fine.'"

Stan struggled with his emotions, letting the words soothe him now as they had back then, easing the pain and frustration of his status of birth, determined it wouldn't affect his status in life. "She always believed in me and before she died she told me to come back here and claim my heritage. 'You deserve it as your father never did,' she said. I won't let her down. I'll live up to all that she wanted for my father and me."

Craig couldn't temper the flood of relief, and having been in Stanley's shoes, the admiration. He struggled inwardly. He didn't want to like the boy and he certainly didn't want to admire him! But he did. Added to basic affection, it totaled confused understanding. "So, what exactly do you plan to do?"

"I'm going to claim my inheritance. In fact, I've already begun that task. I'll build it into something good."

A thought tugged at Craig's mind. It made sense now, perfect sense. And it would give him the ultimate reason to bar the boy from their lives. Oddly, he hoped he was wrong. "I guess marrying Amber would be a real asset to your plans."

Stan couldn't control his reaction this time. Anger fueled by hurt erupted in him like a time bomb. He spit out a curse and faced off with Craig. Head high his chin jerked up a notch while his hands clenched into tight fists by his side. "I should have expected that from the likes of you, and I ought to belt you for it!"

Craig waited, hoping he hadn't underestimated the boy. Hoping Stanley wasn't that stupid.

Stan knew he couldn't take a swing at Craig. No matter how tempting it was. The one thing his grandmother had taught him and taught him well was respect for his elders, and respect for other's opinions. Even if they were wrong, as in this case, dead wrong. His chin jerked up another notch.

"My grandfather sold insurance. My grandmother may have lost faith in him but she firmly believed in having it. I have money. Maybe not near as much as you," he sneered. "Or Amber for that matter, and maybe not enough to do what I want, but definitely enough to get me started. I'll work for the rest," he hissed.

Feeling an absurd amount of pride in the boy, Craig raised his hands in defeat. "I believe you," his voice was soft, sincere. "And I apologize if I've insulted you. But, understand, Stanley, I had to know."

Stan accepted that with a curt nod of his head. His stance relaxed, but his fists stayed clenched and eyes continued to flash.

"How exactly, do you plan on building something out of that run down piece of property?" Craig asked. "It's not a very big ranch if I remember correctly."

"It's not," Stanley admitted. "But it's big enough for what I want to do. I'll raise horses. Not many, but well bred, well trained, high-quality horses. Quarter, Thoroughbred, Walkers, and Arabians; horses for speed, strength, show and beauty." His eyes widened at Craig's quick shout of laughter.

"Horses? No wonder Temper adores you," Craig said with a chuckle.

Anger abated. Stan's reply was a wry grin. "We've had some pretty interesting conversations on the issue. Why do you call her that?"

"Temper? It's been her nickname since she was a child. She has one, too. Don't ever let her fool you. So does Amber," he felt compelled to warn.

"I've seen that."

Craig shook his head in quick denial. "What you've seen is an indication of a passionate nature. Anger is entirely different, especially when it's aimed at you. Those eyes are like jeweled daggers of ice and they'll rip you to shreds."

Stan smiled again. "I'll try and remember that. Look, Mr. Harris, I know it doesn't seem like much more than empty words and big dreams. Especially considering where I come from. But I do love Amber and I'll do my best by her."

Craig heaved a sigh, raked his fingers through his hair and shook his head, unable to fathom the boy's feelings could be that deep or true. Stanley's unwavering gaze had him doubting himself and at a loss for words, but Craig knew he had to say something.

"Well, it's a good thing I learned a long time ago to judge a man by his character and not by his family's skeletons."

Elation swept through Stan. It was more of an acceptance than he'd hoped for.

Craig sighed again. "All right, Stanley, where do we go from here? I still think you're both too young to be this serious. Amber's barely seventeen and you're only twenty. I've never met a twenty much less a seventeen-year-old who had a firm grip on what they wanted out of life and how to get it. Besides, as I've already mentioned, Amber still has a year of high school, then college."

Overwhelmed with relief, Stan dared to tease. "And as I've already mentioned, I haven't asked her to marry me, yet. But since you've decided I'm not such a bad guy after all, I'd like to take her out for supper."

Unable to do otherwise, Craig laughed. "You really are an arrogant little brat, aren't you?"

"From what I hear, I guess you would know."

Craig shook his head with a chuckle. "Touché. Okay," he resigned. "I'm trusting you with one of my most precious possessions, Stanley. Damage it and you'll answer to me."

Stan read between the lines, knew he'd been justly warned, and considered himself the luckiest man on earth. He extended his hand to Craig. Man to man. "Yes, Sir."

Craig sighed. "I'll probably regret this the rest of my life," he muttered. Accepting Stan's hand he eyed him with a meaningful, pointed look. "I'll be keeping my eye on you, Boy," he warned.

"Wouldn't expect less of you, Sir, wouldn't expect less."

Amber sighed with relief when the two men walked around the barn. "Well, no one's bleeding or bruised," she remarked, relief evident in her tone. "In fact, they're smiling."

"Sit down, Amber."

"Right, don't want them to think I was worried."

"Don't want Stanley to think you had no faith in him," her mother corrected.

"Stanley's not the one I was worried about."

"And that's even worse. Your father loves you, Amber," Tamera chided. "He only wants what's best for you."

Amber frowned. "I know, Mama. I know. And I'll try and keep that in mind whenever I feel like strangling him."

Tamera laughed and put the coffee on to warm. "You do that," she remarked, as the two men walked in.

Craig hunkered down beside his daughter. "Now, let me get a better look at that rock."

"Daddy," she chided, extending her hand for him to see the ring. "It's not a rock. It's not even a diamond." She kissed his cheek and risked a wink at Stan. "Yet."

"Better be a long time before it becomes a diamond. If ever," Craig remarked with a warning look at Stan.

Stan chuckled. "Don't start planning the wedding just yet," he teased, enjoying the color which rose to Amber's cheeks, as she lowered her eyes demurely.

Later that evening they sat on the porch swing. Stan had taken her out to eat and to a movie. He glanced toward the door knowing without a doubt Craig was waiting for Amber to come in. They'd been back for nearly an hour, yet he was reluctant to leave her. Raising her hand to his lips, he smiled. "Guess I'd better get going. You, My Sweet, look a little tired."

Tugging at their hands, she rubbed his against her cheek. "I am," she admitted. "But I don't want you to leave yet."

He pulled her against him with a laugh.

"Did you and Daddy have a good talk this afternoon?" Though curious, she hadn't asked earlier.

Stan grinned. "You're just dying to know what we said, aren't you?" He felt her blush even as she shook her head in denial.

"I'm just curious to know what he said when you told him about the kiss."

"What kiss?"

"You know, the one all lips and teeth and tongue." She heard his sharp intake of breath and felt him tremble as his arms tightened around her automatically.

"I was wise enough not to share that tidbit of information with him. Especially since it didn't, and isn't going to happen."

The most delightful of visions had teased her imagination ever since he'd mentioned the kiss. "You know, it's pretty mean of you to say something like that and not follow through," she remarked, a definite pout in her voice.

He grinned, pressing a tiny kiss on her forehead. "And it's not nice of you to tempt me to do so." He rose, pulling her up with him. "Walk me to the truck. It's time for me to leave."

Amber turned so that she blocked his way into the truck. "Just once," she whispered, pulling his head toward hers.

Desire, ever ready, sprang to life. "Once would never be enough," Stanley muttered burying his lips on hers.

Taking control, he softened the kiss to a mild version of what she asked for. Of what he wanted. Swallowing her soft whimper of frustration he grinned against her mouth as she pressed more firmly against him.

"What was that?" she demanded unable to disguise the dissatisfaction she felt.

He chuckled. "Good night, Amber," he whispered moving her gently out of his way. "I'll call you tomorrow."

She rolled her eyes. "I never dreamed you were all talk and no action," she challenged.

He laughed, determined not to give in to her baiting. "Tease."

"Chicken."

"Witch."

"Jerk," she accused desperately wanting him to kiss her that way and yet, surprisingly glad he refused.

He kissed her again, lightly. "Night, Sweetheart." He started the truck but waited until the front door closed behind her before leaving.

Once parked at the gate of the old Morrison homestead, Stan let loose the torrent of emotions which had roiled in his soul that day. Anger, desire, need, hope, acceptance, relief—feelings raced through him, tumbling one into the other, battering him like a thousand tiny tornadoes until all that remained was an overwhelming joy and unsurpassed peace.

Kneeling in the dirt of the land which would one day be his, he thanked God, wishing only one thing was different: That his grandmother was there with him.

"Oh, Grammy," he whispered. "I can still hear you warning me to watch out for those blasted Harrises." He chuckled. "The man I know isn't like the one you knew. And he's got the most beautiful daughter."

He took a deep breath letting a handful of dirt slide between his fingers. "She reminds me of you," he admitted.

Feeling her love so deep and so alive in his heart, Stan knew his grandmother was, and always would be, with him.

Chapter Eight

After their vacation the rest of summer seemed to fly by. Before Amber or Ace was ready, the time for them to return to school had arrived. Once adjusted to the idea of going back to class, excitement overwhelmed Ace at the thought of entering the third grade. No one was more surprised than Craig when Tamera handed the car keys to Amber the first day of school.

"You're not bringing them?" he asked.

Tamera shook her head. The Lord had been dealing with her as much, if not more than her husband on letting go. Still, tears stung her eyes and clogged her throat.

Craig walked with her to the door to wave goodbye and to watch them leave. Once the car was out of site, he turned her in his arms. "What is it?"

Her smile trembled. She laid her hand against his cheek. "I realized this summer that it's time to start letting go. Besides," she continued, her words muffled against his chest when he pulled her closer. "Amber's schedule is so light I'd be getting home just in time to turn around and head back to pick her up." As a senior, Amber went to class only a couple of hours in the morning.

"Ride with me today," Craig urged, brushing his lips across hers. "I know the perfect place to play hooky," he added, his mouth curving into a grin, a seductive gleam lighting his smoky eyes.

Tamera couldn't help but smile, a shiver of anticipation dancing along every nerve ending in her body. "Well, looks like the kitchen floors will have to wait another day to get stripped and waxed," she purred, much to her husband's delight.

Amber had wondered how her mother would handle school this year since her classes only took up three hours of the day and was relieved when Tamera gave her the keys with no fuss. Taking Ace to his class, she made sure he didn't forget anything then drove on to the high school building. As soon as her classes were over she talked with her guidance counselor to see if there was anything she could do to improve her credentials for college. Finding that she wanted a job working with children possibly as a teacher, the counselor suggested she volunteer as an aide for lower-grade instructors. Without the slightest doubt of her parents' approval, she set things up. Three days a week she would work on special projects, tutor struggling students, or share story time with Ace's third grade class. On the days she didn't need to be there, she would spend the afternoon at the library, shopping or whenever possible, at the Bar S with Stanley.

Though she and Stan were seldom alone, the relationship between them held all the promise and hope of young love.

* * * * *

Amber left school with a sigh of relief that she didn't need to be at the elementary education building, positive she wouldn't be able to concentrate anyway. Today was the day Stan would get a final answer on his inheritance, if the case wasn't postponed again.

What Stanley thought and she assumed would be an easy task, was proving to be not only difficult but complicated and expensive. Stan was forced to hire an attorney to file succession on his grandfather's estate and instructed to run an ad in every newspaper within a one hundred mile radius announcing his intentions of claiming the property. Once the ninety-day ad campaign was over, he then presented the courts with the evidence he had to support his claim. He had birth and death certificates, letters his grandmother had saved from her father and affidavits that he was an only child as well as the only living relative of the late John D. Morrison. The judge postponed the case for an additional ninety days to allow any long-lost relatives the opportunity to stake their claim to the property. So far no one had shown up and today was to be the final decision of the court based on Stanley's evidence.

Amber opted to go home, hoping while there she could find something to occupy her thoughts until she heard from him. She drove up to the house, surprised at the quietness surrounding it and within. Walking slowly up the stairs, she stopped herself from calling out. Peeking in their room, she was surprised but unconcerned at finding her parents curled up in each other's arms, sleeping in the middle of the day.

Remembering the remark her mother made while on vacation about nurturing, she smiled to herself, and felt a little tug at her heart as she imagined a future when she could enjoy an intimate morning with her husband. *With Stanley.* Careful to be quiet, she closed the door behind her, and went into her own room. Sitting at her desk, she booted up the computer and poured out her feelings in the form of a story. Fueled by the feelings and dreams in her heart and a vivid imagination, she picked up the romance novel she started writing before the summer began and flowed with it well into the afternoon.

Craig awoke with a start. Listening to the stillness he wondered what had awakened him. Somewhere in the quiet of his mind he heard the sounds of activity. Careful not to disturb his wife, he slid from the bed and into a pair of jeans. Passing his daughter's room, he glanced in, surprised to find her already home.

"Amber? Is something wrong?"

She looked up, her eyes glazed with concentration, bright with excitement. A look he'd grown used to seeing whenever he interrupted her work. It took a moment for her to focus on what he said.

"No. I couldn't concentrate at school so I decided to come home. Has Stan called?"

"No. Why?"

She sighed. "He should have an answer about the property today. I can't wait to hear from him."

"That's no reason to skip class, Amber," he chided.

She laughed. "I didn't skip class, Daddy. I just skipped extracurricular activities. And you're a fine one to lecture. Who played hooky from work to spend the day in bed?"

He snorted and threw a pillow at her. "Watch your mouth," he warned to which she merely giggled.

Going back to his room, Craig kissed Tamera awake. One of them would have to go into town and pick up Ace. He opted to do so, taking advantage of the opportunity to spend some quality time with his son. They'd been home a few minutes when Stanley drove up. Amber bounded down the stairs and flung open the door before he could knock.

"Where've you been? I've been waiting all afternoon to hear from you."

"I was waiting for you to get home from school."

"I came home early today. I passed by the Bar S and you weren't there. Well?"

He grinned. "Well," he hesitated just a moment to tease as the family gathered around to hear his response. "It's mine!" He picked her up, swung her around. "All mine! Legally mine, down to the last spoonful of dirt."

"All right, let's celebrate!" Amber said. Though his face fell, Stan's eyes still shone with excitement.

"We can't celebrate, I'm almost broke."

She laughed. "Well, I'm not. I got my allowance. Root beer floats for everyone!" she exclaimed before he could protest.

Stan swung her around in his arms again as everyone joined in the laughter and congratulated him. "I can handle that. Want to take a ride and look at it?"

"Let's all go," Craig suggested. "Then we'll let Amber buy those root-beer floats."

Loading up in the Suburban they drove out to the old homestead which had once belonged to Stan's great-grandfather and now belonged to him. His hands shaking with excitement, Stanley fumbled with the huge padlock on the gate. Pushing it open as far as the weeds and rust would allow they walked through the gate and toward the house, which was run down and badly in need of repair, but still standing. There were huge windows; some broken from age or vandals and the door was locked. Again shaking with excitement, he fumbled with the keys until it opened with an obstinate groan. They walked through the house, surprised at the sturdiness, despite its state of disrepair.

Humbled, Stan stood in the small foyer. The house wasn't large, two bedrooms, one bath, a living room, dining room and kitchen, but it was solid. And it was his. Pride of ownership enriched his voice when he spoke. "I guess the first thing to do is give it a good cleaning and then see what repairs need to be done."

"The first thing you need to do is get a tractor in here and clean up this yard," Craig suggested. "That way you don't have to worry about snakes and things while you work."

Stan nodded. "You're right."

"When will you get started?" Amber wanted to know.

He shrugged. "I'm not sure yet. I need to speak with Mr. Strickland about rearranging my schedule so I can keep my job while getting this place in order."

"I can come after school and do the cleaning."

Stan shook his head. "Oh, no." He stopped her protests with a finger on her lips. "I know you want to help, Sweetheart, but I don't want you here alone. It might not be safe for a while yet."

"He's right, Amber. Neither do I." Craig insisted, surprised and pleased that Stan put her safety above everything else.

She rolled her eyes when Stanley grinned. "Men!" she huffed.

Craig turned back to Stanley. "You talk with Mr. Strickland, I'll round up some men and a couple of tractors and we'll see about getting this yard cleaned up."

Stan shook his head. "I can't afford men and tractors yet. I'll work something out."

"Who said anything about paying for them?" Craig wanted to know. "It's called being neighborly, Stanley. We always pitch in when someone is in need. It's something you better get used to if you want to make it in this county. I had to learn the hard way. Don't make the same mistake," he urged.

Everyone waited in silence while Stan considered Craig's words and smiled in unison when he nodded.

"Okay."

Craig chuckled and placed a good-natured slap on Stan's back. "Good. Now, I believe Amber promised us refreshments to celebrate."

Set for the following Saturday, the turnout of neighbors was magnificent. The Harrises and Stricklands were the first to arrive. Men appeared with tractors, lawn mowers and tools. Women brought mops, brooms and buckets of cleaning supplies. Some of the old timers brought barbeque pits or gas grills to cook. There was pork, beef, and chicken. Others brought covered dishes to go with the meat. Fifty-gallon barrels hauled water for cleaning and drinking. There was tons of food, gallons of sun-brewed tea and coolers of beer. Some said it reminded them of the old days when everyone got together for a barn raising or a roundup.

Anytime a large group of people fellowship in the light of community, there is usually one who attempts to stir up a little discord. This time, a young man not much older than Stanley, turned out to be the culprit. The men were gathered around tractors discussing what needed to be done and where to start when he turned to Stanley. "Do you even know how to operate a tractor?"

Stan's chin jerked up, eyes narrowed. "No, I'm a horseman, not a dairy farmer," he sneered.

Craig stepped forward hoping to thwart the confrontation brewing. "All right, we're here to help out, not tear each other down," he said, placing a hand on Stan's shoulder.

"That's right," Roy Strickland added, standing shoulder-to-shoulder with them. "And you, Hotshot, can follow me as soon as Stanley lets us know where he wants us," he insisted, putting an end to the unpleasantness and snuffing out the possibility of another flare-up.

"Whenever you're ready, Son," he told Stan. "Just say the word and we'll get started."

Stan looked around at all of the expectant faces and wondered what on earth he'd gotten himself into. His panicked gaze sought Craig's.

The instant their eyes met, Craig's heart went out to Stanley. It was evident the boy had no real concept of family or community. "I think we should start with a prayer," he suggested, his tone soft, reassuring.

Stan nodded. "Me too," he agreed in a shaky voice.

Craig whistled to get everyone's attention. "Let's all gather 'round, folks, it's time to get this show on the road."

Everyone gathered in close proximity. Stan cleared his throat, closed his eyes and thanked God aloud for the turn out of friends and neighbors then prayed for the safety of everyone present. Feeling stronger and more in control he directed his new neighbors.

"Well, as you can tell, the entire property needs an overhaul so anything and everything we do will make a huge difference. And make my work a lot easier from now on. If we can get the immediate area surrounding the house cleaned up, then the pits and grills can be set up for cooking. You guys with tractors can head out in every direction. From what I can understand the entire forty acres is fenced off. Now what shape the fence is in, I have no idea. But if we can get the grass and weeds down and fence up, that'll be a big help. Ladies, if you will get this house cleaned up as much as possible then I'll be able to see what repairs need to be made."

"What can I do?" Ace wanted to know.

Stanley squatted down with a grin. "You younger folks can help me haul trash and once things are pretty much cleared away, I've got a surprise for you."

Of course his statement brought a burst of excitement, a flurry of questions and a round of laughter as Stanley tried in vain to avoid revealing the inflatable swimming pool he'd bought for the children's pleasure. In less than thirty minutes the area surrounding the house was cleaned up.

Tractors headed out in all directions, followed by men on all-terrain-vehicles carrying barbed wire, wood and pliers for mending fences.

Stan was called upon to force windows open inside the stifling house so the women could work a little more comfortably. Barbeque pits and grills were set up and the pre-prepared food set to cooking. Less than two hours of picking up garbage and the youngsters had worked themselves all out. The pool was inflated, set up and filled to keep them occupied and out of the workers' way.

With the first batch of meat nearly ready, the cook fired a shot into the air to signal those on tractors to head in for lunch. Scattered on the porches and lawn, families sat together and enjoyed the feast laid out before them. Though he wanted nothing more than to curl up with Amber someplace quiet, Stanley felt obligated to mingle with his new neighbors while they ate and rested before heading out again for the afternoon.

After hauling yet another wheelbarrow load of trash out to the pile yet to be burned, Stanley stopped by the swimming pool to splash Ace and get splashed in return–a momentary relief from the heat. Glancing up he saw Lori leaning against the barn, a forlorn expression on her face. He'd noticed that she'd worked less and disappeared more as the day wore on. Concerned something may be wrong, he approached her.

"Hey, Lors, what's up?"

Lori shrugged. She hated being stuck here all day with nothing to do but work.

"Are you alright, is something wrong?" Stan asked.

"Just bored," she answered.

"Bored? How can you be bored with so much to do and so many people around to do it with?" His attempt at teasing went unheeded.

Lori snorted. "Exactly. Saturdays are supposed to be for fun and I'm stuck here with a bunch of old hags, old men and young brats with nothing to do."

Stanley saw right through her and stifled a spurt of irritation. Used to being the center of attention, Lori was at wits end on how to fit in as just another one of the girls. "Well, I for one think this is a wonderful thing, Lori. People getting together to help someone is the real definition of community." This statement roused not only another snort out of her but a roll of the eyes as well. Stanley shook his head.

"One day you'll appreciate where you come from, Lori, and the fact there are so many around willing to help out when you're in a pinch." Before he could turn away, she reached for his arm.

"Let's take a walk or something, Stanley. Please," she urged, lifting wide, pleading eyes to his.

"All these people turned out to help me. Do you really expect me to shirk my responsibilities and go play, Lori?"

She pouted. "Just for a few minutes," she pleaded. "No one will probably even miss us."

"I've already spent a few minutes out here with you, a few too many in fact."

She pushed him away, an angry flush filling her cheeks. "Go on back then and leave me alone."

"I plan on it," Stanley assured. "Time for you to grow up, little girl," he added, turning on his heel.

"Watch yourself, Stanley," she hissed. "You still work for my father."

Stanley spun around at the threat and glared at her. "Is that supposed to scare me, Lori?"

Lori shrugged, not the least intimidated by his flashing eyes, clenched jaw and incredulous expression. Before she could answer, Amber walked up.

"Is everything okay?" Amber asked. She'd seen them talking from a window in the back bedroom where she'd been working and thought she'd join them. Exiting through the back door of the house, she hurried toward them when Stanley spun around at something Lori said.

"This is a private conversation," Lori sneered in answer.

Amber arched an eyebrow at Stanley.

"Nothing private about it, the conversation is over," he assured. Taking Amber by the hand he walked away leaving Lori sputtering behind them.

"What was that all about?" Amber asked. "Or is it any of my business?"

Stan shrugged, still seething at the audacity of Lori to threaten him with his job just because he didn't comply to her every whim. "Just Lori being Lori," he told Amber. Turning her in his arms, he brushed his lips across hers in a feathery gesture. "Thanks for coming to my rescue before I said something I shouldn't have or took her over my knee like her father should've done years ago, and regularly since the day she entered this world."

Amber stroked a soothing hand over his cheek, smoothing away the frown on his face. "My pleasure," she assured with a smile.

Soft and warm, her eyes turned a smoky, midnight blue and tempted him to shirk his responsibilities and go play. Stanley grinned and shook his head at the fanciful thought. "Don't look at me like that or I'll be in trouble with *your* father," he teased.

Amber laughed, kissed his cheek and went back to cleaning.

The day was nearly spent, before the place was deemed presentable. Though not yet livable, the house had been cleaned from top to bottom, inside and out. Photos, papers and books were put in large boxes for Stan to go through when he had the time. Appliances were scrubbed, as were ceilings, walls, floors and windows. Furniture which could be recovered, refinished or restored was saved. The rest was burned. Old mattresses, bedding and most of the old dishes were tossed into the fire also. The land surrounding the house was cleared and fences throughout the property were checked and mended as best as they could be.

Once the work was done, the partying began. Stan willingly played his guitar and sang while one of his new friends used the porch rail as a makeshift drum. Tired but happy, husbands danced with their wives and daughters until the sun began to set and night creatures started to rise. Bidding welcome and warm good-byes, people left in small batches and went to their respective homes.

Amber danced with her father for the last song of the evening. "Everyone's just about gone," she murmured.

"Yeah, it's about time for us to head out too," Craig said. He couldn't remember the last time he'd worked so hard nor had so much fun.

"Can I stay a little while longer?"

Craig hesitated in answering. All day he'd taken the ribbing from his colleagues about his "future son-in-law" in stride. Though he liked Stan, he wasn't prepared to consider leaving his daughter here, alone, with the man claiming to be in love with her.

"I don't think so, Amber, it's late."

Amber felt her father stiffen at her question, heard the tension in his answer. "I know it's late, Daddy, but I'm sure Stanley won't mind bringing me home. Please, we haven't had five minutes alone today. Don't you trust me?" she asked, before he could formulate a response.

Craig huffed out a sigh and continued to hold his daughter even though the song had ended. "Yes I trust you, and I'm learning to trust Stanley. But I don't like the idea of you two being alone out here, especially at night. You can never tell what might happen and there's no phone or anything. Everybody's tired and I don't feel like arguing," he added, cutting off her protests with a sharp look.

The disappointment on her face and in those eyes he loved so much tugged at his heart. Craig kissed her on the forehead. "Tell you what, though, I'll round up your mother and Ace and we'll wait in the truck for you. How's that for an offer you can't refuse?" he asked, his tone tender and teasing.

Amber smiled up at him, his offer less than she'd hoped for but more than she expected after the hard look he'd given her. Besides, the truck was parked well out of sight from the front porch. "I don't want to argue either, Daddy, so I'll accept your offer. And I thank you," she added, reaching up to kiss his cheek. Arm-in-arm they walked to the porch.

Stan put down his guitar and stood up when Amber and her father approached, extending a hand toward Craig. "Thank you so much, for coming. Don't know what I'd have done without you all here."

"Had a great turnout, got a lot accomplished," Craig said, shaking the proffered hand. Reaching down, he picked up Ace who was half-asleep on the porch and motioned Tamera with his head.

"Guess we'll see you tomorrow," Tamera said, hugging Stanley.

Stan brushed his lips over her cheek. "Probably, at some point in time tomorrow."

"Why don't you plan on having supper with us," she invited.

He grinned. "Love to, thanks."

Linking her arm with Craig's, she glanced at her daughter. "C'mon, Sweetheart, let's go."

"We'll wait for her in the truck," Craig said to his wife, then turned to his daughter. "Five minutes, Amber."

For the first time in his life, Stan felt like he belonged, really belonged, to a place, to a community, something he was sure his grandmother never felt or great-grandfather ever wanted. All day he'd heard stories and legends of his family, some delighted him, some saddened, but all were welcome snatches of insight into his heritage. Considering society at the time of his situation, most people sympathized with his great-grandfather. Many felt they would do things a little different though, especially in these enlightened times. But all of them felt sorry for the old man whose pride got in the way of knowing his grandson and great-grandson. Overwhelmed, he gazed down at Amber wanting to take her in his arms, yet unwilling to test her father's patience. Running his hands down her arms to clasp hers, he lifted them to his mouth in a tender caress.

"I don't know how I'll ever thank everyone."

Her smile was tender as was the light in her eyes. "I'm sure the day will come when your help will be needed. It's then and only then, you can repay in kind. What's the next step?"

He shrugged. "I don't know. There's the wiring and repairs and painting. I need to get the well and sewer system checked." He paused, overwhelmed at the work still ahead.

Laying her hand on his cheek, Amber smiled into his eyes. "You'll do it. We'll do it," she promised. "It'll be magnificent."

He chuckled. "You are so good for my ego. Thank you," he whispered, cupping her cheeks in his palms. "There's nothing I can't do as long as you're on my side."

Brushing his lips across hers, he pulled her against him in a brief hug then walked with her to the truck. After they left, he closed up the house and drove to the Bar S.

Weeks passed and the days grew shorter. Stan found himself with less and less time to work on his property. Mr. Strickland understood his need and gave him the weekends off. He used them wisely, even though the loss of time cut a hole in his paycheck.

Between court costs, filing and legal fees, property taxes and inheritance taxes, his limited resources ground down to a bare minimum. The house had to be totally rewired as well as re-plumbed and he needed a whole new sewer system, but the well, after minor repairs, was primed and running. That, at least, gave him water to work with. Careful use of industrial extension cords gave him some light, enabling him to work late into the evening. But it wasn't enough.

What he needed was money and that was slow in the making. Every dollar from his paycheck was gone before he earned it. Stanley found himself aggravated with the slow process and discouraged clear down to his weary bones. While repairing some shelves in the living room, the ladder wobbled. Stan grabbed the shelf for support, slashing his hand on a nail. Amber heard his bitter curse and came running.

"What happened?"

He groaned, sliding weakly down the ladder. "I cut my hand."

She reached for his hand. "Let me see," she urged. Jerking the rag out of her back pocket, she wiped away some of the blood, concerned by the amount of it. The cut was deep and jagged and beyond her abilities. "Oh, my God, Stan, it's bad. You'll probably need stitches. Come on. I'll take you to the hospital."

He shook his head. "Just get the first aid kit out of my truck," he ordered between clenched teeth.

"Nonsense!" she argued, wrapping his hand securely with the rag. "Unless you have sutures in your first aid kit and know how to stitch it up we'd better get going."

"Stop it, Amber. I'm not going to the hospital."

"But...

"But, nothing," he hissed. "I can't afford to. This place has cost me every penny I've ever saved and then some," he confessed.

Amber heard the frustration in his voice and sighed. "Okay then, let's go to my house. Mama will know what to do."

"What can she do that can't be done using my first aid kit?"

Amber shrugged, feeling an overwhelming sense of inadequacy. "I don't know."

Stanley ground his teeth. "Just get the kit and let's see if we can fix it."

Closing her eyes for a moment Amber took a deep breath and prayed for calm. "Okay, but sit down. You're losing a lot of blood." Pulling the rag out of his pocket, she replaced her blood soaked one and helped him lower himself to the floor then retrieved the first aid kit from his truck.

Returning to his side, she opened the box and rummaged through the assortment of alcohol swabs and medicine samples. Un-wrapping his hand, she tried to clean the wound while attempting to stem the flow of blood. "God, Stan, I sure can't close this cut up enough with this junk for it to heal properly. Heck, I can't even clean it well. I really think you need stitches." She tossed the box aside and stood up. "C'mon, we're going to the hospital."

Stan jerked away and rose shakily to his feet, leaning against the wall for support. "I already told you, I can't afford to go to the hospital!"

"Well, if you won't go to the hospital, then we're going to my house. Mama or Daddy will know what to do."

"Don't you dare," he growled. "I did not confide in you so you can go running to your father about it. I don't need his money!" he insisted. "Nor your charity."

She glared at him, shocked he would consider her offer of help, charity. "I wasn't going to ask him for money, I was going to ask for advice. But I can see you're too proud for that," she seethed, turning on her heel.

He grabbed her arm, swung her around to face him. "Don't you dare walk away until this is settled, Amber."

Her chin lifted in defiance, eyes narrowed into sparkling slits. She jerked free of his grasp. "What's left to discuss?" she challenged. "Besides, what would you do if I dared to walk away, Stanley? We both know you're all talk and no action."

The taunt was the overload to his emotions. Torn between the desire to shake or kiss, Stan jerked her against him, crushing her lips in a bruising kiss.

Hurt and angry, she stiffened in his arms. His body, hard and unyielding, held her trapped against the firm wall of his chest. His mouth clamped onto hers. His lips demanded a response as the kiss deepened. Amber struggled against the onslaught of emotion rushing through her system as hurt and anger gave way to something else, something deeper and more primitive.

With a soft whimper she wrapped her arms around his neck, her passion igniting, and rising to meet his. Her body swayed in unconscious surrender, melting into his. The moment her mouth slackened, welcoming the possessive weight of his, everything changed. His embrace softened, arms cradled. His teeth nibbled at her lips, tongue teased and tasted. Emotion burst to life within her and swarmed through Amber until it overflowed, warm and wet down her cheeks.

Stan tasted her tears and groaned. Loosening his hold he broke the kiss, burying his face against her shoulder. "God," he mumbled, lifting his head to meet her gaze. "I'm sorry."

She looked at him wide-eyed and trembling. Anger, desire, and wonder warred in her eyes. She rolled them in an exaggerated gesture.

"Now, he apologizes," she muttered then leveled her gaze on him. "Why haven't you kissed me like that before?"

His breath heaved while he struggled for control. "Didn't think it was proper, still don't."

"So that's what you meant by all lips and teeth and tongue?" she asked, her voice quivering with awe.

He stepped back, touching her cheek with his uninjured hand. "Yes." His voice was raw, eyes fierce. "But not with anger. Never with anger. I'm sorry."

Grabbing his hand, she pressed a kiss into it. "Show me," she urged her eyes soft and warm. "Kiss me again, Stanley."

"No, Amber." But she was pressing against him, her arms sliding around his neck. Senses dulled by fatigue, resistance clouded by pain, control ravished and weakened by desire, Stanley succumbed with a groan. Hauling her gently but firmly against him, he buried his lips on hers, this time with devastating tenderness.

His mouth embraced hers tasting, teasing, savoring her lips as though he were a starving man biting into his first meal in weeks. His teeth nipped at her lip, tugging a moan from deep within her. Amber clung to him weakly as they slid to the floor.

Aware of only the need to touch, to taste, he tugged at the buttons of her shirt while his lips continued their exploration of her mouth. His hand throbbed with the movement, seeping fresh blood. Muttering a curse he pushed away commanding control to his raging senses.

They heard the sound of a vehicle in the drive, doors opening and closing and scrambled to their feet.

Stan leaned against the wall, heat pouring through him. His heart pounded and head throbbed. Blood dripped from his wound. Taking deep, calming breaths he inwardly cursed his loss of control while praying that Amber's parents didn't notice his state of being or her flushed cheeks, rumpled clothing and kiss-swollen lips.

Amber's hands trembled when she straightened her clothes and smoothed her hair. Never in her life had she been moved by anything as she had by that kiss. One look at Stanley's taut features and she knew they were in trouble. His face was flushed, his fists clenched, and breathing labored. She could almost see his heart pounding against his shirt and instinctively knew they'd crossed the line to a level of intimacy he hadn't intended to venture.

With tears in her eyes and a soft, trembling smile she whispered gentle, calming words, and reached for his injured hand, shielding him from close scrutiny as her parents walked up on the porch then entered the house. Once in control of her spinning senses and assured Stanley was in control of his, she called out her father's name to give heed to their location.

"Hey you guys!" Craig greeted, when they walked into the room. "We figured you two could use a break and thought we'd all go grab a bite to eat." He stopped, paling at the sight of blood on Amber's clothes. "Amber! Good God, what happened?"

"It's not me, Daddy," she exclaimed, holding Stan's hand against her while applying pressure to the bandage. "Stan cut his hand."

"Let me see." Tamera grabbed Stan's hand and unwrapped it, examining the cut. "You need stitches."

Amber avoided Stan's eyes. "Stan's a little low on funds. He's worried about the doctor bills."

"Amber!"

His eyes flashed in protest. Ignoring the anger and pain in them, Amber gazed up at her father. "He cut it on a rusty nail," her voice trembled. "I have my credit card."

Instinctively Craig knew she was trying to salvage Stan's pride. He nodded in understanding. "Not a problem," he assured. "We'll let you pay the bills," he informed Stan, his glare daring the boy to argue.

"Do I have a choice?" Stanley muttered then turned back to Tamera. "You're a veterinarian. Can't you just stitch it up?"

"What about a tetanus shot?"

"I'll take my chances. I don't think it's been too long since I had my last one."

"No!" Amber protested. Fear made her voice tremble. She turned a worried gaze back to her father.

"You're outnumbered," Craig insisted, giving his daughter a reassuring hug. "Don't trade your life for a few shreds of pride, Stanley. It's not worth it."

Stan ground his teeth in frustration. "You are the most hardheaded bunch of people I've ever met in my life."

"Well you should feel right at home then," Amber hissed through clenched teeth, swallowing hard the lump of fear lodged in her throat. "Please go," she pleaded.

Her eyes, wide and dark with worry, shone with devastation and tears.

"Amber," he shook his head. "Don't look at me like that." He groaned. "How am I supposed to say no?" he asked Craig, trying hard not to crumble.

Craig shrugged. "Start now, building a wall of defense against it." His gaze cut to Tamera who snickered. "Because I've never been able to," he admitted with a chuckle.

"Give me your keys, I'll drive. Amber, you and Mama lock up. Go home and change then meet us at Harry's for supper." He put his hand on Stan's shoulder and led him out, leaving Amber and Tamera to do his bidding.

Tamera watched the men leave then turned to her daughter. "Are you all right?"

Amber looked down at the bloodstains on her clothing and felt the color drain from her face. Passing a trembling hand over her blouse, she swallowed the lump in her throat. "I'm not hurt if that's what you're asking," she admitted, raising a tearful gaze to her mother.

Tamera enfolded her daughter in her arms. "It's not cut that bad, Honey. He'll be fine."

"I know, but how long will he be angry with me for saying anything?" Her mother smiled and hugged her tighter.

"I'm sure he'll get over that just as quickly as he'll heal from this cut," Tamera answered, brushing the hair off her daughter's face.

"I sure hope so, Mama. I've never seen Stanley so upset."

Tamera cocked her head, concerned at the tone of her daughter's voice. "How upset, Amber, did he hurt you in any way?"

Amber shook her head in quick denial. Heat filled her cheeks. "Oh, no, Stanley would never hurt me, not like you're thinking and I didn't mean it to sound that way," she assured, her mind replaying every moment of the incident.

"He's just so frustrated over money and he refused to go to the hospital. I couldn't make him see reason." Blinking back tears she took a few steps then bent down and picked up the first aide kit. "I tried to fix his hand using this but I couldn't. I've never felt so helpless," she admitted, her breath hitching on a sob.

Once again Tamera enfolded her daughter in her embrace. She could just about imagine the scene that had unfolded. "This may be the first time you two have butted heads over an issue, Sweetheart, but I can promise you it won't be the last. Life is full of little challenges, things which will test your relationship and try your patience to the limit. You'll just have to learn to work through them. Remember what the Bible says...*'many are the trials of the righteous man, but God will deliver him out of them all.'* You and Stanley will be just fine."

Relief poured through her. Amber hugged her mother. "Thanks, Mama," she whispered. "We'd better get going."

Tamera chuckled. "Yeah, cause if they beat us to Harry's, we'll all be butting heads."

Amber rolled her eyes then grinned. "Men," she remarked. Within a few minutes they'd closed up the house and were on their way home so Amber could change clothes before heading over to Harry's Diner.

Chapter Nine

Stan threw the book into the trash so hard it tipped the container over. Taking a deep breath to calm down, he walked over and righted the cardboard box. His hand throbbed from the exertion.

Forced to take time off of work due to his injury only added to the frustrations he already had, making him irritable and not at all nice. When complaining to Amber on the phone again last night, she challenged him to stop feeling sorry for himself and to figure out what he *could* do. Initially ticked off at her lack of understanding, he later realized she had a point and decided to go through the boxes of papers and books the women had put aside during the initial cleaning. The task was proving to be all the activity his hand would allow and more than his strained emotions could handle. Grumbling at that last thought, he sat back down where he'd perched himself before, picking up a photo album, so old and raggedy it nearly came apart in his hands.

Picking through the pages with as much care as possible, his heart ached at the few pictures he found, and rejoiced at the ones he could see well. His grandmother had not been a raving beauty as a young girl, a little on the plump side, and poor. But he knew how beautiful she turned out. She had a heart of gold, a tender one that wanted only one thing: unconditional love. He could imagine how easy it was for his grandfather to take advantage of her, and it angered and hurt him to be reminded of the truth. But, had Arthur Stanley not taken advantage of her need and the desires in her heart, Stan knew he wouldn't be here. Nor would he have been blessed growing up in her love and goodness.

At the bottom of the box Stanley uncovered a family Bible beneath a pile letters sent by his grandmother to her father. He sat a moment just holding the book, dusting the cover with gentle strokes, amazed his great-grandfather had kept it, and the letters. From what he'd heard of John D. Morrison, he never would have imagined the old man keeping letters from a daughter he'd cast out, much less a Bible. His biggest surprise came when he opened the cover to find not only his father's birth recorded there, but his marriage and Stan's birth also. He thumbed through the pages, finding a wealth of scriptures underlined with notations in the margin, words which spoke of pride and pain, disappointment and regret.

Words leapt out at him from the pages of the book and the corners of his mind. Things like *with prayer and supplication let your requests be known to God.* And *with God all things are possible.* As well as, *My God shall supply all your needs....* Things he'd been taught as a child. Expressions of truth and promise his grandmother had lived by and had instilled in him as far back as he could remember.

Closing his eyes, Stanley realized he had started out doing not only what his grandmother wanted, but what he believed was God's will. But, somewhere between the beginning and where he was now, he'd left God out. He'd forgotten His faithfulness by not seeking His direction and wisdom, or asking for His help.

Clutching the book to his chest, Stan asked for forgiveness. He thanked God for his successes so far and asked for His guidance and wisdom in deciding what to do next and how to do it. Opening his eyes he looked around at the other boxes and decided to get as many of them sorted through as he could.

Going through the next one he came across some old papers and things belonging to his great-grandfather. He noticed some faded check stubs from Evans Oil, one of the wealthiest oil companies in Texas. The stubs showed that his great-grandfather had once opted to invest a portion of his pay in profit sharing.

Stanley's hands trembled and heart pounded as he searched through the papers to see if the shares had ever been traded, cashed in, or sold. Excitement curled in the pit of his stomach when he found no evidence that they had. Unless he overlooked it or no record was kept, there were stocks somewhere which belonged to him. From what he guessed, a small fortune in them!

Placing the check stubs in the Bible, he thought about his discovery. His heart pounded, afraid to hope. Yet, somehow, Stan knew this was the answer to his prayer. God was showing him that his needs were and would continue to be met.

"Thank You," he whispered. Peace enveloped his soul, assuring Stanley once again that he was doing God's will. In the silence of his heart, he vowed to never leave Him out of his decisions again.

Hearing his name called, he arose when Lori walked into the room. "Where's Amber?" she asked.

Stan smiled. "Ace's class had a field trip or something so she stayed in town today.

"What are you doing?" she asked, glad to finally have a chance to be near him without Amber hanging around.

"Just going through some boxes," Stan answered. "What about you, everything okay?"

She shrugged and took a step closer. "We haven't seen much of you lately."

"Been busy, Lors."

Placing a hand on his chest she lifted wide, innocent eyes to his. "I know, but I miss you," she said, pursing her lips into a well-practiced pout.

Stanley saw through her ploy to the dark emotions reflected in her eyes. A tender smile tugged at his lips. "Are you sure that's all that's bothering you?"

Again she shrugged.

"C'mon Lori, fess up. You've been fighting with your family again, haven't you?"

She nodded.

"Want to talk about it?"

Lori shook her head, dropped her hand from his chest. "No, I don't want to talk about it. You'll just take their side."

"When have I ever taken sides?" he asked, amazed at how quickly she changed from sweet innocence to spoiled brat.

She frowned, took a step back. "You always agree with them that I'm too young for anything."

Stanley tucked a curl behind her ear. "You're in too big a hurry to grow up Lors, and those who love you don't want to see you get hurt or make some heavy mistakes."

"It's my life isn't it? I should be able to live it as I please and if mistakes are made, well then, they're mine to make," she insisted, hating the gentle, chiding tone he used with her.

Stan shook his head, positive with her attitude, she'd be making plenty. "Well, don't say we didn't warn you. Now, how about I take you home and see how you and Sampson are doing?" She brightened, amazing Stanley again at how swiftly her mood could change.

"Really?"

Stan nodded. "Yeah, not much I can do over here with this bum hand," he remarked, leading her out of the house and helping to put her bicycle in the back of his truck. A companionable silence accompanied them back to the Bar S as each immersed in their own thoughts. Stanley marveled at what he'd discovered.

Lori wondered how she could use the fact that they'd been alone to her benefit.

She despised the way Stanley treated her, like she was his baby sister or young cousin, and not at all like the woman she considered herself to be. Closing her eyes, she dreamed of the day when she could show him who she really was and what she felt for him. Too soon they arrived at the ranch, but not before she'd formulated a plan. Helping him unload her bike, she hurried and saddled Sampson so Stan could see how well trained he was becoming, and how fast on the barrels. Reining the horse to a stop beside him, she leaned down and brushed her lips across his.

Stan stepped back, wiping his mouth with the back of his hand. "What the hell?"

"For luck," she replied, her voice sticky sweet.

"You might be fifteen now, Lori, but you're still too young for anyone beside your father to be kissing you, for any reason."

She laughed and twirled the big gelding around. "That's what you think," she replied, kicking Sampson into a dead run.

Stan watched the display noting the jerky motions of the horse and rider and shook his head with a sigh. No matter how skilled or well-bred the horse, Lori would never be a champion rider, he thought, though he'd bite his tongue off before stating that aloud. No sooner had the thought crossed his mind than Sampson tripped and Lori tumbled from his back. Grabbing the fence with his uninjured hand, Stanley jumped it and raced over to them. Sampson stumbled away from his mistress, favoring his left foreleg. Stanley knelt beside Lori.

"Are you all right?" he asked, giving her a gentle shake. Before he could ask again, she was in his arms, her lips plastered to his.

Stunned into immobility, shock raced through Stanley, then anger. "What do you think you're doing?" he demanded, pushing her away.

"Don't you think I'm pretty, Stanley?" she whimpered, sidling closer.

"Pretty?" he snorted, rolling to his feet and dragging her to hers. "You tripped up your horse to pull a stupid stunt like this and you want to know if I think you're pretty?"

Lori shoved away from him. "It's just a stupid horse," she muttered, turning on her heel. "Who cares anyway?" Stanley whirled her around to face him, his eyes narrow and glittering like the hot blue of a flame.

"I care," he spit out through clenched teeth, his hands curled into fists by his side. "You could have crippled him! And as far as you being pretty, Lori, there's an old saying that pretty is skin deep but ugly is to the bone. I suggest you think about that." With a deliberate swipe of his sleeve across his mouth, he turned away and went to tend to Sampson, thankful to find that his injuries appeared to be minor.

* * * * *

Two weeks later Stan sat talking with Craig while waiting for Amber and her mother to get ready for homecoming festivities.

"Mr. Craig, I need some help. Do you know anyone who knows anything about investments? Stock? Dividends? Someone you trust?"

Craig shrugged. "I know a little. What's up?"

Stan's eyes widened in surprise, "You do?"

Craig laughed at the look on Stanley's face. "A wise man always invests in his future. You never know when you'll need something to fall back on."

Stan grinned. "I guess you're right. I just assumed you'd leave that aspect of the business in someone else's hands."

"If I don't know what's going on, how will I know if I'm being cheated?"

Stanley nodded in agreement. "True."

"Now, you want to tell me what's going on?"

Stan showed him the copies of the check stubs he found, and the certificates of stock he'd obtained. They were worth about twenty thousand dollars. "It's not much considering I probably need ten times that much to get set up. But, I'd like to use some and invest some. Like you said, for the future."

Craig nodded his approval. "I'd say that would be a smart move."

"My question is how much? How much should I keep to use and how much should I invest?"

"What you need to consider is how soon you'll be able to show a profit. Do you have enough to hold you until then? If not, how much will it take to reach a certain point in getting started? And how long do you plan on, or need, to keep working elsewhere?"

"Well, if I get it plowed up and plant grass now, this summer I should be able to maintain a few head of horses."

"Will the house be ready by then?" Craig asked.

Stan sighed. "I doubt it."

"Can you properly take care of your animals and not live on your land?"

"I think so, for a while. At least until I'm ready to start working and training foals."

"Is that what you want?"

"I don't know," Stan sighed, pondering the question, carefully considering his answer. "Not really. What I really want is to live there, to have *my* house on *my* land and be able to work at building a business."

"Want advice?" Craig offered, and continued at Stanley's nod. "Get some figures on the cost of fence, grass and material for barns. Then decide what you want the most and invest accordingly, at least half either way.

"If you want to live there and build your business slowly while working elsewhere, then work on the house. It'll take time, but you can fix it up a little at a time even after you're living there. If you want to try and build a business while living and working elsewhere, get ready for horses.

"If I were you, I'd go with the house. It'll be easier to build a business if you're there more than gone. And you could invest more and draw on it in a year or so. If you have to work all day elsewhere as well as work on the house and worry about your animals, something will suffer, probably you or your animals.

"If you want to talk again, feel free. And remember, Stanley, there is a season for everything. I know you think I have a lot here, and I do, compared to some. But it took a long time. It's a slow and often frustrating process, Stan. Sowing and reaping always is."

Stan sighed. He had a lot to think about. Before he could say more, Amber walked into the room. Desire surged through him at the sight of her.

Craig didn't have to turn around to know his daughter had made her entrance. Stanley's expression said it all.

"Watch yourself, Boy," he warned, his voice soft, his snapping gray gaze commanding compliance. Satisfied his meaning was clear, he pasted a smile on his face, rose from his chair and turned to greet his daughter. The smile disappeared and his jaw dropped. "Amber," he breathed.

Dressed in shimmering blue silk, the dress slid over her form, clinging in all the right places and slit on one side to mid-thigh. Her hair, caught up at the crown with a silver barrette, hung in thick curls down her back with a few tendrils curled around her face. Her cheeks were flushed and her eyes sparkled with excitement.

Amber smiled, not sure whose expression touched her more. "Like it?"

They nodded mutely.

Stan's gaze sought Craig's when he stood up and took Amber's hand. "I think you'd better stay on and chaperone the dance."

"Why?" Amber demanded.

"Because someone has to beat the boys off so I can dance with you."

Craig chuckled. "Just think of all the pretty girls you can dance with if she's dancing with other boys."

Amber's eyes narrowed into shimmering slits. "You'd better not," she warned Stanley.

Stan's chuckle died in his throat when Tamera entered the room draped in a silver dress similar to Amber's. Her hair fell in silken waves over her shoulders and down her back. "On second thought, you'd better round up a whole slew of chaperones," he suggested, grinning broadly at Craig, "Or a truckload of bodyguards."

Amber smiled at her mother. "I think they like our dresses. Wouldn't you say, Mama?"

Tamera's laugh was silky, seductive. "I'd say so," she murmured, reaching for Craig's hand.

He turned her in a slow circle, his eyes sweeping over her in blatant approval. Images crowded his mind, images of removing the dress slowly, revealing the silk undergarments he knew she'd be wearing. He knew how she'd smell. How she'd taste. His body tightened with need.

"It's going to be a long night," he muttered, pulling her against him.

Stan laughed.

Amber giggled.

"How on earth am I supposed to keep my eyes on him when I won't be able to get them off of you?" Craig asked his wife.

"Oh, I'm sure you'll manage," she assured him, winking at Stanley.

Later, at the dance, Stan pulled Amber as close as he dared; having the distinct impression that Craig somehow kept a close watch on him without even having to take his eyes off of his wife. "You know it's really cruel of you to wear something like this just to torture me," he teased.

She gazed up at him with wide-eyed innocence, fighting hard not to smile. "I thought you liked it."

He grinned, leading her across the floor, away from her father's probing gaze. "Oh, yes. I like it. Even if it is driving me crazy," he assured, his voice husky. Risking a caress up her spine, he sank his fingers in the silken mass of curls down her back. Pressing her closer, he indulged them with a tiny kiss.

"You know, it's been a while since you've really kissed me."

His arms tightened automatically, bringing her into dangerous proximity with his hard frame. He chuckled. "Oh, I'm sure your father would just love to see that," he teased, knowing without a doubt the kind of kiss she was referring to.

She glared in the direction where her parents were dancing. "I wish they'd leave."

"Why?"

"So you can relax and hold me tighter, closer, and kiss me like you really mean it."

"Sweetheart," he breathed, his lips brushing over her cheek to whisper in her ear. "Every time I kiss you I mean it," he assured her in a husky whisper.

"Well, I know you don't think it's proper," she continued, referring to the kind of kiss they shared the day Stan cut his hand. "But I doubt it would hurt every now and then. Would it?" she purred, moving her hands up his back in a subtle caress while pressing against him.

Hot flames of desire licked his belly. "Amber," he mumbled with a strangled little laugh, deliberately stepping back from her enticing embrace. "You, My Sweet, are getting entirely too good at tempting me."

"Oh really?" she queried in a soft, silky voice.

"Yes, really," he admitted with a wry grin. Her eyes sparkled with mischief. She pressed her lips to his cheek.

"I'm sorry," she whispered.

"Are you?"

She nodded smiling a sweet, innocent smile. "Sorry it's not working."

Craig's eyes sought them out in the crowd at the sound of Stan's husky laugh. He frowned down at Tamera. "I think it's time I danced with my daughter."

Tamera giggled. So far she'd been successful in keeping Craig away from Amber. She nodded slightly and allowed Craig to lead her across the floor where the kids were dancing and waited while he cut in on them. With a slight, apologetic smile, she danced with Stanley.

Stan smiled down at Tamera and thanked her. She gazed up at him, the sparkle in her eyes belying the innocent expression on her face.

"For what?"

He grinned, glancing over at Amber and her father. "For having such a beautiful daughter, and making it possible for me to dance with her."

She laughed. "Craig can be overprotective sometimes."

"Oh?" he teased. "Is that what you call it? And I thought he didn't trust me." His eyes danced merrily, waiting for her to continue.

Tamera smiled as though revealing a deep, personal secret. "We trust you. Even though, as her father, he doesn't want to. Don't let us down."

Catching the serious note in her voice, he gazed down at her a moment before declaring, "I won't."

The dance ended. Tamera drew Craig's attention back to her and Stanley reached for Amber's hand when the next song began. "Let them dance," she whispered, despite her husband's frown.

"You really like him, don't you?" Craig asked, leading his wife out on the gym floor. She smiled and nodded. Arching an eyebrow expressively, he waited for her to elaborate.

"He's so charming and adorable."

She gazed over to where Stan was smiling intently into Amber's eyes. Her smile and the light in her eyes reflected pure tenderness.

"And he reminds me of you."

Craig grunted. "All the more reason to keep him away from *my* daughter."

"Nonsense. Most girls want a man who reminds them of their father. It makes them feel special, loved, and secure," she assured him.

Taking his hand, she led Craig out of the building. Turning in his arms she pressed her lips to his. "I think it's time we went home," she suggested in a husky whisper. "They'll be fine."

The look in her eyes convinced him she was right, for the moment.

Amber heaved a sigh of relief when her parents finally left, but the feelings were short-lived when Lori arrived at the gym with a group of her friends. She sidled up to them and slipped her arm around Stanley's waist.

"Let's dance," she suggested, her words nothing more than a suggestive slur.

Stan pulled away. "You're drunk," he accused. "What's with you, Lori?"

"It's homecoming, time to celebrate," she reminded, turning in a shaky twirl and giggling when she nearly lost her balance.

Stanley grabbed her by the arms to prevent her from ending up on the floor in an unladylike sprawl. Taking advantage of the attention, Lori slid her arms around his neck and placed a sloppy kiss on his mouth. "Dance with me, Stanley. Please," she urged, pressing against him.

Stanley shook her loose. "Dance? You can barely stand up. Geez, Lori, what in the world's wrong with you?"

She jerked away. "I just know how to party," she slurred. "Unlike some people I know," she added, her eyes cutting to Amber in a scathing look.

Amber's eyes narrowed when she rubbed herself against Stanley in an inviting gesture and remarked, "You'd have more fun with me."

Stanley rolled his eyes in disgust and grunted. "Well, the party's over," he insisted, taking Lori firmly by the arm. He turned to Amber.

"I can't let her stay here like this."

Lori jerked loose before Amber could respond. "You're not my father," she snarled. "Not my big brother or even my keeper, and you have nothing to say about what I do."

Stan took her by the arm again, pulling her up short. "No, and you'd better thank your lucky stars I'm not, because if I had the slightest say over you, you'd be grounded for life. Now stop acting like the brat you are and let's go." He turned back to Amber.

"I'm sorry. Do you want me to take you home first, wait here, call your parents, or what?" Before she could answer Lori moaned and passed out. Muttering a curse, Stanley picked her up.

"I'll be back as soon as possible," he told Amber.

Carrying Lori out to his truck, he dumped her in the passenger side and drove her out to the Bar S. Knowing he could not get her into the house without making enough noise to rouse her parents, he put her in his bed until he could figure out what action to take. Returning to the gym, he stalked in only to find Amber on the dance floor with one of her classmates. Raking his fingers through his hair, he considered cutting in on them when his eyes met hers.

Even in the dim lights, Amber saw the frustration on Stanley's face. Sending him a reassuring smile, she turned her attention back to her dance partner and prayed the song would end soon. When it was over, she thanked her classmate and allowed him to lead her off the dance floor to where Stanley waited.

"Everything okay?" she asked.

He shrugged. "About as well as can be expected," he muttered, stifling a quick spurt of jealousy when another of her classmates asked Amber to dance, and grateful when she refused.

"You don't look like you're in the mood to party anymore," Amber remarked, trying not to sound as disappointed as she felt.

Stan took her hand in his, raised it to his lips. "I'm sorry. Leave it to Lori to spoil what should have been a perfect evening."

"You get her home okay?"

"Sort of," he replied, then continued when her eyebrow arched in question. "I didn't know what to do, so I dumped her in my bed. Guess I'll try and sober her up some when I get home before sending her to her own."

"You did what?" Amber exclaimed.

"Shhh, lower your voice," Stan urged when people stopped dancing to stare.

Turning on her heel, Amber stormed out of the door.

"Amber, wait," he demanded, following in her footsteps. "Where are you going?" he asked, grabbing her by the arm and turning her around to face him.

"I can't believe you put her in your bed! What were you thinking? Do you know how that's going to look to her father?"

"What was I supposed to do?"

"I don't know, but putting her in your bed is just plain stupid!"

"Roy Strickland knows I would never disrespect him or his daughter in any way, regardless of what the situation looks like," he insisted.

Amber glared up at him. "How can you be so naïve? That girl was all over you when she got here. One hint, even a whisper of wrongdoing to her father and you're going to be nothing but a memory."

"Oh, Lord," Stan muttered. "I never thought of it like that. What in the world am I going to do?"

Amber shook her head. "I don't know but you'd better think of something, and it had better be good." Swallowing the lump of dread in her throat, she turned away. "Take me home, Stanley. I've had enough of this evening."

A tense silence accompanied them on the drive to the Rockin' H. Stanley wondered what to do and Amber worried over the outcome no matter what he decided.

Pulling up to the house, he put his arm around her shoulders and pulled her close. "I'm sorry, My Sweet, that things turned out the way they did tonight," he whispered, hating the way she stiffened in his embrace.

"Just take care of the situation, Stanley. And watch your back," she answered, pulling away. Opening the door for herself, she exited the truck and left him sitting there.

Chapter Ten

All the way home, Stanley debated about what to do. In the end, he figured the truth always worked best and woke Mr. Strickland.

"Stanley, what's wrong, Son?"

Stan swallowed hard. "Mr. Strickland, I don't know how to tell you this, but Lori is passed out in my bed."

Roy shook his head, positive he'd misunderstood Stanley's statement. "Excuse me?"

Stan noticed the way his eyes narrowed and hurried to erase any misguided thoughts. "No, wait, Sir, let me explain. She showed up at the homecoming dance, drunk as all get out. I tried to make her leave, but before I could get her out of the gym, she passed out. Not knowing what else to do and not wanting to abandon Amber, I brought her here, put her in my bed then went back to take Amber home."

Roy shook his head and sighed. "That child's going to be the death of me," he muttered, raking his fingers through his hair. "I'll be right back," he assured Stanley, and went upstairs to change clothes.

Stanley waited until Roy returned then walked with him to the room he'd called home for the past year-and-a-half.

"Do you know where she got the alcohol?" Roy asked.

Stan shook his head. "No, Sir, but if I ever find out, they'll answer to me. That is, after you finish with them," he assured.

"You're a good boy," Roy answered, putting his hand on Stan's shoulder. "How's Amber this evening?"

"Beautiful and furious," Stan answered, looking his boss straight in the eye. "She's concerned about how all this will look to you. I assured her you know I'd never disrespect you, your wife, or Lori in any way, but she's still worried."

"Tell her not to worry," Roy said, gazing down at his daughter sprawled in a drunken heap across Stanley's bed.

"This one, on-the-other-hand…" his words trailed off when he bent down to pick Lori up.

Stanley held the door open for them wondering at the words left unsaid. Kicking off his boots, he shucked the dress clothes and climbed into bed then phoned Amber, noting right away the weepy sound of her voice when she answered.

"Hello?"

"Hi, Sweet. Are you okay?"

Amber sniffed back tears as she'd done for the past half-hour and muttered, "I guess."

"I'm really sorry, Amber. I know this is your final homecoming dance and I hate the thought of it being ruined."

"It's not your fault. You did what you had to do."

"Thank you for that. Mr. Strickland said the same when I woke him up and told him what happened."

"Well, I'm glad everything turned out all right," Amber remarked. "Guess I'll see or talk to you tomorrow?"

"Yeah, but I want you to promise me something tonight."

"What?"

"Promise you'll never again send me packing without a goodnight kiss, no matter how angry you are."

The disappointment in his voice pricked Amber's heart. "I'm sorry," she whispered. "If you want to drive back over, I'll be happy to give you one."

Stan sighed. "Sounds nice, but answer me this; should I ring the doorbell and risk waking your father or climb the trellis outside your bedroom window?" Amber giggled as he hoped she would.

"There is no trellis outside my bedroom window, so I guess you'll just have to ring the doorbell and take your chances, especially considering my hair isn't quite long enough to braid for you to use as a rope."

"Just my luck," Stan muttered, trying to sound disappointed in spite of their teasing. "Knowing your father if there was a trellis it would be covered in barbed wire and if

I ring the doorbell this late, he'll answer with a shotgun in his hands."

Amber laughed. "Probably so."

"Well, guess I'll just have to pass on this one, if you promise it won't happen again."

"I promise," she whispered. "'Night, Stanley."

"'Night, My Sweet."

* * * * *

"You seemed to enjoy yourself today," Amber remarked after she and Stanley curled up together on the porch swing.

Stan chuckled. "I did. Thank you for goading me into coming," he teased, remembering the way she had bullied him into attending Ace's birthday party.

"I didn't goad. I merely convinced you that you needed some time off."

He grinned. "I always take Sunday's off and I had to take time off when I cut my hand. If I keep taking time off, I'll never get finished. Besides," he continued to tease. "You are so beautiful when you're angry," he admitted with a chuckle, and then winced when she tugged lightly at the hair showing through the open collar of his shirt. "Ouch!"

"You're a jerk," she accused, snuggling closer to his hard frame. Her fingers stroked the curls she'd tugged and fingered the gold cross she'd bought him while on vacation with her parents.

He pulled her closer to his body, cradling her in his arms, sharing his body heat with her. "I love children," he admitted, remembering the games they played that day. "Hope to have several of my own someday." He felt her nod.

"Me, too. Mama had such a hard time having Ace. She had a couple of miscarriages and one baby was born dead."

Her voice deepened and eyes darkened with the emotions which gathered in them. Stan stroked her hair and waited for her to continue.

"I remember seeing her after she'd had a miscarriage. Scott smuggled me into her room. She was so pale. Her eyes were huge and red-rimmed, with dark circles beneath them. She held me in her arms and cried and cried. Everyone cried. Daddy held us both and Scott left the room in tears. I tried to comfort her, saying that I would always be her baby and that when I grew up, I would get a baby for her." Amber swallowed the thick lump of emotion clogging her throat and gave him a wobbly smile.

"I know now, it's a little more complicated than that. But I'd still like to give them a whole slew of grandchildren someday."

Stan felt the sting of tears in his eyes; his heart swelled realizing again how beautiful she was, how loving and generous. How special. And how blessed he was to have her in his arms. They sat, cuddling to keep out the fall chill. Amber absently outlined the cross, nestled in the soft curls covering his chest. The warmth of her touch heated his blood as though he were seated in front of a roaring fire, so intense he shivered in the cool night air. Grabbing her hand, he kissed the fingertips which were driving him crazy.

Amber's fingers traced the sensual fullness of his lips and the hint of mustache that grew there. It was baby fine, and soft, like the hair on his chest. Desire trembled awake within her. Not a white-hot flash but a slow burn. A fire simmering in her blood tempered by the innocent feelings she had for him. In that instant her heart confirmed she wanted their love to last forever. She wanted to curl up in his arms on cold winter evenings and wake up in them on warm summer days. His eyes glowed warm and bright like a flawless summer sky. Desire darkened the pupils like storm clouds. She smiled up into them.

"I love you," she said, her voice soft, full of emotion.

Stan's breath caught on a hiss. His heart squeezed with emotion then opened up. The love he felt for her poured through him. Pulling her closer, he covered her lips with his in a tender caress. "Oh, Amber," he breathed, not knowing what to say.

He'd promised Craig he would take it slow, that he wouldn't push her. And he hadn't. He'd withheld his own declaration of love from her in order to fulfill his vow to her father. Now it hovered on his lips, still afraid to encourage or push her tender feelings.

"Sweetheart," he began, his voice soft. "You know I care about you a lot." He halted at the hurt which crept into her eyes. He couldn't lie to her, or hide it from her any longer. *The devil hang Craig Harris.*

Stan smiled tenderly tracing her lips with his thumb. "I love you, too, Amber. I've loved you since the moment our eyes met homecoming eve a year ago."

"Why haven't you said anything before now?"

"Because I didn't want you to feel obligated to return the words. And because I promised your father I would take it slow and not push you into something you're not ready for."

She rolled her eyes. "My father refuses to face the fact that I'm growing up." With a triumphant little laugh, she cupped his face in her hands.

"Say it again, Stanley, then kiss me."

Stan grinned at her boldness. "I love you, Amber Nichole Harris," he whispered, each word punctuated by a feathery brush of his lips over hers. He trembled when she shyly traced his lips with her tongue then tentatively dipped into his mouth. His breath escaped on a groan when she pulled him closer, getting bolder with her searching lips. Dragging his fingers through her hair, the kiss deepened until he was breathing heavily, grasping for control. She whimpered, clinging when he dragged his lips from hers to brush kisses over her face.

Confused and excited at the feelings coursing through her, Amber shivered, pressing her lips to the skin showing through the open collar of his shirt. She heard his soft moan when his arms tightened around her. Desire poured through her like hot, molten lava as evidence of his feelings pressed intimately against her and his heat enveloped her. Her lips traveled with exquisite slowness to feel the pulse throbbing in his throat.

His fingers tightened in her hair and he stopped her torturous journey. "Jesus," he rasped. "Amber, stop," he ordered through clenched teeth. "If your father finds us like this he'll kill me. Or at the very least, geld me."

She tried but couldn't suppress the giggle. "I won't let him," she promised in a silky voice. A reluctant grin played along his sensuous lips.

"It's time for me to leave." He sighed, and untangled himself from her tempting embrace. The wind picked up and she tugged the buttons of his jacket closed. Insisting that she get out of it, he paused just inside the door for one last, fleeting brush of his lips over hers then left.

* * * * *

Craig wandered up the stairs toward his daughter's room. For the third day in a row Amber was not helping her mother with supper as expected. He sensed something amiss. There had been a subtle change in her, and in Stanley, in the weeks since Ace's birthday. They were quieter, closer. Their eyes met and gazes lingered, whenever they were together. His heart thudded with fear and anxiety when he wondered what could have transpired between them. But he knew. Somehow, somewhere deep down inside, he knew their feelings for each other were maturing sooner than he expected, or wanted. He cursed himself for not throwing the boy off his ranch months ago.

Reaching Amber's door he entered without knocking and found her writing. "How come you're not downstairs helping your mother?" he asked, his voice rougher than he'd intended. She looked up, confused, her eyes glazed with concentration.

"I'm sorry. I lost track of time," Amber answered, when her father stalked into the room. She hesitated in shutting down the computer when his gaze shot to the screen and the writing there. She heard his sharp intake of breath as

124

he read the tender love scene she'd been working on all afternoon.

Craig's eyes widened when he read the poignant, passionate words. Blood pounded through his veins, sharp and hot, at the sweetly innocent yet somehow erotic hints of love and romance secluded in exotic prose. Images crowded his mind. She was an excellent writer. You could see the scene unfold, feel the depth of love and desire between the characters, understand their hunger and need. There was love there, and desperation, quiet, suffocating desperation. He felt it now. Fear thickened in his chest.

"I hope this is imagination and not experience talking?" he queried in a suffocated voice. Her shy blush and hesitant gaze gave him his answer.

"Daddy, of course it's imagination," she admonished, her cheeks a delicate shade of crimson. "Is it like that for you and Mama?"

The question floored him. Feeling suddenly weak-kneed, Craig sat on her bed. Innocence shimmered in the question and in the dark depths of her eyes. He nodded slowly, knowing she wanted and needed a direct and honest answer, and that he'd never given her anything less whenever she asked him something.

"If what your mother and I share could be put into words that would come pretty close, but Amber, there is a lot more to love than pretty words," he warned. "There's often pain and heartache and situations where no one really wins."

"I know that, Daddy." Her voice was soft, confident. "I love Stanley that way."

He groaned, shaking his head in denial. "Sweetheart, I know you care about him a lot..."

"I love him," she insisted.

"You're too young to know the meaning of real love," he remained adamant, suddenly angry. It was too soon. She was his! His daughter, his baby. She couldn't have the feelings of a grown woman!

Amber stiffened, surprised and shocked at her father's tone of voice. Turning away from him, she saved her work and shut down the computer. Rising, she glared at him, her eyes sharp with pain and anger.

"I'll go help Mama now."

"Amber, wait," he reached for her, suddenly afraid. Afraid he'd said all the wrong things, pushed the wrong buttons. Afraid he was losing her. He sighed heavily, his eyes searching hers, wondering what on earth he should say now. He cleared his throat and tried to breach the gap of angry silence which had sprung up between them.

"Sweetheart, I'm trying to accept the fact that you have feelings, strong feelings," he amended at her mutinous expression. "For Stanley, but I..."

He hesitated at the word doubt. He'd never doubted Amber in her life. She always knew her heart and mind. He'd taught her to do so. "I'm not sure you, either of you, really understand the commitment behind the word."

"I do." She said it simply, honestly. "I can see you're not ready to believe that yet. But Daddy, the day will come when you'll have to accept it," she said, a subtle hint of warning in her voice. Turning on her heel, she left her father sitting on her bed and went downstairs to help her mother.

Tamera took one look at the expression on her daughter's face and the pain in her eyes and asked what was wrong.

Amber shook her head. "Just Daddy, being Daddy."

"Which means?" Tamera queried, her eyebrow arched in question.

"I've been working on a love scene in my novel and was just finishing up when he walked into my room demanding to know why I wasn't down here helping you. I'm sorry about that, Mama, I just lost track of time like I normally do when writing. Anyway, he read the scene and asked if what I wrote was imagination or experience." She shook her head.

"Don't ask me why he'd think it would be anything other than imagination. However, when I asked him if the love between you two was similar to what I'd written, he said if what you share could be put into words that would be pretty close. Then he went on to tell me that love is more than pretty words, as if I don't already know that," she huffed.

Taking a deep breath, she continued. "And, when I told him I love Stanley that way, he got all bent out of shape, saying I'm too young to know the real meaning of love and that he didn't think either of us understands the commitment behind the word. How could I not know the commitment behind the word growing up with you two?" she demanded, her voice reflecting the anguish and confusion in her heart.

Tamera hugged her daughter and chose her words with care. "Just because you've witnessed love doesn't mean you understand it to the fullest, Sweetheart. Do you honestly think the feelings you have for Stanley could withstand what your father and I have been through in nearly twenty years of marriage?"

"I don't know about all that, Mama. I only know I love him and I want to have a future with him. Is that so wrong?"

"No, it's not wrong, but only time will tell if what you two feel for each other is real and strong enough to withstand the tests of life. In the meanwhile, don't be too quick to assume it is and don't rush things. And, as I've said before, don't expect your father to understand much less accept those feelings easily or soon. You're his baby, Amber, and he's not ready for you to be anything else yet. Be patient."

"Humph," Amber grunted, "Easier said than done."

Tamera laughed. "It sure is, but patience is a virtue and, like all virtues, it takes time and testing to develop. If you can't be patient with your father whom you've lived with for over seventeen years, what makes you think you can be patient to any degree with Stanley? He's a lot like your father, you know."

Amber rolled her eyes knowing her mother's words were true. "Is that good or bad?" she asked, a teasing lift to her brow, a smile tugging at her lips.

Again Tamera laughed. "Like I said, only time will tell. In the meantime reassure your father of how much you love him as often as you can."

"Think that'll work?"

Tamera smiled. "It certainly won't hurt," she remarked, before calling Craig and Ace to the table.

Supper was quiet compared to normal. Though enlightened by the conversation with her mother, Amber still resented the fact that her father doubted her feelings for Stan. He'd always taught her to know her heart and mind and now he accused her of not doing so!

Craig watched his daughter throughout the meal. He could all but feel the disappointment radiating from her. When she asked to be excused, he nodded his approval but caught her hand when she passed by his chair after putting her dishes in the sink.

Amber saw the emotions in her father's glittering gray gaze and felt a tug at her heart. Smiling, she bent down and brushed her lips across his cheek. "I love you, Daddy," she remarked.

"Love you, too," he said.

"Love you more," she declared.

Remembering the game they played when she was but a baby, Craig couldn't help but chuckle. "Love you first."

Amber smiled and shook her head. "Na-ah," she insisted, exiting the room before he could argue further.

The following Sunday afternoon Amber and Stanley stretched out on the floor in the den, playing cards with Ace perched between them. Craig watched through lowered lids over his newspaper as they laughed and teased, noting the light in their eyes and the gentle way Stan touched her cheek. Always the perfect gentleman, always! He suppressed a frustrated growl. Part of him wished Stanley would give him an excuse, any excuse, to throw him off the ranch. His eyes narrowed when Stan whispered something to her and Amber laughed. He folded the paper shut with a snap.

"Amber, why don't you go and see what Mama's doing? I think she was baking. Maybe she could use your help."

Amber tossed down her hand of cards. She couldn't concentrate anyway. Besides, she was losing. Rising, she ran her hand through Ace's hair then walked over to kiss her father. "I love you," she whispered, her lips brushing over the hair-roughened skin of his cheek.

The sweetness of her gesture eased the frustration in his heart. Craig grabbed her hand, pressing a kiss into the palm.

Stan gestured slightly to get Craig's attention. Craig arched a questioning brow at him. Stan grinned.

"Mr. Craig, I need to ask your advice on the house. I've been thinking about adding central air and heat since I have to rewire it anyway. What do you think?"

Craig nodded still holding onto his daughter's hand. "Sounds like a good idea. You might think about the future too. If you plan on raising a family there someday, you may want to go ahead and remodel now."

Stan nodded. Craig's words were just the opening he needed. "Amber, maybe you can help. What would a woman want done?" he asked, halting her departure from the room.

Craig noticed the light in Stanley's eyes and the way he chewed on his lip, fighting back a smile and caught on to what was going on. He grinned and shook his head. Lord, but he liked the boy's spirit and courage. That remark was about as loaded as a twelve-gauge shotgun in prime hunting season!

Amber's heart jumped into her throat. She turned to face Stan, a flush rushing to her cheeks. "Why are you asking me?"

Stan shrugged. "You're a woman, aren't you?" he asked, and continued at her nod. "I'm sure most women want pretty much the same things in a house."

Her eyes narrowed at the remark. "Well, I'm not most women, what if your future wife doesn't like my ideas?"

Stan rolled his eyes. "Just answer the question. What would a woman want done, in general I mean?"

"Well, for starters, a bigger bathroom."

Stan chuckled. "Imagine that," he remarked, a hint of sarcasm in his voice.

She smirked at his tone. "A fireplace and a utility room. What about colors?"

He shrugged. "I'm leaving everything white. That way my future wife can decorate however she wants." Her eyes narrowed into tiny slits of shimmering blue. Stan smothered a grin.

"You know," he began in as serious a tone he could muster considering his next statement. "I could paint everything a deep, dark, green. You know Jade, or that new shade...Jealous I think they call it."

Amber realized she'd been had. She walked over and shoved him onto his back. "You are a jerk," she accused, when he burst out laughing. She glared at her father whose shoulders shook suspiciously. "And you shouldn't encourage him," she admonished, shaking her finger in his face.

He grabbed her by the arm, jerking her onto his lap. "And just what do you intend to do about it?" he queried in a soft voice.

"I'll think of something I'm sure." Pushing herself out of his arms, she headed toward the kitchen.

"Jeans are a little tight don't you think?" her father asked, slapping her firmly rounded bottom with his paper. She smiled a sweet, innocent smile that belied the hint of mischief in her eyes.

"Discourages roaming hands, huh, Stanley?" she queried in a soft, smug voice, savoring the sweet taste of revenge.

Stan groaned, burying his head on his knee. "Getting me murdered is pretty nasty revenge just for my teasing you, Amber."

She snorted, turning on her heel.

Craig eyed Stanley a moment. Convinced the boy was innocent of her allegations, he grinned. "You hold her down and I'll beat her," he offered.

"Deal!" Stan scrambled to his feet as Amber ran for the kitchen.

"Mama! They're ganging up on me," she cried, hiding behind her mother, which was ridiculous since she was a full head taller than Tamera.

Tamera stood between her daughter and both men. "It's a pity it takes two of you to control one headstrong girl," she taunted.

Craig chuckled reaching for is wife. "Get out of the way, Darling. She's needed this for a long time."

Tamera stiffened protectively for a moment then grinned. "You're right," she admitted, stepping away from her daughter.

"Mama!" Amber squealed, making a mad dash around the table only to be caught in Stanley's arms. She struggled for a moment then changed tactics. Slipping her arms around his neck she snuggled against him and whispered in his ear.

He glared at Craig. "Child abuse is a crime in this state," he warned.

Craig tossed back his head with a laugh. "She's got you whipped," he teased.

Stanley grinned. "No more than you."

Craig accepted the barb for the truth that it was.

Chapter Eleven

Stan walked through the house thinking about all he'd accomplished and all he had yet to do. Compiling the advice of many, he'd reinvested half of the stock back into Evans Oil commodities. The rest he invested in more accessible CDs and market funds. Using those invested funds for collateral he opened a line of credit, making sure the payments could be met with his paycheck from the Bar S.

He'd plowed and planted grass knowing that being able to feed horses was the first and most important step. He could divide the property with fences and barns one section and one breed at a time.

He then sank money into the house. Instead of enlarging the existing bath, he added another bedroom and bathroom. He had the foundation built for a utility room and a wall designated for a fireplace. He ran the plumbing and gas pipes and would rewire the place, run central air and heat, and blow insulation in the walls whenever the improvements were finished. He painted everything white, leaving further decorating for Amber to choose after they were married.

Unrolling the sleeping bag which served as his bed when he worked late in the evenings and on weekends, he stretched out, thinking of the days to come.

Tomorrow was Thanksgiving. He'd already promised to have dinner with Amber and her family and dessert and coffee with the Strickland's. Then he would come home. Home, was exactly what he considered the place which bore his name. The old brand, the letter M displayed as the back of a swing, would once again be the trademark for the Swinging M Ranch.

Thanksgiving Day dawned bright and clear, but cold. Getting up, Stan's first prayer of thanks was for hot water to shave and wash up and for the small heater that had kept him warm during the night. Thinking about the day ahead and what it meant, he recognized all he had to be thankful for, all he wanted, and all to come. Heating up water for coffee, he spent a few minutes in silent contemplation with God. Later, Amber met him at the truck bundled up in her warmest jacket.

"Take a walk?"

"It's cold," he warned, the wind cutting straight through his well-lined denim coat.

"We won't stay out long. I just want to spend a few minutes alone with you."

"Okay," he nodded, taking her hand in his and walking toward the shelter of the barn. At the first available stall, he pulled her into his arms. His lips covered hers in a gentle caress. Stanley pulled her closer when she shivered, her breath catching in a soft sob. "What's wrong, My Sweet?"

"It's Thanksgiving."

Stan eyed her, a curious lift to his brow. "And?"

Her smiled trembled. "I always get a little depressed on Thanksgiving. Sometimes I feel so guilty that I have so much and so many have so little."

"Amber," he soothed, stroking her hair off her face. "It's no shame you have so much. The Bible says God blesses the works of our hands. Your father has worked hard to build all this and to provide for you."

"It also teaches us that to whom much is given, much is required."

"Didn't you bring a truckload of groceries to every shelter in three counties yesterday with extra sweets and gifts for every needy child for miles around?"

She nodded smiling at the memory and the fun she'd had. She did that every year out of a portion of the allowance she'd saved. This along with her other charity works was her way of giving back.

Stan laughed, loving her more by the minute. "You know what my grandmother used to say?" At the shake of her head he continued. "She used to say that when you've done all you can do, and given all you can give, the only thing left to do is to pray."

"She sounds like a beautiful person."

"She was. Sometimes I miss her so much," he admitted, tears stinging his eyes. "She was generous and loving and compassionate. I've seen her empty out the refrigerator of leftovers, before they went bad, and make a huge pot of soup then stand in her yard serving it to anyone who asked.

"'Stanley'," she'd say, "'when you start thinking you don't have enough or that you need something more, just look around and you'll see how truly blessed you are. Nothing humbles a person more than seeing and helping someone in need.'

"She never had much money to give, but she always gave so much of herself. You remind me of her a lot," he observed.

Amber smiled, snuggling against him, aching for him. "I'm honored you think so. I love you, Stanley."

He pulled her closer, kissed her again, lingered over it. "I love you too, Amber," he mumbled, nibbling at the corners of her mouth. "We'd better go in before your parents start to worry," he whispered, with a reluctant sigh.

She stood firm, wrapping her arms around his waist. "In a minute. I want to feel you strong against me. I want to hear your heartbeat and feel your arms around me." She nuzzled his cheek, her voice lowering to a husky whisper. "I want to taste your lips. Kiss me, Stanley," she insisted, pressing her mouth to his.

Desire poured through him, galvanizing in its wake. His hands got lost in the luxurious thickness of black silk trailing down her back. He moaned pulling her closer, covering her mouth in a hungry kiss. His lips clung to hers, molding and shaping them to his—tender, searching, tasting greedily of her sweetness and fire.

Amber clung to him as his lips assaulted her senses. A soft moan escaped when he drug his mouth from hers, pulled her against his hard frame, and buried his face in her hair. She felt a twinge of feminine satisfaction at his labored breathing and thudding heart.

"Lord, Amber, you drive me crazy," he mumbled in a thick voice, thinking he needed to have another talk with her father. Soon.

She stroked his chest in a soothing caress, brushing feathery kisses over his face and neck. Stepping out of his arms she smiled. A tender, loving light shone deep in her eyes.

"That should keep you warm for a while," she teased.

His replied with a throaty chuckle. "Or make me catch pneumonia when we walk out in the wind again," he countered.

Taking both of her hands in his, he pressed them to his lips then turned her toward the door. He paused at the barn entrance, pulling her to him once more, reveling in her lips. One more hug, one last taste. Stanley forced himself to stop and take her in the house while he still had the sense and strength to do so.

Dinner was a lively affair. They laughed and talked, sharing past experiences and old jokes. Stan couldn't remember when he'd had a nicer Thanksgiving. Not since his grandmother died two years ago. When Amber and her mother started clearing the dishes away for desert, Ace escaped into the den.

Stan eyed Craig with a pointed look. "I don't know about you, but I need to walk off dinner before dessert."

Craig's eyes narrowed and he wondered what the boy wanted. With a curt nod, he rose from the table. "Me too, let's go. We'll have desert in the living room later," he informed Tamera.

Amber walked out of the kitchen to gather more dishes. "Where are they going?"

"Taking a walk."

She eyed her mother with wary suspicion. "Why?"

Tamera's smile was tender. "Amber, don't question their every move. And don't worry so. Your father likes Stan. They're taking a walk. Okay?"

Amber's smile was relieved. "Okay, now, how about some ideas on a Christmas present for Daddy, and for Stan."

Tamera laughed and they went into the kitchen tossing ideas back and forth.

Stan waited until he and Craig were well out of earshot from the house before broaching the subject uppermost in his mind. "I need some advice on a gift. What are you getting Amber for Christmas?"

Craig's smile was sly, smug. "A car."

Stan choked on a laugh. "A car? Oh. Well," he swallowed the lump of nerves in his throat. "I'd like to give her an engagement ring."

Craig's face paled then flushed with anger. "Hell no. I thought we agreed just a few short months ago, this relationship would develop slowly?"

Stan met his gaze unwaveringly. "Things happen. Things change."

"What kind of things?" Craig demanded, his eyes narrow slits of steel.

It took less than a heartbeat for Stan to realize what Craig was thinking. He shook his head, wary, sad. "Not that. I haven't slept with your daughter, Mr. Harris," he insisted, opting for more formal tone in lieu of the usual 'Mr. Craig.'

"I thought you were beginning to trust me by now. Will you ever?"

His relief was so profound, Craig grinned. "Probably not until I've known you a while."

"How long a while?"

He shrugged. "A hundred years or so."

Stan risked a grin into the ominous gray gaze. "We'll be married long before then."

Craig snorted. "Stubborn, aren't you?"

"Yes, Sir. I love her. I want to marry her. I'm requesting your permission to *ask* her to marry me because it's the proper thing to do. But," he hesitated, not wanting to appear overly threatening but determined Craig know *and accept*, the fact that he loved Amber. "I can wait until she's eighteen. We won't need your permission then."

Craig suppressed the urge to punch the kid, to grab him by the shirt and throw him off his ranch. He should have done so months ago. "You gave me your word you wouldn't push it. She's not even out of high school yet."

"I kept my word. I kept my feelings from her until the night of Ace's party. And I told her *after* she told me she loves me."

"Amber's young. She's innocent and romantic..."

"Bull," Stan interrupted. "Are you telling me you don't trust your daughter to know her own feelings?"

Anguish ripped at his conscience and showed in his eyes. Craig swore, softly, violently.

"No," he admitted, his voice sullen, his expression grim.

"I just want to give her the ring," Stan said. "We'll wait as long as we have to, as long as we can. But I want to marry her."

"What about college?"

"I would never stop her from going to college if she wants to go. People get married and still go to college all the time."

"Yeah, but they usually never finish. Or the marriages don't make it through," Craig argued.

"Ours will."

"I don't want her hurt. And whether you believe it or not, I don't want to see you hurt either. I think you're both too young for this."

Stan held his ground and Craig's gaze. "I know you do. But we're not."

Craig heaved a weary sigh, raking his hand through his hair in an agitated gesture. Damn the boy was confident, determined. A pity he liked that in a man. Still, this was his daughter they were talking about, his baby. He eyed Stanley, willing to see how far the boy could be pushed, tested, trusted.

"I'd rather wait until she turns eighteen. You can give her a ring for her birthday, or as a graduation present."

Stan rolled his eyes and ground his teeth in frustration. "Why? What difference would a few months make except give her more time to set a date and plan a wedding? I'm going to marry her, Mr. Harris, if I have to do it the day she turns eighteen," he insisted. "I'd rather not do that. I'd rather have your blessing."

"I could throw you off this ranch until then," Craig warned through clenched teeth, his voice deceptively soft.

Stanley's blistering gaze never wavered. Craig felt the heat of it.

"I'm sure you could, but would you?" Stan challenged, his voice level, gaze unwavering. "Would you do that because you're too selfish to want her happiness or too jealous share her? I wouldn't force Amber to make a choice, Mr. Harris. Would you?"

The truth will set you free. Craig knew it. But by God, did it have to hurt so much?

Pain darkened, tears shimmered, intensifying the glint of anger in Craig's steely eyes. Stan took a step closer, his voice softened.

"I love her, Mr. Craig. I will never purposely hurt her or rein her in. And I'll do the very best I can to see to it all of her dreams come true," he promised.

Craig sighed, remembering the talk he'd had with Amber not too long ago and how she had insisted that she loved Stan. He knew he had to make a decision and it had to be the right one. More than Amber's happiness depended on it. His relationship with her hung in the balance. If he fought against them, he'd lose. He may be able to hang on for a few months, but in the end, he would lose and very possibly lose his daughter in the process. Still, he hesitated. "I have absolutely no peace about this, Stanley."

"The flesh is always at war with the Spirit."

Craig grunted. "Yeah, and right now my flesh wants to run your sorry little butt plumb out of Texas or better yet, out of the country." Stanley wisely forced back a smile but couldn't stop the flash of laughter in his eyes.

"I'm sure it does," he admitted, taking another step closer to Craig. "And I'm sure you could. But it wouldn't change anything. I'd still love her and I'd come back."

Tension mounted and stretched, taut, anxious, and wary. Craig pleaded silently for wisdom. *Like golden apples in silver settings are words spoken at the proper time.* Craig knew his next words would change his life forever. He took a deep breath, shook his head and opened his mouth to speak. No words came.

He swore again, more viciously than the first time, swallowed hard the lump in his throat and shrugged with a heavy sigh. "I believe you love her, Stanley, and I believe that Amber believes she's in love with you. Give me a few days," he pleaded.

Stan retreated with a sigh and took a step back. It wasn't a yes but it was a sight better than hell no. "Okay. I've got something picked out. Whether she gets it now or later, I'd like your opinion on it." He really didn't care if Craig liked the ring or not, but he did value his opinion of whether or not Amber would like it. And he wanted Craig to feel like he had a say in the matter.

Craig nodded. "A few days."

Amber noticed the tension in her father's eyes the minute the two men walked through the door. She turned to her mother, her eyes wide and pleading.

Tamera noticed the tension also and shook her head in silent warning to her daughter to let it go. "Ready for desert?" she asked her husband.

Fearing he couldn't swallow a gnat without choking to death, Craig shook his head. "Later. Where's Ace?"

"In the den."

Craig nodded and headed out of the room. Tamera followed. Amber turned to Stanley. "What happened?"

"We were discussing some things."

"Like what?"

"Personal, private, guy things," he answered with a grin.

Amber felt a little thrill of excitement and was tempted to push the issue, but knew by the look in Stan's eyes she would get no further explanation. She frowned, forced back her questions with a muttered "whatever" then asked if he wanted desert.

Stan shook his head. "Think I'll take mine to go, I'd like to work a while this evening."

"Aren't you coming back for supper?"

He shook his head again, smiling tenderly at the disappointment in her eyes. "Just fix me a couple of sandwiches and I'll eat later. Besides, I promised the Strickland's I'd stop by for coffee and desert this afternoon." He stopped her protests with a finger against her lips. "Spend some time with your family, My Sweet."

"You mean spend some time with my father."

He nodded. "Especially with your father. And that's all I'm going to say so don't even ask," he warned with a chuckle before brushing his lips across hers in a tender caress. "Now, about those sandwiches?"

"Jerk," she mumbled, and set about making his sandwiches and packing them up along with huge helpings of pie and cake.

Stanley took the bag of food in one hand, slid the other around her waist and pulled her close. "Thank you. I'll talk to you later, or tomorrow."

She smiled up at him, her eyes shimmering like flawless jewels.

"Okay. Be careful, Stan. I love you," she whispered against his lips.

"Love you too," he answered in a husky breath, his lips capturing hers in a gentle caress once more.

Closing the door on his departing figure, Amber went to the den where she found her father stretched out on the couch, his head in her mother's lap. Their eyes met, Amber's heart stuttered at the myriad of emotions clouding his gaze. She smiled, relieved when the corners of his mouth turned up.

"Thought I'd run over to the soup kitchen and help serve supper. Anyone want to join me?"

Craig glanced up at his wife, noting the approval shining in her eyes then nodded at his daughter. Donning jackets, hats and gloves they headed over to the county courthouse where a tent had been set up to serve the needy. Hours later, a poignant silence accompanied them back to the ranch. As disturbed as he'd been to see hopelessness in the eyes of so many, he was equally proud to witness firsthand the way his daughter treated what others would deem the dregs of society. The love and compassion radiating from his child filled him with a sense of awe and wonder at the young lady she'd become. A woman any man would be proud to call wife, he thought, anguish stabbing his heart. Later he sought the advice and consolation of his wife.

Tamera felt a thrill of happiness for her daughter, a flash of pride in the boy she'd grown so fond of and was already beginning to think of as a son, and a tug of empathy for her husband. "What did you say?" she queried with a tender smile.

"First I said no. We talked some more and I asked him to give me a few days to decide if I'll allow it or not."

"You can't say you're surprised. We've both suspected this was coming."

"Yes, Temper. But, damn it, I still think this is happening too fast. These kids are too young to be this serious."

"Maybe that's because Amber's never been attracted to many boys. She hasn't gone through the typical teenage crushes. But, Craig, what's meant to be will be. You know that," she chided, her tone gentle. "What's the real problem?"

He pulled her in his arms, burying his face in her hair. "I feel like I'm losing my little girl," he admitted in a choked whisper.

She stroked his shoulders and back in a soothing caress. "You're not losing her, Darling. She's growing up. You know the old saying: *you're not losing a daughter but gaining a son.*"

"I have a son, thank you," he said, glaring at her with eyes of shimmering steel.

She chuckled and kissed him. "Yes, and it'll be quite a few years before he grows up and takes a wife. I'm sure you've also heard the saying: '*A son is a son until he takes a wife but a daughter is a daughter all of her life.*' She'll always be your little girl, Craig," she assured him with another kiss.

"But you have to let go. Stanley is a good man, boy," she amended at his snarl. "You've said so yourself. And you like him. I think that's what makes this so much easier. Nicer. Believe me it's extremely difficult when your father disapproves of the man you're in love with." She smiled remembering what she'd thought was her first love and how wrong she'd been. Tears shimmered in her eyes even as she smiled and kissed her husband again.

"Trust your instincts about Stanley, you know they're right. He's as perfect for Amber as you are for me."

"What if I allow it and it all falls apart around her ears?" Craig asked.

"You can't protect her from life, Craig. Do you really believe Amber would take such a commitment lightly? If you remember correctly, she informed you a year ago she had met the man she was going to marry. Somehow she knew even then how special Stanley is."

Craig knew she was right. But it didn't make it any easier. Four days later he met Stanley at the jewelers, gave his approval of the ring, and mourned, cursing Stanley, fate, and life in general that his little girl had grown up so soon.

Chapter Twelve

The time between Thanksgiving and Christmas shortened and Craig's decision wavered, his heart divided. The thought of giving his daughter away had him ripped with indecision and torn between happiness and hopeless resignation. His confidence in Stanley grew when he watched them together. Love, appreciation, and gratitude, were reflected in Stanley's gaze every time the blue eyes met his gray ones. Stan had the most expressive blue eyes he'd ever seen, next to Tamera and Amber of course. Nothing could compare to the brilliant gaze his wife and daughter shared.

However, he did find relief in the fact that he still had several months before the marriage would actually take place. A lot could happen in those months. Though he doubted Amber would change her mind once she said yes, and he knew without a doubt she would say yes, he still harbored the hope that she would decide to wait until after college before tying the matrimonial knot.

Watching Stanley with Ace Christmas Eve day, he couldn't help but admire the boy's nerve.

Stan had arrived early, his arms loaded with gifts. Enlisting Ace's help, he curled up with him under the tree. Craig chuckled when he heard Stan say in a conspiring whisper, "The trick is to make them think you're rearranging the gifts," thereby giving Ace the perfect excuse to shake and rattle every box under the tree. He watched with a smothered grin when Tamera walked in the den and Stan scrambled into a sitting position to shield Ace from her view.

"What's going on?" she queried, her eyes narrowed in suspicion.

"Nothing," Stan replied with an innocent grin. "Ace is helping me make room for my gifts."

His eyes glittered with mischief. Tamera's eyes narrowed another notch. "Stanley," she chided. "You're just giving him an excuse to play with them."

"Not me," Stan insisted with a vehement shake of his head. A guilty grin gave him away.

Tamera's rueful gaze turned on her husband. "You should be watching them," she insisted.

He laughed pulling her onto his lap. "I am." He grinned at her snort of disbelief. "Don't be a Scrooge." His voice lowered into a husky whisper. "You above all should know anticipation only enhances the excitement," he teased, chuckling at the flush which rushed to her cheeks.

Tamera rolled her eyes, snuggled into his chest and relented.

Stan watched in silence, wondering what Craig could say that would make Tamera blush like that after so many years of marriage, thrilling at the glimpse of what his future with Amber would be like. As usual he left not long after supper in order to get in a few hours of work at his house.

* * * * *

Scott and Katrina arrived at the Rockin' H late that evening and it was well after midnight when he and Craig wandered up the stairs to say goodnight to the women.

"I find it utterly amazing how they can be stunning, brilliant, alluring women one minute and giggling little girls the next," Craig drawled, leaning against the door to Amber's room where the three of them were huddled together laughing and talking.

Scott chuckled in agreement. "Yeah, and that in turn, makes us feel like macho men or wicked little boys," he replied, and had them all doubled over again.

Craig held his hand out to his wife. "Come on, Temper, time for bed."

"It's early," Amber protested.

Craig laughed. "Yeah, early in the morning," He eyed his wife, a meaningful lift to his brow; his arms open wide in invitation. "Come on, Darling, I think I'll give you your present early," he teased.

"Daddy!" Amber squealed.

"What?" He asked, all innocence. "And where is your mind young lady?" He demanded when color rushed to her cheeks.

Regarding him with laughing eyes, Amber leaned over the bed, pretended to lift the lid off the sewer tank and called for her mind. "And bring my heart with you," she insisted, reducing everyone into a helpless mass of chuckles and giggles once again.

Tamera hugged both Amber and Trina then walked into her husband's outstretched arms. Offering her cheek to Scott, she waited for his kiss then took her husband's hand.

Craig hesitated with a sly grin. "Ace's room is just down the hall," he told Scott, nodding to the door of his son's room.

"Thanks, Buddy, I'm sure I can find it," Scott remarked, his voice tinged with laughing regret. As of yet, he hadn't enjoyed the pleasure of Trina in his bed. And, even if he had, he wouldn't exploit her, their love or Craig's friendship by exposing his children to the fact. He waited until Craig and Tamera's door closed before joining Amber and Katrina for another hour of teasing and laughter.

* * * * *

Christmas Day dawned bright and cold. Stan knocked on the door, tucked his hands into his jacket pockets to keep them warm and waited for someone to answer it. Preparing to knock again, his hand froze in midair when the door opened. His eyes widened and jaw dropped. Standing in the doorway was none other than Craig Harris's double. Stan grinned.

"Dr. Hensley, nice to meet you, Sir," he greeted, hand outstretched. He'd heard rumors and seen pictures of how much he and Craig resembled each other and therefore knew instinctively who he was.

Scott chuckled, no doubt in his mind who he was. "Hello. You must be Stanley," he remarked, letting him in.

Two pair of eyes swept over Amber when she bounded down the stairs dressed in tight, green jeans and a cheerful, Christmassy silk blouse. One gaze glowed with parental admiration, the other with total adoration. Throwing herself in Stan's arms she hugged him, her eyes glistening.

"Merry Christmas," she greeted.

"It is now," he replied, his voice husky, his lips brushing over her cheek.

Eyes aglow with love and laughter, she pointed to the mistletoe hanging above their heads. Stan chuckled and kissed her again, his lips covering hers in a gentle caress.

Scott watched in silence while everything about the boy softened—his stance, his expression, and the look in his eyes. A sharp stab of panic enveloped him. No wonder Craig was in a tizzy. As a man he'd recognize the signs of love. As a father he'd rebel against it. Scott grinned; glad he didn't have a daughter. Hearing Trina's high, tinkling laugh coming from the kitchen, he envisioned her delicate, fragile beauty, and wished desperately for one.

"What about me?" he teased Amber, opening his arms for a hug when Stanley moved out of her embrace.

Amber lingered a moment and then moved into Scott's arms kissing his cheek. Scott held her close, remembering the day she was born. With a sigh, he let her go. They grow up too fast, he thought when Stan stepped up and took her hand.

Alive with love and laughter, lunch simmered with excitement, especially since the time for exchanging gifts got closer with each tick of the clock. Ace squirmed with anticipation. The moment the meal was over, he tugged on Stan's arm. "Come on Stan, we've got to make room for Scott's gifts."

They laughed at Tamera's warning glare. "Stanley..."

"Ma'am?" he queried, his eyebrow arched in innocence, his eyes dancing with humor.

He kissed her cheek before allowing Ace to drag him into the den. "I swear he's got the world beat at spoiling Ace," Tamera remarked with a tender smile.

Craig grinned over at Scott then winked at his wife. "Not the whole world," he teased. The flush which rushed to Tamera's cheeks confirmed she knew he was referring to her.

Gifts were exchanged amid laughter, hugs and kisses until all that remained were those for Amber and Stan.

"I'm afraid your gifts couldn't fit under the tree," Craig remarked, gathering them together and leading them outside.

Amber shrieked with pleasure at the sleek, sporty Mustang which had been parked in front of the porch sometime during lunch. Throwing herself into her father's arms she kissed him.

Craig welcomed her hug, clung for a moment, relishing the strength of his daughter's embrace. With a brief nod toward the barn, he urged everyone's attention in that direction when Sam led two yearlings out. He smiled when Stanley's eyes widened in comprehension. "We thought these would be an appropriate gift for you since you plan on raising high-quality horses, a colt and a filly out of my best cutting stock. They should get you started."

Stan's eyes filled with tears of gratitude and love. "Oh, man," he exclaimed, jumping off the porch and running an appreciative hand over each. "They are beautiful!"

Walking back to them he hugged Tamera and shook Craig's hand. "Thank you."

Craig responded by pulling the boy in his embrace for a brief hug. "They can stay here until you're ready for them," he offered, as Stan slipped his arm around Amber. She glowed up at him.

"Now, it's time for me to give you your gift. I'll be right down," she remarked, heading upstairs while everyone retired back into the den. Hurrying to her bedroom, she retrieved his gift. Excitement colored her cheeks and brightened her eyes when Stanley eyed the huge, oblong, box.

He shook his head. "Amber, no," he breathed, when she held it toward him. *Only one thing would come in a box that size.*

"Open it, then tell me no," she challenged. Stan's eyes registered pure pleasure when he lifted the shiny new guitar out of its case.

"Oh, Amber," he breathed. "It's...God, it's beautiful! Wow!" He chuckled, hugging her against him. "I don't know what to say."

She laughed, thrilled at his reaction. "There's a condition to the gift, Stanley. You have to play and sing for me every day."

He stroked the strings in a loving gesture. "You've got it, Sweetheart." Reaching under the tree, he retrieved the last tiny, gaily-wrapped package and handed it to her. "I hope you're not disappointed," he said. Glancing up, he winked at Craig.

Anticipation shimmered around the room while she opened it with trembling hands. Lifting the lid, she found a small ring box with tiny, intricate flowers carved all over it. She looked up at Stanley, her eyes wide and glittering with hopeful tears.

Stan bit back a grin when she opened the empty box. Amber gasped, her gaze searching his. "I could only afford the box," he said, trying for an apologetic smile.

Craig's chuckle cut off her reply. "Boy, you are either foolishly brave or incredibly stupid and I've yet to figure out which."

Amber struggled for composure, knowing she was being teased. "It's such a lovely box. Isn't it, Mama?" She held it out for Tamera's inspection and kissed Stan's cheek. "I'm sure I can find something to put in it."

Her laughing eyes belied the deadly expression on her face when she turned to Scott. "How big is the human heart?"

Laughter roared throughout the room.

"Amber!" Stan gasped, clutching his heart. "I thought you, of all people, would understand my finances right now." He tried to look disappointed. He really did. The grin gave him away.

Emotion clogged his throat as her expression changed when she noticed the tiny ring on his finger, a lovely, petite diamond flanked by two tiny but sparkling sapphires.

"Oh!" she gasped, covering her mouth with her hand, tears rushing to her eyes once more.

"There's a condition to the gift, Amber."

"Ah, no, no, no. That's not how it's done," Craig and Scott cut in simultaneously.

Stan flushed but willingly got on one knee, reaching for her hand.

"Will you marry me, Amber?"

"Don't answer that."

Amber whirled around waiting for Scott to explain. He did, his brown eyes dancing with humor.

"After what he did to you with the box, I'd make him sweat for an answer."

Amber smiled, turning back to regard Stanley, her gaze glittering. "How long should I make him sweat?"

Scott chuckled. "Oh, a day or two at least, a week maybe."

"A year," Craig interjected. "A century."

Stan glared over at them. "I can grovel with the best of them," he assured, willing to do just that. The love shining in Amber's eyes convinced him he wouldn't have to.

He stood up, changed tactics. Brushing her hair off her face, he caressed her flushed cheeks with trembling hands.

"I love you, Amber," he whispered, brushing his lips over hers as her eyes brimmed over. "Say yes," he urged, slipping the ring on her finger then raising her hand to his lips.

"Make this the happiest Christmas of my life. Say yes."

She nodded with a sob, wrapping her arms around his neck.

"Is that a yes?" he teased.

"Yes," she whispered, soaking his shirt with happy tears. Getting her trembling emotions under control, she gazed up at him. "When? Today? Tomorrow? Next week?"

Silence filled the room when Craig and Tamera's eyes met in surprise. Suddenly she laughed. "She's just like you."

He grinned. "Did you tell her?"

She shook her head. "No."

"What?" the others in the room demanded in unanimous question.

Tamera giggled. "Those were the exact words Craig said when I told him yes."

Once again laughter filled the room and everyone gathered around to see the ring.

Stan's gaze met Craig's. "Thank you," he mouthed, his eyes revealing the depth of his gratitude.

Later they laughed and sang Christmas songs while Stanley played his guitar. His rendition of *Silent Night, Oh Come All Ye Faithful*, and *What Child is This?* brought tears to everyone's eyes.

Scott sighed, brushing a tear off Trina's silky cheek. "Do you know 'All I want for Christmas is You'?"

Stan nodded. "Yeah, but I can't do it justice like she does," he remarked, and then promptly did it better.

"Can't do it justice, huh?" Craig asked. "You missed your calling, Boy. You should be in Nashville."

Stan grinned strumming his strings. "Are you saying that because you think I'm good?"

His gaze glittered into Craig's.

"Or because you'd rather I be anywhere but here?"

"Both," Craig admitted with a chuckle.

Chapter Thirteen

Amber stopped papering and watched out the kitchen window while Stan worked on the fence enclosing the back yard. She could already envision a swing set there and a sandbox.

A thrill of desire raced through her as she watched the strong muscles in his back and shoulders ripple and flex with every swing of his hammer. The sun bounced off his bronzed skin and shone in subtle blond streaks through his chestnut hair. He needed a haircut, she thought with a smile when he brushed a lock off his forehead, put his hat back on and went back to work.

A frown of concern creased her brow when the hammer broke and he threw the handle down with a muttered curse. *He's working too hard.* She told him that often, worried at his obvious frustration. Putting down her tools, she brushed her hands on her jeans and walked out the back door, pausing just behind Stanley when he laid his head on his arm with a weary sigh. "Stan?"

"What?" he growled, turning on her in an angry huff.

Her eyes widened. She held her arms out to him, her palms raised in a gesture of supplication. "I love you," she whispered. He grinned, his expression softening.

"That makes everything all right," he assured, pulling her close for a quick kiss. "There are only two things I need in my life. The rest can fall by the wayside."

Amber waited, wondering what else he held equal to, or above, her love.

He smiled. "God and you, nothing else matters as long as I have you on my side."

She smiled with obvious relief. "I thought you were going to say horses," she teased, reveling in his quick shout of laughter.

"Well, three things," he amended with a grin.

"You want to tell me what's bothering you?" she queried.

Stan sighed, pulling her down beside him on the stack of lumber nearby. "I don't know, Am. It's all going so slow," he complained.

"Sweetheart, you've done wonders with this place. Look at what all you have accomplished. The house is beautiful; it's almost ready to live in. And I'm glad you didn't paint anything deep, dark green," she added, nudging him with her shoulder.

"The barn is looking good; it's nearly finished. The weather will soon let you complete that and the fence. Daddy will be bringing your foals soon and you can start working with them. The rest will follow," she assured him.

He sighed again. "Yeah, but look at what all else there is. I still have to blow the insulation in the house, run the air and heat, finish the barn, rebuild or repair fences over the rest of the property. Build more barns. Buy more horses. One pair of Quarter horses is not going to be enough."

"But it's a start," she argued, her tone gentle. "But you know that already. What's really bothering you, Stanley? Can't you tell me? How do you think we'll ever make a life and marriage if you don't confide in me?"

He smiled. "I just don't want you worrying."

She rolled her eyes. "I worry now because you're not talking to me. And I probably assume worse than the truth."

He sighed again, knowing she was right, but still embarrassed at the truth. The truth being, he was broke. He couldn't earn enough, fast enough to have them up and running by the summer. Though they hadn't talked about it, he hoped they would marry over the summer and he wanted to be able to support her when they did. A dark flush crept into his cheeks. He eyed her with a rueful smile.

"I just don't think I can get it together, Amber. I don't have enough money to pull it off."

She felt his embarrassment and ached for him. Chewing on her lip she considered their options. She knew he would never go for financial help from her father. But, maybe there was another way. "I could get a job," she offered. "Something part-time after school, the money I earn can go toward this place."

He shook his head in quick denial. "No way, I won't have you working to support me."

Anger flared in her eyes. "I will not settle for being just your wife, Stanley," she hissed, getting up to pace. "I want a full partnership in this marriage. Like my parents have. They share things, hopes, dreams, and disappointments. This will be my home too. I don't see anything wrong with me helping to get it going."

"Yes, but your mother does not have to work. I don't want you to either."

"You forget how they met," she fumed. "They met when she came to work for him."

"That's different."

"Why?"

"She's a veterinarian. You're not even out of high school yet. Then you have college to consider. What kind of job could you get now? I won't have you waiting tables or slinging hash."

"And what would be wrong with waiting tables or slinging hash?" she demanded, hands on her hips, eyes flashing. "They're both respectable, honest endeavors."

Stan smothered a grin. God, she was beautiful when angry! And to have all that passion focused on him...He shook his head forcing his mind back to the conversation at hand. "But they're not for you, My Sweet," he assured, his tone placating, reaching for her hand.

She snorted, jerking away. "You're a jerk, an old-fashioned, chauvinistic jerk. The twenty-first century is barreling down on us and you are acting like an idiot. Besides, school is not a problem. I could not attend another day and still graduate with honors."

He scrambled to his feet, glaring down at her. "A jerk, am I? Is it wrong for me to want to take care of you?"

She sighed, knowing he just wanted the best for her, for them. And he was proud. But too much pride was wrong. "No, Stanley, it's not wrong. But is it wrong for me to want to help? The day will come when I can stay home and raise children while you raise horses. Is it wrong for me to help until then, to want to invest in my, in our, children's future?"

He knew she was right. But he didn't like it. Old fashioned and chauvinistic though it may be, he wanted to provide for his wife and children. And he didn't want to see her slave away in some grease pit for less than minimum wage like his grandmother had. He didn't want to fight with her either.

Stan sighed, raking his fingers through his hair. "No, Sweetheart, it's not wrong for you to want to help. Look, let's just play it by ear for now. Finish school and don't worry your pretty little head about it. We'll see how things go this summer and we'll discuss it again."

She eyed him, her eyes narrowed in doubt, sure he was just pacifying her for now. Like her father would. "Promise?"

He grinned. "Lord, but you're stubborn."

She crossed her arms over her chest, determined to wring a promise from him that he would talk to her when he was in trouble and let her help if she could. "Promise me, Stanley, that you will take me seriously. I'm not some pampered little girl. I'm not afraid to work. And I want to help," she insisted.

She saw the admiration in his eyes, and something else. They glittered with amusement. "What?" she demanded, nearly stomping her foot in agitation.

He couldn't suppress the chuckle. "You are so beautiful when you're in a huff," he teased. "And so easy to get a rise out of."

She growled, wanting to punch him. Her eyes narrowed into glittering slits, her fists clenched. *Easy to get a rise out of, huh?* The thought infuriated her. Tossing her head, she stepped closer to him. *We'll just see,* she seethed, her mind searching for a way to retaliate. The idea came to her in an instant.

Her arms went around his neck. Pulling his lips down on hers she kissed him before he could protest, her lips boldly searching his mouth. Her hands traveled down his back to his waist then hips, brazenly pulling his hard thighs against her soft frame. She pressed against him in an intimate gesture.

Desire erupted in him like a volcano, spewing lava through his blood. Stan groaned in surrender. The moment his arms wound around her, she stepped back.

His eyes registered confused excitement. Desire darkened them like thunderclouds against a brilliant summer sky. His breathing was labored, his body tense. His face was flushed, taut with need. Amber's mocking gaze swept over him, her lips curled into a smug, chiding grin.

"Looks like I'm not the only one who's easy to get a rise out of," she taunted, turning on her heel.

Shock then surprise registered in his heat-fuddled brain, as Stan realized she'd succeeded in bringing him down a notch. Or two, he conceded silently, his mouth curving into a grin. He chuckled. "I'll get you, you little witch."

The playful threat carried on the breeze to her ears. A giggle escaped when she broke into a run. Graceful though they were, her long legs were no match for the speed and strength, which had enabled him to play wide receiver in high school football. He overtook her as she raced up on the porch. His arm swung around her waist, tackling her to the floor. Cushioning the fall with his body, he rolled over, pinning her down with his long frame.

"Want to play grown up games with me, little girl?" he queried, his lips capturing hers in a thorough kiss. One hand held her arms imprisoned above her head while the other caressed her body from the hip upward to cup her waist.

Amber struggled against his hold, wanting to wrap her arms around him and pull him closer. Wanting desperately to show him this was no little girl he was holding in his arms.

"What are you going to do now?" he taunted. His lips traveled down her throat, teasing a responding moan from deep within her. He moved against her in a tender, intimate way pleased at the flare of passion in her eyes,

Struggling for some semblance of control, Stanley watched desire turn her eyes from brilliant sapphire to smoky midnight blue. His hand brushed over her firm abdomen to rest just below her breast. His mouth watered with the desire to taste the sweet flesh he held. She whimpered and trembled, wringing an answering groan from him.

"The question is what *you* are going to do now?" she challenged, feeling the strength of his need even though he held himself tightly in rein.

Stanley struggled between what he wanted to do and what he had to do. What he wanted to do was throw out common sense, forget every ounce of morality he'd been taught, every lesson he'd ever learned and bury himself in her love.

What he had to do was stop now, let her go while he still maintained enough control to do so. Lingering over one last kiss, he loosened his hold on her. He groaned when she wrapped her arms around him, arching against him sweetly, lost in the passion of their embrace.

Burying his hands in her hair, his lips softened then left hers. "Amber," he breathed, pushing away from her with the last shred of control he possessed. "I'm going to let you go," he whispered stroking her cheek, smiling into her eyes. "For now. But one day, My Sweet, I'll make you mine," he promised. "But not here, not like this. You're much too precious for that."

Tears filled her eyes, rolled slowly down her cheeks. "I love you," she whispered, her voice achingly tender.

He pulled her in his arms again. "I love you, too, Amber, so much, too much to treat you like some over-sexed teenager in heat, enough to wait until we're married."

"I'm sure you have plenty of experience with over-sexed teenagers," she remarked. "Especially since you're barely twenty-one yourself."

He heard the question and the jealousy in her voice and chuckled. "I think I've enough experience to know how to please you, My Sweet," he promised. "But not as much as you think. There's been no one since long before the night I fell in love with you. And we both know when that was."

Her eyes widened in surprise. "Really?"

A nagging feeling started in his gut and Stanley wondered if she doubted him, and if so, why? He nodded. "Really. What's up, Amber?"

She blushed, burying her face in his shoulder. "It's just that," she hesitated. "Well, I've heard talk and, you know...."

"What kind of talk?"

Her blush deepened. "About how difficult it is for a man to do without sex and that, if he's not having sex with his girlfriend because he wants to marry a virgin, he's having it with someone on the sly," she admitted, embarrassment evident in her voice.

"I love you, Stanley. I know waiting until we're married is the proper thing to do, but if you...." Her voice trailed off at the look of surprised understanding dawning on his face.

She was offering herself to him.

Stanley swallowed hard, fighting the demands of his heart and body. Desire clawed through him, sharp and painful. His hands clenched into fists as he fought to smother the need boiling through his blood. God help me, he pleaded silently.

Amber pulled away from him, embarrassed to the core. "I'm sorry. I just thought...."

He pulled her in his arms, holding her against his chest. "Oh, Sweetheart, God, Amber, I want you so much," he admitted with a strangled little laugh, wondering how to talk with her about this and not increase her embarrassment.

"Listen to me," he urged, cupping her hot cheeks in his hands. "I love you. And believe me, I want you. But I can *and will* wait until we are married. Regardless of what you've heard, man is not controlled by flesh alone. What you've been listening to is people trying to legitimize their excuses for having sex. Period. It's not as difficult to do without as you've imagined or the talk you've heard has convinced you."

A teasing grin tugged at his lips. "Except in moments like these. Then it's very difficult to let you go. Only the thought of cheating you and myself out of the most important night of our life makes it bearable. Not to mention the disappointment it'll cause your parents if we act irresponsibly." He kissed her tenderly then chuckled.

"Added to that, is the fact your father would kill me. I'd like to live long enough to hold my children and watch them grow up." She smiled relief evident in her glowing gaze.

"Maybe I should tell Daddy you're all talk and no action. Then he won't worry as much," she teased, feeling better.

He laughed and hugged her. "Oh, Sweetheart, you don't know how tempting it is to prove you wrong," he admitted with a wry grin, moving the temptation of her out of his arms.

"Tell me about it," she urged, her expression curious yet shy.

"About what?"

She slid behind him, wrapped her arms around his waist, and pulled him against her. Her hands caressed the firm muscles of his chest. "About your first time."

He grinned. "Why would you want to hear about it? It wasn't as romantic as you might think."

She laughed. "I'll bet you've had to fight the girls off since you were five," she teased, feeling his muscles contract when a throaty chuckle rumbled through his chest.

"Well," he hedged. "A little older than that," he confessed. "I can't believe we're sitting here talking about this like it was the weather."

She nuzzled his cheek. "But it is like the weather." Her voice softened to a husky whisper. "Hot, sultry." Stan choked on a strangled laugh and tried to pull away from her. She tightened her arms around him

"I want to hold you," she whispered.

He relaxed with a sigh. It felt good to be held by her, to have her arms wrapped around his waist and her cheek snuggled sweetly against his. He could hear the thick thudding of her heart, feel it strong against his skin. His voice was soft as he remembered, with quite some embarrassment, his first time with a girl.

"I was fifteen, and stupid." He chuckled. "And ready. She was every boy's dream. An older woman, girl really, it was awkward and embarrassing and it only happened once."

"And after?" she queried, jealous at the thought, yet curious.

"The second time I was a little older and got my heart broke. She was much older, and as it turned out, liked young boys," he admitted, feeling as angry and insulted as he did back then.

"I felt dirty and used. I decided after that, sex wasn't all it's cracked up to be. Not without love. Oh, I'd heard it all before. My grandmother taught me well about the facts of life and right from wrong. But it wasn't until that happened I began to listen, really listen, to what she was saying.

"Then I began searching God's truth on the matter and I'm convinced, love is the key, the difference, between having sex and making love. I've fancied myself in love a time or two," he admitted, grinning at her glare.

"But not like this, not enough to try again and I've waited. I've never felt so strongly about anyone and I know it'll be so much different, so much better, between us. Believe me, it's sheer torture to be here with you like this and not make love with you," he confessed, looking up into her sparkling eyes.

"I love you, Amber. So much," he breathed, pulling her lips down on his. Her smile was tender, as was the light in her eyes.

"Do you know what it does to me to know that? And to hold you like this?" she queried, her cheeks flushed.

Her eyes glowed with love, sparkled with desire. "Do you know how hard, difficult," he amended, a hot flush covering his face at her grin. "Difficult it is for me?"

She laughed, a tender, teasing sound that vibrated clear through him.

"Which is why we're not alone like this much?"

He nodded, his silky hair rubbing against her cheek. "And why I work so hard," he admitted with a grin. "Hard, physical, labor is the best way I know to work off the tension."

She giggled. "Oh, I do love you," she admitted, hugging him again.

He laughed, tightening her arms around his waist. "Speaking of not being alone, how did you manage to be here today without Ace?"

"I have my ways," she teased.

He chuckled. "I'm sure you do, My Sweet, but I'd sure like to know how you convinced your father to let you come here alone."

She laughed. "I didn't have to convince my father. When Mama asked what we had planned for today and I told her I would be hanging wallpaper, she knew Ace would be more of a hindrance than help so she didn't send him. Since Daddy was already gone there wasn't much convincing to do. Of course, I got the whole responsibility lecture and all, but she's just not as overprotective as Daddy."

"For that I'll be eternally thankful," Stan remarked. Taking her hand in his, he raised it to his lips, savoring the taste of her skin, thrilling at the tiny shiver which raced through her. "So, now it's your turn. Tell me what your dream lover is like."

"You."

"Aw, c'mon now, play fair," he teased.

She heaved an exaggerated, lusty sigh. "Romeo."

He chortled. "As in Romeo and Juliet?"

She nodded. "I became a full-fledged romantic the first time I read it."

"When was that?"

"When I was thirteen."

He looked at her in surprise. "You read Shakespeare when you were thirteen?" He laughed when she nodded. "What do you want to be when you grow up, little girl? A doctor? Lawyer? Rocket scientist?" he teased, flinching when she pulled the hair on his chest.

She shook her head. "A wife and mother, maybe someday a published author, or possibly a teacher or daycare worker. I'm not sure yet, but I know I want to work with children, watch them learn, feel their excitement at a new discovery, help them if they're having trouble. That's the ultimate high. Children are such a blessing and a joy. They're our hope, our future, and the future of our families, communities, and nations. Even watching Ace catch on to a new game or discover something exciting is a thrill."

She shrugged and nuzzled his cheek. "Anyway, Romeo and Juliet is a beautiful story, so romantic, so sad. And it's not that hard to understand. Then when I saw the movie and the actor was so sexy."

She sighed again, giggling when he glared at her. "I swore then I would find my own Romeo some day. And I've waited, until now. I knew the moment our eyes met that same homecoming eve, I had finally found him."

Her voice softened as she remembered. "I told my father the very next morning, I'd met the guy I was going to marry."

He laughed. "I'll bet he was just thrilled beyond reason to hear that. What did he say?"

Her eyes danced merrily. "He said I couldn't date until I was twenty-one or marry until I was thirty-five. Then he bet you wouldn't hang around that long."

"And what was your reply?"

"That by the time I'm thirty-five, he would be a grandfather," she answered, her grin smug.

Stanley laughed. "I bet that went over big," he said with a chuckle. "What, exactly, made you believe I *would* hang around?" he challenged with a grin.

She shrugged. "I just knew, in my heart, you would." Her eyes narrowed into icy shards. "And if you ever think of doing otherwise..."

"What will you do, little girl?" he taunted.

"Sic my father on you," she assured her smile confident, cocky.

"That should keep me in line," he gasped between chuckles.

Speak of the devil. They heard a loud bang as the front door slammed, and Craig calling for them through the house. Scrambling out of the embrace, they sat an arms-length apart.

"Kiss me, quick," Amber teased, hearing her father's footsteps in the kitchen. "And I won't tell him you're all talk and no action."

Stan laughed and kissed her, then looked innocently into Craig's steely gaze.

Craig's eyes narrowed at seeing his daughter's flushed face and sparkling eyes, she looked sweetly rumpled. Anger and fear collided in his chest. "What's going on?" he growled.

Amber giggled regarding him with wide, innocent eyes. "We're just taking a break. Stan broke his hammer."

He glared at the boy. "I know there's more than one hammer around here."

Amber sighed. "My hero." She extended a hand toward Craig in an elaborate gesture. "Ever the doting, overprotective father," she teased. "Where's Mama?"

"She wanted me to come and tell you that dinner's ready. You're going to have to get a beeper or phone or something," he told Stanley.

Stan risked a grin. "Then you won't be able to surprise us and check up on me."

Craig obviously didn't think that was funny in the least. "Boy," he remarked, his tone ominous, gray gaze flashing with barely suppressed fury.

Amber laughed. Jumping to her feet, she hugged her father. "I'll go shut things down inside."

She glanced at Stan, her eyes warm and tender. A look neither man missed.

"Put on a shirt."

"Yes, Ma'am."

Craig watched her leave and turned back to Stanley. "Look, I know Amber is a very beautiful..." he hesitated a second. "Woman," he admitted, sounding as though he'd realized it for the first time.

Stanley noticed the stunned look on Craig's face and smothered a grin. It obviously still surprised him Amber wasn't a little girl any more. "Yes, Sir, that she is. And I'm doing my level best to avoid the temptation she presents."

Craig eyed the boy in wary confusion, trying to believe, to trust. "Would the threat of castration make it easier for you to avoid temptation?"

Craig's eyes were a dark, dangerous gray, his tone deadly serious. Stanley reached down and retrieved his shirt off the porch rail where he'd laid it that morning. Pulling it over his head, he smoothed the grin off his face.

But he couldn't hide the laughter in his eyes.

"Yes sir. It just might at that."

Chapter Fourteen

Craig and Tamera came in after an early morning ride to find Amber pouring over the newspaper. "What'cha doin', Sweetheart?"

"Looking for a job," she answered her father, not glancing up.

He frowned. "A job? Why do you need a job?"

She sighed. "I don't need a job, Daddy. I want a job."

"Why? If you need money, you know all you have to do is ask."

She smiled. "I know. But," she hesitated, not wanting to say too much about Stan's financial situation, but needing their support. "There are some special things I want to do with the house and I need a job in order to do them."

"I think that's a wonderful idea," Tamera remarked.

Amber smiled again, grateful at least her mother was behind her.

"Did you discuss this with Stanley?" her father wanted to know.

She grunted in a very unladylike manner. "Stanley thinks I should finish school and not worry my pretty little head about it."

Craig chuckled at her tone. "I, for one, agree with him."

She glared at him. "I hate it when you two gang up on me."

He tossed back his head with a laugh. "Hey, Boy," he barked playfully at Ace who ran in and slid his arms around Tamera's waist. "Get your hands off my wife."

Ace grinned over at him. "She's my mama," he challenged. This was an old joke, adopted when Ace was a three. Everyone smiled remembering the incident as though it were yesterday.

Feeling exceptionally generous after hours in his wife's presence, and arms, Craig laughed. "I had her first," he insisted, with a wink at Tamera.

"Yeah, but she loves me most," Ace retorted. "Huh, Mama?"

Tamera laughed, hugged Ace and refrained from comment then she set about making breakfast. Craig turned back to his daughter. "What kind of job were you looking for?"

"I was hoping to find something in an office or daycare or maybe baby-sitting. But there's nothing, unless I want to be a dancer." Her eyes laughed into his.

"I'll bet Stanley would just love that," Craig remarked with a grin.

She rolled her eyes with a grunt. "Stanley won't hear of me waiting tables or slinging hash, I can promise you he wouldn't even discuss me dancing, even if I was old enough to do it."

Craig grinned at her. "I think I just might like that boy after all. When did you two discuss this?" he queried, imagining how the discussion went.

"Yesterday."

"So," he urged. "He doesn't want you working. What did you say to that?"

"Craig," Tamera warned, her tone telling him to butt out. He grinned, winked and ignored the warning.

"I said he was acting like a jerk." Amber replied.

Craig roared. "So that's what you were doing when I got there, fighting?"

Bound by honor to return his teasing, she shook her head, flushing. "No. When you got there, we were making up," she admitted, raising a triumphant gaze to his.

His eyes narrowed, but continued to glisten with humor. "I'm gonna kill that boy."

Her husky, sensual laugh had him grinning in return. "Oh, Daddy," she drawled, tossing the paper at him. "What's wrong with a little hugging and kissing? You and Mama do it all the time."

"Your mother and I are married. We have a license to do that."

"And you didn't do any of that before you were married?" she asked, arching an eyebrow in interest.

Craig glanced over at his wife who was waiting for his reply, her eyebrow arched in teasing. He grinned. "That's different." Amber's shout of laughter made him smile.

"Why?"

"Because you're my daughter and I say so. You're to do as I say, not as I do."

She snorted, raising wide, pleading eyes to her mother. "Why do men have to be such jerks?"

Tamera giggled. "I don't know, Darling. I've been trying to figure that one out for years.

"All right," Craig interrupted. "Let's get back to the subject at hand."

"What subject is that?" his wife asked all innocence.

"Any subject besides male bashing," he remarked, reducing both of his females to a helpless mass of giggles. Craig shook his head when they continued to taunt him.

"Where's Stanley when I need him? You two are impossible."

"Huh!" Amber huffed. "You and Stanley are impossible." Her father grinned. A cocky, arrogant, heart-stopping grin that still worked it's magic on women of all ages.

Rising from the table, he slipped his arms around his wife. "Am I impossible?" he queried in a soft, husky tone of voice, which still had the power to weaken her knees.

Leaning against his broad chest Tamera nodded. His smile tender, he covered her lips in a sweet caress then winked at his daughter.

"Let me know if you find a job you're interested in, or have any other ideas."

"Well, there is one other solution," Amber began, his comment just the opening she needed.

Craig poured another cup of coffee, sat back down, and waited for her to continue.

"Do you think I could use part of my college fund?"

"Amber, that money is put up for a reason."

She sighed. "Daddy, you have enough money put up to send my children to college."

He chuckled. "I put up enough for you to go to college no matter what you decided to be, a doctor or lawyer maybe."

"Or a rocket scientist?" she teased.

He grinned. "Whatever."

"What if I told you, all I want is to be a wife and mother?" she asked, locking her gaze with his. "I don't need a degree for that, do I?"

Craig fought back his fears and bit back his arguments. *So much for hoping she would wait until after college to get married.* "Sweetheart, if that's what you want, it's fine. But you still need to go to college for something. You need some skills and training to fall back on should something happen to Stanley."

"I know that, Daddy. And I will go to college at least for the basics until I decide what I want to do. But there's no way I'm going to need all of the money you have put aside."

"Well, after college, it's yours."

Amber held back a frustrated groan. "Why not now? I promise to use only what you allow."

Gazing into her pleading gaze, Craig cursed inwardly. *Damn that look again.* He relented with a sigh. "Okay. Your mother and I will discuss it. We'll talk again later."

Amber's smile was tender, her eyes brilliant. "Now, if I can find a way to get around Stan's pride to use it."

Craig chuckled. "That's your department, Sweetheart. I could transfer it over to your checking account. He wouldn't even have to know," he hinted, testing her loyalty.

She shook her head. "That's not honest. It would never work and it would only cause more problems."

"Good for you," Tamera congratulated her response.

Craig nodded in agreement. "Keep that attitude and you'll have him eating out of your hand," he teased.

She smiled. "Oh, I doubt that," she remarked, in a voice that assured him otherwise.

That evening, Craig approached Stanley himself, thinking maybe he would be more reasonable if the offer was changed to one of a matter between them. Man to man. He set the scene in the den while the women were doing the dinner dishes. Placing a check on the coffee table between them, he regarded Stanley with a serious expression. "I have a proposition for you."

Stan saw red, bright, hot, furious red. "Amber talked to you, didn't she?" he insisted, jumping up to pace.

"Something wrong?" Craig drawled, anticipating the storm.

"Yeah, something's wrong. When I confide in my fiancée I expect it to be confidential."

Like lightening across a stormy sky, his blue eyes flashed while Stanley continued his tirade, stopping just short of cursing Amber for her betrayal and damning Craig for his interference.

Craig waited in calm, lethal silence until he stopped pacing. In that moment he realized why Tamera insisted Stanley reminded her of him, and wondered how his grandfather had ever put up with his attitude. He hoped to handle Stanley as effectively as Gramps would have handled him. "Are you finished?" he queried in a quiet voice.

Stan fumed. "Yeah, I'm finished." He turned on his heel and stormed out of the house. Determined to leave before he lost complete control, he cursed at finding his tire flat. Kicking it, he started walking.

Amber came in from the kitchen, unaware of the situation. She'd agreed with her father it would be a good idea for Stan to regard their help as a business deal, thinking it would be easier on his pride. "Where's Stan?"

"He left."

Her eyes widened. "What did he say?" Craig repeated enough of Stanley's words to infuriate her.

"Oh, really?" Turning on her heel, she followed in Stanley's wake. "Where in heaven's name are you going?" she demanded of his retreating form.

He turned on her in an angry whirl. "Where am I going? I'll tell you where I'm going," he bit out as she approached him. "I'm getting the hell off this ranch."

"Why?"

Stan ground his teeth in frustration. "Amber, when I confide in you the last thing I want is for you to go crying to your daddy."

"Did you even listen to him?"

"I don't have to listen to him, to know you told him my business," he hissed. "Grow up, little girl. Daddy won't always have the answer," he sneered, too angry to see the hurt in her eyes.

She all but growled in response. "Maybe you ought to grow up and lose some of that stubborn, arrogant pride of yours."

Her eyes narrowed into icy shards. Stanley snorted, fighting the effect her raging beauty had on him.

Rolling her eyes, Amber dug in her pocket. "If you're so determined to leave, take my car. It'll be faster," she hissed, tossing her keys at him.

He caught them. "When I want something from you, I'll ask for it," he snarled, dropping the keys in the dirt.

Too furious to think, Amber turned on her heel. *Let him walk!*

"That's it, Amber, run back to daddy," he taunted.

She clenched her fists, fighting to calm down. His words tore at her heart, the intentional slur more than she could tolerate. She turned on him in an angry whirl, her palm connecting with his cheek.

Stanley grabbed Amber's arm, twisting it in his firm grip and pulled her against him, fighting for control. "You know," he told her in a soft, lethal, voice. "When you hit a man, you put yourself in a man's place. Don't you ever slap me again," he warned, all but shoving her away.

They glared at each other; both determined the other would back down first.

Amber took a deep, trembling breath, blinked back tears of anger and pain and fought the urge to rub her wrist.

"For your information, I did not go whining to my father," she said, her voice thick with unshed tears. Turning on her heel, she stalked toward the house.

Stan turned in the opposite direction. He took about three steps when a still, small Voice got his attention.

"He who answers before he hears, his is the folly and the shame."

Glaring at the heavens, he argued with himself, and God, knowing deep down inside, he was wrong. He hadn't even heard what Craig had to say, before jumping to conclusions and flying off the handle.

"The quick-tempered man displays folly at its height," the Voice reminded.

Stanley sighed. "I hear You, Lord," he muttered, accepting the guilt as the Lord convinced him of the truth. "You're right. I'm acting like a fool. I'm sorry," he whispered, and then felt the wave of relief and peace that always accompanies repentance and forgiveness.

"What now?" he asked, although he knew.

Pride was a huge, bitter pill to swallow and took a few minutes to get down. Turning, he picked up Amber's keys, tossing them in his hand. "A little wisdom now wouldn't hurt, Lord," he pleaded.

Craig met him at the door, nodding at her bedroom when he asked for Amber. Stan waited for permission before going up then paused in the doorway. She sat in a chair by the window, an open Bible in her lap. He watched her wipe a tear off her cheek. Remorse washed over him in sickening waves.

"Amber?" She looked at him and the devastation in her eyes tore at his heart. He took a step forward. "I'm sorry."

Her smile was tender and her lips trembled. She took a deep breath and held a hand out to him. "Me too, Stanley," she whispered.

He went to her, took her outstretched hand in his, and knelt at her feet while her eyes searched his.

"Do you think I care so little about your feelings that I would trample on your pride by running to my father?" she asked.

He shook his head. "No," he admitted in a soft, bitter voice. "You're right; I didn't even listen to him before flying off the handle."

"I love my father, Stanley. He's been my whole life." She fought the urge to stroke the cheek she'd slapped.

"Until you entered it," she admitted in a soft voice, her eyes boring into his. "I'm sorry if you feel threatened by that, or jealous. I love you, but if you truly resent him that much, maybe we'd better rethink our situation."

Stan's heart thudded with fear. "It's not that, Amber. I love your parents and I respect your father. But, I'll be your husband. I want you to come to me and I want to be able to confide in you and know whatever is said between us, remains between us."

Glancing down, Amber blinked back tears and fought down her response to the accusation in his voice. Proverbs 15:1 caught her eye: *A mild answer calms wrath but a harsh word stirs up anger.*

"I haven't broken your confidence, Stanley," she promised, and then shook her head. "We talked, remember? You want me to come to you, but you refuse to take me seriously."

Stan sighed knowing she was right. *Again.* He swallowed hard, audibly forcing down another dose of foolish pride. "Lord, I hate gnawing on leather," he muttered, making her smile.

"You're right. It's just," he hesitated, his eyes begging hers for understanding and forgiveness. "There are some things a man has to do for himself."

Amber nodded, blinking at the tears which rushed to her eyes. Her lips trembled. She took a deep, shuddering breath. "I thought we'd do it together," she said, suppressing a soft sob.

He lost. If there were any reasons, any reasonable excuses to refuse to listen to their offer, she demolished them with that one word.

Together.

In that moment Stanley realized, man wasn't supposed to go through life doing things alone. God created woman to be his helpmate, his support—emotional, physical, in whatever way she could. And God had blessed him with the love of one of the most compassionate, tenderhearted, generous women He'd ever created.

Stan swallowed the thick lump of emotion clogging his airways. "I don't deserve you," he whispered, cupping her cheeks in his hands. "I love you, Amber. Always remember that. No matter how many times we butt heads."

He heaved a resigned sigh. "I'll listen to whatever your father has to say. And we'll discuss it," he promised. "Together."

"That's all I ask, Stanley," she admitted with a tender smile. "That we do this together. That's what marriage is all about. What *life* is all about."

Pulling her in his arms, he held her a long time, gaining strength and courage from her love. Strength to accept the truth he'd just learned and courage to face her father after acting like an ass.

Craig didn't put him through the embarrassment of an apology and an explanation. He simply nodded his acceptance when Stanley stumbled over the words 'I'm sorry.'

"Stanley," he began, "pride is an honorable thing. But, too much of it is dangerous, and foolish. Even the Bible states that the Lord despises pride and that the proud will be punished. First off, Amber did not come crying to me. I found her pouring over the want ads this morning looking for a job. She said there were some things *she* wanted to do with the house."

He paused a moment, letting Stanley digest that fact. Obviously struggling with his emotions, Stanley got up to pace.

"Sit down," Craig commanded. His tone brooked no argument. Stanley sat.

"However," Craig continued, "It doesn't take a genius to know how difficult and expensive this task you've undertaken is. Secondly, I agree with you that she does not need to take a job. She needs to concentrate on school and continuing her education for some kind of skills to fall back on if necessary." He grinned into the questioning gaze.

"Yeah, we had a very lively discussion when I agreed with you on that," he admitted with a chuckle. Picking up the check, he slid it into Stan's shirt pocket.

"You don't even have to look at this until you put it in the bank. How you and Amber choose to use it is up to you. You can make arrangements to pay it back now, you can accept it as the gift that it is, or you can pay it back later by providing for my daughter and grandchildren."

Stan nodded choking on the urge to refuse. Pride insisted he consider the offer a loan, his heart urged him to accept it as a gift. Only his love for Amber enabled him to accept it at all.

Chapter Fifteen

Stanley walked through the house with Amber, making mental notes of last minute changes in the décor she wanted.

"Humph, I see you managed to paint something dark green," she remarked.

Her eyes sparkled like rare, precious jewels. Stan chuckled. "Seems appropriate with the paneling," he commented, referring to the sheets of off-white wood with scenes of deer peeking through lush batches of forestry. He had to admit, if only to himself, that things went a lot faster and smoother when you had money. In the weeks since he accepted the check from Craig, he'd finished the house and was living there.

Pulling Amber down on the porch swing with him, he kissed her, urging her to set a date for the wedding.

"You're in a hurry all of a sudden," she teased.

He laughed. "Sweetheart, I'd marry you tomorrow if your father would sign the papers. Besides, it's very uncomfortable sleeping in a double bed all alone."

She grinned. "Well, we could take a nap," she offered, her tone sweet, charming. "Just hold each other."

Her eyes sparkled with desire. Stanley grunted. "Right. Your father is due here any minute with my horses and you want me to take a nap with you. No way." His voice lowered to a husky whisper. "Besides, when I do carry you over that threshold and lay you in that bed, I will not have to worry about being shot in the back. Or you leaving to go home," he assured.

"How about sometime this summer?" she asked crawling onto his lap.

"I was hoping you'd say that. When?"

She laughed. "Oh, I don't know. August or September." She was teasing. He fell for it.

"That long? I'll go insane if I have to wait that long. How about June or July?"

She giggled and snuggled against him. "How about tomorrow?"

He rolled his eyes, positive Craig wouldn't agree to that. He wanted Amber safely graduated from high school before she got married. "How about tonight?" he queried. "We can elope."

She paused as if considering the idea. "No. I want a wedding, a real big one, at home. I have this dream of my father walking me down the stairs while you sing."

He grinned. "Have you discussed this with your father?"

"Leave my father to me," she said, her tone assuring him whatever kind of wedding she wanted, she'd get.

He chuckled. "Just name the time and place, Sweetheart, and I'll be there," he promised, his lips covering hers in a tender caress. A groan escaped when she leaned into him, getting lost in the kiss as it deepened. Cupping her face in his hands, Stan regarded her with glittering eyes. "Amber, do you love me?"

She nodded. "Very much."

"Well, then, will you please get off my lap so I can compose myself before your father gets here?" he pleaded in a thick, agonized voice.

She giggled, wriggling closer when he tried to lift her off his lap. Sinking her hands in his thick, chestnut hair, she buried her mouth on his again. Her lips moved to caress his cheeks and ear. She pulled him closer when he trembled in her arms.

"Amber. Please," he begged, a near-whimper punctuating the plea.

"Please what?" she teased, while he removed her arms from around his neck.

Taking her hands in his, he dumped her on the floor. Her eyes widened in surprise and she burst into gales of laughter.

Stanley's eyes narrowed into glittering blue flames.

"You, My Sweet, are an incurable tease. The day will come when you'll pay for torturing me," he warned.

"Right, Mr. All Talk and No Action, I'm terrified."

Her eyes glistened. Rolling to his feet, Stan dragged her to hers, his lips covering hers in a fierce kiss, leaving no doubt to the depth of his frustrated passion.

"Amber, Love," he muttered, pulling her closer, his hands roaming over her back and arms in a restless caress. "God, you tempt me," he moaned, giving in to the need to taste her sweetness and fire again. His arms wrapped around her, pulling her closer.

Picking her up, he wound her legs around his waist, settling her on the porch rail, her back resting against the post. Her soft purr of pleasure burned through him like too many hot irons, branding his resolve, searing his control.

Passion erupted.

His mouth molded and shaped hers to fit his until every ragged breath he took robbed them both of much needed oxygen. One hand held her in place, while the other tugged at her pony-tail, getting lost and tangled in the silken strands.

Swept up in the sea of emotions, Amber clung to him as though he were a life raft and she a drowning woman. She didn't know what to do or what to expect, she only knew that she ached, everywhere—in places she never knew existed and that she wanted...Something. She whimpered his name, not sure if it was a plea for him to stop or an invitation to continue.

The pleading tone in her voice broke through the red haze of desire, revealing need, deep and raw, mixed with fear and uncertainty. Stan shuddered. Taking a deep breath, he dragged his lips from hers, his breathing sharp and painful. He rested his head against her shoulder, commanding control to his raging senses.

Her hands ran over him in a soothing caress. "I'm sorry," she whispered. "I didn't mean to push you. I didn't realize," her voice trailed off, and he shook his head.

"Don't apologize," Stan mumbled. "It's okay." Such sweet misery, he thought, searching for the words to ease her fears and dispel her embarrassment. Making sure she rested safely against the post, he cupped her face in his hands and stroked her cheeks with his thumbs. His lips covered hers in a tender but brief caress.

"I love you, Amber," he whispered. "And I want you with a hunger unlike anything I've known. Passion is all of those things: hunger, need, desire. It's also tender and gentle. And when it's born of love, there's no description. No words can express the depth of what I feel for you. Or how much I need you, and want you." He shrugged, continued to stroke her cheeks with his thumbs.

"I'm sorry if I frightened you. But, when I have you in my arms I get carried away."

Amber smiled, a tender, loving light in her eyes. "I'm not sure if I was frightened or why. I know only that I love you. You make me feel things I've never felt, only read about, heard about, and imagined. I mean, I'm not that naive, or stupid, but," she shrugged, a hot blush filling her cheeks. "I don't know how to explain what happens to me when I'm in your arms, when you're holding me and kissing me. It's so different from anything I've ever dreamed because it's so real and so deep. I'm sorry if I've tempted you beyond your control. I don't mean to and I'll try not to again."

He chuckled, the sound full of joy and longing. "Oh, Sweetheart, just being near you strains my control. When you play with fire, you risk getting burned. But thank you," he whispered, nuzzling her cheek.

She giggled and blushed harder. "Tomorrow you said?"

In control again, Stanley laughed. Pulling her off the rail, he fought the urge to touch her as she smoothed her rumpled blouse and hair. "Anytime, Sweetheart. Anytime," he assured. "And until then, I don't think I'll put the new hot water heater to much use. Not with all the cold showers I'll be taking."

She laughed; a deep, husky, sensual sound which made Stanley ache to take her in his arms again. He deliberately took a step back. And just in time. Craig turned in the drive pulling a horse trailer which carried his yearlings, the first pair of champion cutting horses, the beginning of a dream.

His dream.

Rubbing his knuckles over her cheek in a gentle caress, he brushed his lips over hers then jumped off the porch to meet Craig when he backed the trailer up to the barn.

* * * * *

The incident was a precursor of days to come, of frustrations to follow. As if the excitement of graduation with its parties, invitations, pictures and prom weren't stressful enough, Amber had another issue to deal with altogether. Lori Strickland had taken it upon herself to plant seeds of doubt as to Stanley's fidelity in her mind. What began as minor irritation, turned to utter anger when she got to school one morning to find Lori leaning against her locker.

"Got something to tell you," Lori stated, her voice nothing more than a smug whisper.

"Doubt very seriously I want to hear anything you have to say, Lori," Amber answered, shoving her away so she could get into her locker.

"Oh, you'll want to hear this," Lori purred. "I know you don't believe me when I tell you I've been intimate with Stanley, but I think you'll see in time, I'm telling the truth."

Amber slammed the locker shut. "You know, Lori, when you first started talking all this trash I thought you were just young and immature or maybe even jealous. And I was willing to give you the benefit of the doubt. I mean, Stanley is a wonderful man and I wouldn't blame you or anyone else for trying to break us up. But now I know better. You're not just young and immature, or even jealous. You're downright mean and no matter what you say, I don't believe you."

Lori just smirked, and rubbed her stomach. "Well, we'll just see about that," she remarked, then sauntered away.

The bell rang forcing Amber to stuff her emotions into a tiny corner of her heart. She'd often wondered if she should tell Stanley of Lori's taunting, but with the whirlwind of school activities, and last minute finishes to the house, not to mention deciding on a wedding date their stress levels were already strained to the max. And she didn't want to add to it by falling for one of the oldest tricks known to women. Still, she couldn't stop the sharp stab of pain in her heart at the mere thought of him being with another woman. Though she'd never let it show, especially in front of Lori. The situation came to a tumultuous head one evening.

Taking advantage of the rare opportunity of some time alone, they'd gone out to dinner. Pulling out her chair, Stan waited until Amber was seated before taking his own. Sliding his hand under hers, he lifted her fingers to his mouth, kissing the tips. "Hi, My Sweet."

Amber cocked her head in question. Stan grinned. "We've been so busy lately with parties and crowds, it seems like we've hardly had a moment to actually speak to one another." Her smile took his breath away. Stan pressed his lips into her palm then rested his cheek in her hand.

Amber caressed his face. "Life has been kinda crazy lately, hasn't it?"

He nodded. "I'll be glad when it's all over and things settle down."

"Me too," Amber agreed, as the waitress approached them, her eyes trained on Stanley.

"Hello, Gorgeous," she addressed him. "Y'all ready to order, or do you need a few more minutes."

"I'm always ready," Stan assured. "How 'bout you?" he asked Amber, noting the way her eyes narrowed and honed in on the waitress.

Amber flushed, glaring up at the woman. Jerking her hand away from Stanley's cheek, she snapped open the menu and made her selection. "I'll have the broiled chicken dinner," she answered, her tone clipped.

Once their orders were in and the woman gone, Stan reached for her hand again. "You okay?"

Embarrassment heated her cheeks. Amber smiled and lifted his hand to her face. "Yeah, guess I'm just feeling the strain of the last few weeks." Before she could say another word, the waitress appeared with their drinks.

"Thank you," Stan said, as she placed Amber's iced tea in front of her.

"You're welcome, Darlin'," she purred, putting his drink down with a flourish.

Amber stiffened at the intimate tone and the way she leaned toward Stanley, but refrained from looking at the woman, afraid if she did, she'd end up making a scene. Her hand trembled when she took a sip of her tea.

When the waitress left, Stan reached for Amber's hand, again lifting it to his mouth. "So, are you ready to be done with school?"

Amber forced herself to smile and nodded. They talked a few minutes before the food arrived. Once again, Stanley thanked the waitress who in turn gave him a saccharine smile and winked.

"Anytime, Sugar."

Amber took a deep, hissing breath and forcefully refrained from waving her engagement ring in the woman's face. The green-eyed monster had its claws around her heart and she didn't know how to deal with it.

Stan noticed the change in atmosphere immediately but thought maybe if he gave her the space she needed and didn't press, whatever was bothering Amber would come out in the course of the evening. The notion fled the moment the waitress appeared to refill their drinks.

"Can I get you anything else, Doll?" she asked.

Stan shook his head. "No, thank you," he answered, eyeing Amber when she cleared her throat in an exaggerated manner.

"What's wrong, Sweetheart?" he queried, reaching for her hand once the waitress left. She jerked from his grasp.

"Nothing," she mumbled, hearing and hating the pout in her voice.

He frowned. "Amber?"

She tossed down the fork, like a child about to throw a tantrum. "I'm just not hungry anymore," she mumbled, wishing they were anywhere but here.

"Let's go then."

Hearing the tautness in his voice she sighed, feeling petulant and very confused at her own reaction. "Finish your supper, Stanley," she ordered, her smile tight.

"Sure?"

She nodded, massaging her throbbing temples. "Yes."

He watched, concerned when she pushed the food around on her plate, took a couple of bites and put the fork down with a look of disgust. "How about some dessert, Sweetheart?" he offered, when the waitress sidled up to him again with the desert menu.

She took a deep, hissing, breath and shook her head, excusing herself to depart to the ladies' room. Once there and assured she was alone, she let a few tears fall, tears of frustration and anger, anger which bothered and bewildered her. Washing her face, she pasted on a cheerful smile and went to join Stan once again.

Stan took one look at her face and stood up. Waving for the check, he dropped the bills on the table, took her arm, and left. "You want to talk to me?"

Her frustrated heart and tense mind took his urging as an invitation to explode. "I don't understand you," she exclaimed, a slightly hysterical note in her voice.

"What?" he asked, exasperated.

"It sure didn't seem to bother you that she was hanging all over you!" she accused, her voice raising an octave.

Without thinking, Stanley laughed. "You're jealous." Though it shouldn't have, the thought surprised him. "Why?"

"I don't want you slinging hash or waiting tables, Sweetheart," she mimicked, a hint of nastiness in her voice.

"Now, I know why. Waiting tables is an invitation to flirt or be flirted with by every man or woman who walks in. You wouldn't hear of me doing it, but you let someone else have a great time with her job. And at my expense!"

"Whoa now, I didn't encourage her at all! I don't even know her name," he defended, and then fumed because he had to defend himself at all.

"Wendy," she snorted. "It was plainly and boldly printed over that well-rounded chest of hers."

Hearing the fury in her voice, he smothered a grin. "Well, Sweetheart, that just goes to show what I was not looking at."

She huffed, flinging away from him to the passenger side of the truck.

"Aw, come on, Amber. What in the world is wrong with you? You've been snapping at me for days now. What gives?" When she began to tremble with the effort to hold back tears, he stopped the truck.

"Talk to me, Amber," he urged, pulling her into his arms.

Talking was the last thing Amber wanted to do. She wanted to know that he was hers. Hers alone. And she was his. That he wanted no one else. Not even for a moment, or a night. Wrapping her arms around his neck, she pulled him toward her. "Kiss me, Stanley," she pleaded. "Hold me and kiss me like you really mean it."

Aware of nothing but the need in her voice, Stanley succumbed. Pulling her against him, he tried to stay in control of the situation. She went wild the moment his lips covered hers.

Her fingers dug into his hair, tugging him closer. Her body fit perfectly, against his, making him dizzy and achy with desire. He tried to pull back, to stay in control. She wrapped herself more firmly against him. Her hands strayed to his chest, tugging at the snaps of his shirt. She moaned, whimpering with need as it gave way to her insistent tugging. Her lips traveled down his throat, nipping at his collarbone, touching, nibbling, and grazing on the soft hair and skin covering his broad chest.

"No," he rasped. Sinking his fingers into her hair, Stan pulled her back to his lips, trying desperately to gain control.

"Amber, stop," he insisted with a tortured groan, pushing her away with the last ounce of strength he could muster.

"Why?" she whimpered, her voice was raw, wounded. "Why don't you want me?"

"Oh, Sweetheart," he moaned, cupping her cheek with his hand. "I do want you. But not here, not like this, you're much too precious for that."

"Then lets go home," she whispered, running a hand down his chest and letting it rest invitingly, temptingly, on his thigh.

"God," Stan muttered his breathing harsh and uneven, struggling for control. "Jesus, help me," he begged, then shook his head, moving her hand from his person with a firm no.

Amber took it as rejection, plain and simple. She moved away from him, curling into a tiny corner of the vehicle.

"Amber, wait," he pleaded, reaching for her. She jerked away hissing at him not to touch her.

The ride back to her home was in total, pained silence. Before she could escape from the truck, he tried again to talk to her. She stormed out, slamming the door in his face.

Infuriated, he stomped after her. "What on earth is wrong with you?"

"Nothing. Go back to your little waitress!" Jealousy gnawed at her heart and soul, ravishing her mind and obliterating all common sense.

"She is not my little waitress!" Stan insisted. "Whatever gave you that idea anyway?" He grabbed the front door before she could slam it in his face. Amber mumbled something about the woman hanging on him like a dog in heat and stomped up to her room.

Obviously Craig heard their raised, angry voices and came out of the den in time to hear her parting remark. He glanced at Stan, an eyebrow raised in question. Stan groaned, imagining what her father thought, and shook his head.

"Don't ask," he warned with a bitter snort. "I couldn't answer if you did."

Craig bit back a grin. Trouble in paradise, he thought, wondering if Stanley really understood what he was getting into by marrying the second-most stubborn woman God ever created. Masculine pride insisted he had absolutely nothing whatsoever to do with her being that way.

"Go on up," he insisted with a nod. "Neither of you will rest this night unless you get it settled. But Stanley, it's late, mind yourself," he cautioned at the boy's relieved grin.

Stan nodded in understanding and took the stairs two at a time to Amber's room. Entering, he closed the door behind him.

"Get out of here!" she ordered. "Before my father kills you."

"Your father gave me permission to come in here. Now, I want to know what you meant by that last remark."

"Oh, please, Stanley," she bit out with exaggerated sarcasm. "I know you're not stupid. You don't want me, so go on back to her."

Her eyes shot lightening sparks at him. Stan swore softly. Jerking her to him, he covered her mouth with an angry, bruising kiss, one meant to stop her baiting and unjustified accusations. Dragging her across the floor, he flung her on the bed at an angle, which lent no access to its comfort. They rolled to the floor with a thud.

She began to struggle in earnest, surprised and frightened at the depth of his anger. "Stop it. What are you doing?" she demanded, when he pulled her arms up over her head, holding them imprisoned with one firm grasp.

"I'm giving you what you want," he taunted, tugging at the snaps of her shirt. "A fast, hot, tumble."

She stopped struggling, going still and cold in his grasp. Her breath escaped in a hiss. "That is not what I want," she ground out between her teeth.

"It's what you asked for," he said, his voice hushed with hurt and anger. He didn't move and didn't loosen his hold, watching her lids lower, covering and hiding the turmoil of emotions in those beautiful eyes. A flush warmed her cheeks when he bent to kiss the throbbing muscle in her jaw.

"Look at me," he said with gentle insistence, growling when her chin lifted in defiance. "Amber, look at me," he demanded. She did, her eyes swimming with anger and humiliation.

Craig was right, Stan thought. Those eyes *were* like jeweled daggers of ice. They were ripping him to shreds, tearing at his control, searing his determination to wait and to hold out for the prize, the brass ring. Only the brass ring was a tiny gold band which would bind them together for life and brand her as his, always and only his. Loosening her arms, he pulled her against his chest.

"It's not what I want either, Sweetheart," he assured, stroking her hair in a soothing caress. "I'm sorry," he whispered, when she began to cry.

Each soft sob tore at him. Each tear eroded the thin wall of reserve he'd built around his desire and need. Stanley wondered how much longer either of them could withstand this tension without losing control or seriously hurting the other.

When her sobs subsided into soft, hiccupping sounds, he cupped her face in his hands. "I love you, Amber," he whispered, brushing his lips over hers.

"I love you, too," she mumbled. "And I'm sorry. I should never have doubted you. It's just..." her voice trailed off and another sob shook her slender frame.

"The talk again?" he queried with a sudden flash of insight.

She nodded avoiding his gaze.

Stanley's gut churned with unease. "It's more than that, isn't it?"

Again she nodded.

"Tell me," he insisted.

Amber withdrew from his embrace and hesitated, knowing what she was about to say would hurt. But she had to know! She considered her words with care. "There's a girl at school saying things about you and her."

"Do I know her?"

"Very well if what she's saying is true."

"Who is she?"

"I'd rather not say. She's probably just young and impressionable and jealous. I know it's crazy for me to protect her identity and I'm sorry. I love you Stanley and I don't want to doubt you, but she's been very graphic in what she says goes on between you."

"Young and impressionable? Right," he snorted. "And probably the same person who tried to come between us a year ago."

"Probably," she agreed, still unable to look him in the eye.

Stanley rose to his feet, pulling her up with him. "Look at me, Amber," he insisted, lifting her chin with his finger. When she did the pain and confusion in her eyes tore at his heart and softened his words.

"I can't fight this if you don't confide in me." Tears welled up in the azure eyes he loved so much, spilled over and rolled down her cheeks.

Amber felt the familiar frustration as the mocking voice in her mind argued against the truth in her heart. She searched his eyes then tore her gaze from his, knowing she couldn't hide the facts from him any longer, and the facts would hurt him as much if not more than her doubt.

"It's Lori," she whispered.

"Lori?" *No way.*

Amber nodded.

There had to be some mistake, Stanley reasoned mentally. "Strickland?"

Amber wrapped her arms around her waist, continued to avoid his gaze and nodded again. "She's pregnant you know."

Stanley collapsed onto her bed. *Pregnant?* "And she's saying it's mine," he concluded.

"I'm sorry, Stanley. I want to trust you." She took his hands in hers, knelt at his feet and rephrased her last remark. "I do trust you. But she's been so graphic and adamant that I don't know what to think anymore."

"How long has this been going on?"

Again, Amber avoided his gaze. "She started taunting me months ago, saying how great a kisser you are, and homecoming wasn't the first time, or the last, that she'd been in your bed. I tried ignoring her, figuring if I didn't give in to her baiting, she'd just let it go. But she hasn't. Then once you moved into the house it just got worse."

Stanley swore vilely. "That's why you've been so tense lately."

She nodded.

"Well, she's lying. I have not been with any girl or woman in this town. Hell, not even in this county or this state for that matter. I promise you this much, though, I will get to the bottom of this."

"She even said you'd been together at the house."

"My, house? Our house?" Stan asked his tone incredulous.

Amber nodded.

"Another lie," he ground out. "She hasn't been to that house since I cut my hand and, after what happened homecoming night, I haven't been alone with her. Not even at work." He stood up and pulled Amber in his arms when silent sobs began to shake her slender frame.

"Oh, Sweet, I wish I knew the words to convince you that I want only you. But I don't have them. I can only say it. And I'll say it as often as you need to hear it. But, you've got to trust me, Amber. We have nothing without trust."

"I know," she cried, her voice raw, harsh. "I do trust you. It's just, I want you so much. This need, this desperate ache, is frustrating and it hurts. Everywhere! And all this talk is driving me crazy. I just don't know what to do anymore!" she wailed.

"Just hang on, Darling, and set a date for the wedding," he suggested, his voice gentle, his chuckle soft and throaty. "Real soon," he urged, his lips covering hers in a tender caress.

* * * * *

Stanley prayed all the way home. After Amber had apologized again and walked him out, she made him promise to be gentle when confronting Lori. He had no idea how he would be gentle when such gut-wrenching fury filled him at the thought of what she'd done, so he decided to wait and talk with her after a night of prayer.

He waited at the Bar S until she got home from school the next afternoon. Her eyes lit up when she saw him. Stanley stepped back before she could touch him. "We need to talk."

Lori could tell by his expression Stanley was *not* happy. Anger clouded his sky-blue eyes and she knew it was time to pay the piper. She felt a tiny twinge of fear and guilt, but squashed it with ruthless determination. "What's wrong?" she asked in her sweetest, most innocent voice.

The fury was back, clawing at him. Stan mentally counted to ten. "You tell me." Before she could answer, he exploded. "How could you, Lori? How could you tell Amber those things?"

Her lip quivered, tears trembled on her lashes. "I love you."

"Oh, really?" He snorted, took another step back and fought the urge to shake her. "You've been spreading lies and rumors about me to my fiancée, lies and rumors that could ruin my reputation and send me to jail and you call that love?" he sneered, his breath heaving out in angry huffs as he struggled for control.

"Know this, Lori; I will not bear the brunt of your promiscuity and some young buck's irresponsibility!"

The tears spilled over, running down her cheeks. "I am not promiscuous!"

"Who's the father?"

"There is no father. There is no baby. I'm still a virgin!" Though her cheeks burned at the admission, Lori knew the time had come for truth, the whole truth.

"I only told those things to Amber, knowing she would never, *ever* repeat them and I made sure no one else heard me either. I thought she would dump you then I would have a chance to show you how much I love you."

She's probably just young and impressionable and jealous. Amber's words echoed in Stan's mind and heart. Suddenly he understood why Amber had hesitated in telling him about Lori and why she'd insisted he be gentle when confronting her.

Little incidents began to surface in his mind—the way her eyes lit up at the slightest attention, the smile, the comments, and the innuendos. Suddenly Stanley saw Lori for who she really was, not a child too used to getting what she wanted, but a young girl in the throes of her first crush. Raking his fingers through his hair in an agitated gesture, he cursed himself for not seeing it before.

"Gosh," he muttered. "I'm sorry, Lors, I had no idea how you felt. I do care about you, you're like a little sister to me."

"I know and I hate that the most!" she cried. "You treat me like a child. I'm not a child, I'm a woman and I love you."

"I don't know what to say, Lors. You were thirteen-years-old when I came here and I was eighteen. Your father gave me a job and a place to live how could I think of you any other way?"

"But I'm not thirteen anymore," she insisted.

"I know that, but I still think of you as a little sister. Besides, I'm twenty-one, way too old for you."

"Only six years," she argued. Stepping closer she placed her hand on his chest and looked up at him, her gaze imploring.

"Six years isn't that much, besides love knows no age."

Stan shook his head having no idea how to reach her. Taking her hand from his chest, he kissed the fingertips. "I'm sorry I hurt you," he whispered.

Lori whirled away, angry now. "It's all because of Amber! I wish you'd dumped her when you thought she'd stood you up!"

Stanley's eyes narrowed. "What did you say?"

Realizing what she'd said, Lori flushed and burst into tears.

"You put that note in my locker last year, didn't you?"

Caught, all Lori could do was nod and cry. "I've loved you since the day you came here," she wailed.

Angry all over again, Stan sent a silent plea to God for help, her continued weeping dousing the sparks of fury.

Speak the truth in love. The scripture floated through his mind, giving him direction and the courage to say what he knew he had to say. Lifting her chin, he gazed into her tear-drenched eyes. "You asked me one time if I thought you were pretty, you remember that?"

She nodded. "You said I was ugly to the bone," she sobbed.

"That's not what I said, Lors," he corrected, pulling her against his chest. "I think you're a very pretty girl, but your attitude tends to be less than pretty. Half the time you're not even nice. If you're not careful, the only types of boys you're going to attract are those who'll hurt you and leave you heart broken," he warned.

When her sobs subsided, he pushed her gently out of his embrace. His smile tender, he brushed the hair off her flushed cheeks. "This may sound lame to you right now, Lors, but one day you'll meet your Prince Charming, and you'll be glad you waited for him."

"I hope he's as great as you are," she whispered.

Stanley smiled. "I'm sure he'll be an even better man than I am. There's probably some cowboy just sitting on the fence waiting for you to notice him," he remarked, and then continued when she didn't comment.

"Regardless, hold out for the best, Lors. Even if you think you've met Mr. Right, hold out until you're sure and then make him wait until you're married. Don't ever settle for less."

He stroked her cheek. "Forgive me for being insensitive to your feelings?"

She nodded. "If you'll forgive me for what I've said and done I'm really sorry, Stanley."

He nodded. "Okay, but Lori...."

"I know," she interrupted. "I owe Amber an apology, too."

This time when she looked up at him, her eyes were wide with fright. "What do you think she'll do?"

Stan smiled and tucked a curl behind her ear. "Knowing Amber, she'll probably hug your neck and offer to be your best friend."

Stanley's eyes glittered with emotions, leaving no doubt in Lori's mind as to the depth of his feelings for Amber. Lori knew she was blessed indeed that her childishness hadn't cost her more than a few angry words between them. She vowed to apologize to Amber, to never make the mistake again, and hoped God would send her a man as bighearted as Stanley Morrison.

Chapter Sixteen

Stan walked Amber to her car, his hand resting on her waist. In the days since the situation with Lori had been resolved, he'd spent as much time with Amber as their schedules would allow. Though careful with his kisses and caresses, he did everything he could to assure her that she held the key to his heart and all of his affection. They both agreed to call it an early night tonight. Guiding her onto the driver's seat, he closed the door, nodding in approval when she buckled up. Leaning in the window, he kissed her.

"Call me the minute you get home, Sweetheart. Sleep tight. I've got a full day tomorrow but Sunday's all yours," he promised, with a smile.

She smiled and sighed, pulling his head down for another kiss. As promised, she phoned him the minute she walked in the door then went in search of her family. Her mother and Ace were curled up in the den reading while her father wandered around the house looking for something to do. She met him on the stairs and he followed her up to her room for a quiet chat. Unbraiding her hair, she handed him the brush and sat at his feet as she had when she was little, and hadn't in a long time. Amber felt herself relaxing under his tender administrations and a contented sigh escaped her lips.

Craig chuckled. "Thought you were getting too old for this, or had someone else doing it for you." Unspoken questions hung between them. She smiled leaning against his knees.

"No. Not yet. I'm sure I'll have to delegate the chore to Stanley after we're married, but it's yours until then."

He kissed the top of her head. "Or I could come by your house every evening around bedtime and do it for you." He ran his fingers through the thick silken mass of black hair, one of the many traits she'd inherited from him.

"It'd be my pleasure. And it's not a chore," he argued when she giggled, replying to the negative. They sat in companionable silence for a moment.

"You've been awfully tense the last few days, weeks really. Is everything okay?" he asked, inviting the intimate conversations they used to share.

She sighed again, letting the soothing stroke of brush against scalp ease the tension from her mind and body. "Mmm, mm."

Craig grinned, kissed the top of her head again, and waited for her to initiate conversation. When it was evident she had nothing pressing to discuss, he spoke. "What do you want for your birthday, Amber?"

Amber closed her eyes and thought for a moment. A tiny smile tugged at the corners of her mouth. "A trip to the Bahamas."

Her father laughed. "Is that all?" he queried, his tone reflecting that he didn't believe her. "Sounds nice, maybe we can go there instead of Mississippi this summer."

Taking a deep breath, Amber turned to face him. "It could be a combination birthday present, graduation present, and honeymoon," she said, gazing up at him her eyes wide and imploring.

Craig felt his heart stop then start again, thudding in his chest. "You're not serious?"

His voice begged her not to be. She nodded. Rising to her knees she took his hands in hers. "Yes Daddy, I'm serious. What I want most for my eighteenth birthday is to get married."

"No, Amber. You're too young. It's too soon. What about college? What about graduation?"

"Graduation is only a few weeks after my birthday. I'll be out of school within a few days of my birthday. I'll graduate. And I'm not too young."

"No. I'm sure." He snorted. "It's ridiculous. This whole conversation is ridiculous. It's out of the question."

"Why, Daddy? Why is it ridiculous?"

He tossed the brush down with a growl, his voice harsh, his eyes anguished. "Amber, you'll be eighteen, barely out of high school. You've got your whole life ahead of you. Why do you want to rush into marriage at such a young age? Neither you nor Stanley, have experienced anything life has to offer. I think it's a mistake, a big mistake. And I won't allow it."

"You can't stop it," she declared. Suddenly tired of arguing with two men she loved she sighed, rubbing her throbbing temples.

"Okay, fine." She threw up her hands in exasperated defeat. "I won't marry him. Tell Mama to make me an appointment with her gynecologist."

He paled. "What?"

"I want to get on birth control. I won't marry him, Daddy, if you insist. But I'm tired of waiting to be with him."

"Don't you dare threaten me with that, Amber," he warned, lunging to his feet to glare down at her, his voice taut with barely controlled fury.

"I'm not trying to threaten you, Daddy," she insisted, grabbing his hands. "I'm trying to make you understand how I feel. I love him. We love each other. I want to marry him. We've been successful so far in not giving in to the desire we feel for each other, but I'm not sure how much longer we can wait."

"Oh, I see," he snarled, his eyes narrowed into shimmering slits of steel. "You want a license to have sex."

"No!" Amber's eyes narrowed and teeth gritted with the anger she felt toward her father at that moment. She clenched her fists, barely controlling the urge to slap his face.

Craig saw the temper flash in her eyes and met the challenge head on. He took a step nearer. "That's what it sounds like to me."

Amber whirled away, fighting the urge to strike out at him with each trembling breath she took.

Grabbing her by the arm, he flung her around to face him. "Don't turn away from me when I'm talking to you, little girl," he warned in a soft, deadly voice.

Her clenched fists rose to his chest, pushing him away. "Get out," she snarled. "Get out of my room and leave me alone."

"You forget yourself, Amber," he ground out, pulling her against him and giving her a furious shake. "You forget who you're talking to."

"Craig?" Tamera's questioning voice seeped through his anger. He turned his expression a mixture of misery and fury.

"What's going on?" she asked.

Craig stepped away from his daughter with a muttered oath. "Ask your daughter," he spat, storming out of the room.

Tamera turned to her daughter disturbed by Amber's hardened features, heaving breath, and clenched fists.

One glimpse of the fear and concern on her mother's face and Amber crumbled, sliding into a shattered heap on the floor.

Taking her nearly hysterical child into her arms, Tamera held on while Amber clung to her, sobbing in anguish. She rocked her while Amber told of the situation with Lori, the fight she'd had with Stanley a couple of nights ago and the fight with her father moments ago.

"Do you believe there was never anything more than friendship between Stan and Lori?"

Amber nodded. "Stan and I have both talked with Lori and I honestly believe there was nothing more than that. She had a terrible crush on him and didn't know what to do about it. Or so she thought. What it really boiled down to is that she's an only child and he's been like a brother to her and she felt he would forget her entirely when we get married. That and the fact she's spoiled rotten," she added, and shook her head.

"She's really a sweet girl, just young and immature. I trust Stanley completely, Mama, but I'm confused about what's really right and wrong!"

"Confusion is not of God, Sweetheart."

"I know that," she insisted. "But I am. One minute I'm praying for God's wisdom and direction and the next I'm talking and acting like a harlot."

Tamera chuckled and stroked her daughter's hair. "Oh, Darling, you're not acting like a harlot, you're acting like a woman in love."

"Then why doesn't Daddy understand? Why is he so dead-set against this?"

"Your father is having a difficult time in letting go, Amber. Pray for him."

"I do. I pray all the time and I still end up fighting against everything and everyone I love! I fight against God's command to be holy and abstain from sexual immorality. I fight against Stanley's desire to wait and I fight with my father over everything," she cried, burying her face against her mother's breast, seeking comfort and guidance.

Tamera prayed silently for the words to give both. When Amber's sobs subsided, she lifted her chin and gazed into her daughter's eyes. "It sounds to me like you're fighting against everything and everyone because you are relying on your own strength to get you through these battles instead of allowing God's Spirit to work in you and to handle them for you," she chided, her tone gentle.

"I love Stanley so much, Mama," Amber said, her voice hushed with emotion. "I love everything about him. I want to crawl inside his heart and mind, know all of his thoughts and dreams and I want to be as close to him as I can get—mentally, emotionally, physically. Is that really so wrong?"

Tamera chose her words with care. "No, it's not wrong, Sweetheart, it's perfectly natural and beautiful for you to feel that way and to want to do those things. But love like that is meant to be expressed within the bonds of marriage. True love waits."

"Whose decision is it on how long we should wait, Mama? God's, yours and Daddy's, or mine and Stanley's?"

"The law has determined, you are a minor until you're eighteen- years old. Until that time, it's up to your father."

"Well, he's being ridiculous! Women have been getting married much younger than me for ages."

"Your father wants what's best for you Amber and he's afraid getting married at such a young age is not the best."

"Who is he to say what's best for me? Shouldn't *I* be allowed to say what's best? Maybe we should just elope," she muttered, emotions coloring her tone.

Tamera's heart constricted. "I don't think that's the answer either, Sweetheart. It would tear your father's heart out. And mine. Like I said, your father is having a difficult time in letting go. I'll speak to him, Amber, but let's take things easy. You have to promise to take it slow. And don't do anything rash."

Amber knew her mother was right and vows spoken without the blessing of her family and friends was not how she wanted to start her life with Stanley. "Okay, Mama, I'll take it easy. I'll let you handle Daddy and I promise not to make any rash decisions."

"Thank you, Sweetheart." Tamera left her daughter and went in search of her husband. She found him in the den. Pacing. Furious.

"We need to talk."

"The only thing we need to discuss is whether or not I should take a belt to her and a shotgun to Stanley."

Tamera forced back a smile. "Kind of late for that, don't you think?" She picked the Bible up from where he'd tossed it aside in frustration and noticed it was opened to Proverbs.

"You're reading the wrong Scriptures, Craig. Maybe you should try Ephesians, chapter six to be exact." She opened to the passage and handed him the Bible.

Children, obey your parents for this is right...Fathers, do not provoke your children to anger...

"Are you telling me I should just walk away and let her get by with such blatant disrespect?"

"I'm telling you that you should lighten up. You have raised her up in the Lord and you should trust her to know and do what's right. And you shouldn't provoke her so."

"Great," he snarled. "Now, when she's seventeen-years old, you presume to tell me how to treat my daughter."

Tamera felt the words like a slap in the face and fought against her rising temper. "Oh, so now she's just your daughter? Heaven forbid I should tell you anything even after all these years," she insisted, cringing inwardly at the sarcasm in her voice.

"Fine, Craig," she threw up her hands in exasperation, "I won't say another word." She walked to the door.

Craig reached for her regretting his ill-tempered response. "Temper, wait."

She slapped his hands away. "No, you wait and you'd better listen to me, Craig! Keep pushing and you might as well cut her heart out and leave her wide open and bleeding all over the place. Just don't be so arrogant as to assume you're going to walk away unscathed," she warned, the door slamming in her wake.

Craig sank down into his chair, buried his face in his hands and wept.

Later that evening, unable to sleep, Amber tiptoed downstairs to find her father too, was having a restless night. Wrapping her arms around his waist, she apologized.

"I'm sorry Daddy. I don't want to fight with you. It hurts too much when we fight, and I don't mean to be disrespectful. I've just been under a lot of pressure lately with graduation and the house and everything."

Her eyes begged his forgiveness and understanding. Craig hugged her close, feeling as though this would be one of the last precious times he'd be able to do so. His evening stubble rubbed against her silky hair. "It's okay, Darling, I know you don't and I'm trying to understand," he assured, his voice raw with emotion.

"I love you, Daddy," she whispered, tightening her embrace.

Craig buried his face in her hair and swallowed the lump in his throat. "I love you, too, Sweetheart."

Saturday dawned bright and beautiful. After a long talk with her father the evening before, Amber slept late for the first time in weeks. She crawled out of bed just before noon and spent the rest of the day visiting and riding with her family. She even got in a couple of hours of writing. Though she enjoyed the day immensely, she missed Stanley and stayed on the phone with him deep into the night.

Though a few dusky clouds danced on the horizon, hinting at, but not threatening rain, Sunday dawned as lovely as Saturday. Stan arrived shortly after breakfast to spend the day with Amber. After an hour of romping around with Ace, he begged off, keeping his promise that he was all hers for the day. After some discussion, they packed a lunch, saddled up and took off for an afternoon of riding and relaxation.

They rode for hours, stopping occasionally to rest the horses and stretch their legs. Like two kids on a date, they laughed and talked, held hands, teased, and flirted and made plans for their future without taking too much too serious. After one such break, Amber flung herself into the saddle.

"Race you," she challenged, kicking her horse into a gallop.

"Hey!" Stan yelled, jumping into the saddle and urging his mount into a run. Pulling his horse alongside of hers, he leaned over, grabbed her reins and slowed them to a trot then walk.

"Not fair," he huffed, his breath nothing more than ragged pants.

Amber laughed and shook her hair off her shoulders. "You'd have let me win anyway," she taunted. "Not that I couldn't beat you if I wanted to."

Stan grinned and brushed his lips across hers. "You're right," he conceded.

Well into the afternoon, they took a break, feasting on the lunch Tamera had packed for them that morning. Pulling Amber into his arms, Stan rested in the peacefulness of joy and the joy of love. Two hours later he awoke, surprised at the sudden darkness which overtook the bright afternoon sky. His eyes widened when huge thunderclouds moved in from the south. The air was thick with the smell and feel of rain.

"Amber, wake up," he urged, rolling out of her embrace. "We're about to get wet!"

The words had barely left his mouth when the sky opened up. Lightning flashed and thunder roared catching them unaware and unprepared for the sudden storm. Fighting to control his high-strung mount, he heard Amber yelling his name.

"Come on!" She hollered, mounting her horse in a single fluid motion. "I know just where we can wait it out!" Seeing his nod, she kicked her horse into a gallop turning in the saddle as he rode up beside her. She pulled up at a deserted cabin. Reining her horse to a sliding stop in the small corral, she jerked the saddle from his back, carrying it inside and dumping it on the floor, leaving Stan to do the same.

He followed her, dripping muddy water in his wake. Glancing at her, he grinned. "You, My Sweet, look like a drowned rat," he teased, brushing wet strands of hair off her flushed cheeks.

She laughed. "And you look much better, I'm sure," she commented, her teeth chattering. Both were soaked to the skin and chilled to the bone.

Stan glanced around the tiny cabin surprised to find dry firewood stacked by the fireplace. Rubbing his hands together, he walked toward it. "I'm going to start a fire. You see if there's something we can use to dry off with. We've got to get warmed up or we'll catch one heck of a cold."

Nodding in agreement, Amber went to do his bidding.

Stan piled wood in the fireplace. Getting the fire started, he fed it until it roared, warm and welcoming. Pulling off his boots and socks, he placed them where they would dry. Tugging his wet shirt off, he laid it over the back of a chair; feeling that it would dry and he would warm up quicker without it on. Choosing to leave his undershirt and jeans on, he stood by the fire waiting for Amber's return.

"This place looks lived in," he called out.

The acoustics in the tiny cabin were super. He could hear her chuckle from what he supposed was the bathroom, where she'd disappeared several minutes ago.

"This is Mama and Daddy's hideaway. They spent their honeymoon here," she informed him, walking out of the bathroom carrying her clothes in one hand and toweling her hair with the other.

"I got these." Dropping her boots next to his, she spread her clothes over a chair and held a towel toward him. "There's another robe in the bathroom if you want it."

Stan's eyes widened when he reached for the towel. Amber resumed drying her hair, which hung in a tangled mass over her shoulders and down her back. It was evident that she wore very little, if anything beneath the thick, plush robe which reached ankle length on her long, slender legs.

His outstretched hand dropped. The towel slipped to the hearth. His breath caught in his throat with an audible hiss. Clenching his now trembling hands into fists at his sides, Stanley smothered the urge to drag her into his arms. Struggling for control, his teeth clenched as he fought the desire roaring in his blood. The frustrated moan he tried to suppress escaped in a near whimper.

Amber realized their predicament the same moment he did. A flush covered her cheeks. Her hand stopped in mid stroke with a visible tremble when Stan dragged his gaze from hers. Her eyes widened when he grabbed the front of her robe and jerked her to him.

"You're killing me," he complained in a thick, husky whisper.

His lips covered hers in a scorching kiss. Wrapping his arm around her, Stanley held her, her arms imprisoned at her sides. Just as quickly, he pulled away. Turning on his heel he walked over to the bed and jerked the quilt off of it. Returning, he wrapped it around her, again imprisoning her arms at her sides. Picking her up, he headed toward the bed.

"What?"

"Be still," he ordered, his voice terse. "You're going to stay put and I'm going to sit over there." He indicated by the fire with a curt nod of his head.

Amber giggled. "Stanley, if I don't comb the tangles out of this mop, I'm going to have to cut it just below my ears."

His eyes raked over her, noticing how snarled the thick tresses were. Turning around he walked back, depositing her in nearly the same spot she'd occupied a moment ago. She smiled up at him, a tender light in her eyes.

"There's a comb in the bathroom, a big one with wide teeth."

Going into the bathroom, Stan took advantage of the space between them to restore some semblance of control to his raging senses. "God, Jesus, help me," he pleaded. "Even a saint would have a problem here."

And with every temptation He will make a way out...

Stanley waited for that way out. He heard the rain pounding on the roof, saw it spray against the windowpane like bullets of ice, felt the chill on his skin and shivered. The heat in his blood cooled. "Nothing like a cold shower straight from heaven," he muttered in a soft, chuckling under-breath. He retrieved the comb and returned to her side.

"What took so long?" Amber asked. "Have trouble finding the comb?"

He eyed her with a pointed look and shook his head. "I was praying."

She flushed. "Oh. Me too," she admitted. "It's hard, isn't it? Trying to do what's right."

He nodded. "Especially when we're stranded together, alone in a deserted cabin in the middle of nowhere and you're dressed like that."

Amber glanced down at her bare feet, a hot blush stinging her cheeks. She pulled the quilt more tightly around her. "I'm sorry. I wasn't thinking about that when I changed. All I was thinking about was getting out of my wet clothes and into something warm and dry as quickly as possible."

His eyes narrowed into dangerous slits of simmering blue. "Sit," he ordered. "And don't you dare lose that blanket."

"Yes, Sir," she complied, her tone meek. Turning her back to him, she sat at his feet when he took the chair.

Stan chuckled. "Will you always obey me so meekly?" She turned, her blistering gaze answering for her. He grinned. "Thought so."

With painstaking gentleness he combed the tangles out of her hair. The warmth from the fire was more effective than the best blow dryer, he thought as the silky strands began to dry and curl around his fingers. The chore worked its soothing magic on both of them and they began to relax. Tossing the comb aside, he picked her up again and carried her to the bed. It creaked in protest when, bracing himself with one knee, he laid her in it. She gazed up at him. Her eyes wide and innocent, smoldered with longing.

"Hold me. Just for a moment. Like earlier. There was nothing wrong with that was there?"

He groaned, doubting she understood just how precarious their situation was. "Amber," he breathed. "I," he shook his head. "No."

One hand buried in the folds of the blanket, keeping it tightly closed, while the other sank into the luxurious length of her satiny tresses at the same time he swallowed her protests with his mouth. His lips covered hers in a hungry kiss, drinking deeply, greedily, of her sweetness.

Amber's hands clench into fists at her sides as desire swept through her. She felt trapped, unable to move, robbed of the opportunity to sink her fingers in his thick, chestnut locks. Forcing herself to relax, she welcomed his embrace. His lips clung to hers; molding and shaping them to his until each ragged breath he took robbed her of her own. Her heart thudded thickly in her chest, desire poured through her, infusing her with lethargic warmth. Her breathing was sharp, almost painful as the kiss deepened briefly before he drug his lips from hers.

"I want," he began...Shaking his head as if to clear it, he continued. "I want to hold you."

A triumphant gleam lit her eyes. She smiled. "Me, too."

A soft grunt escaped him. "Just hold you, Amber, blanket and all."

She pouted prettily. "That's not fair. I want to hold you too."

He shook his head. "If you touch me, I'll lose it, Amber. Take it or leave it. Otherwise, I'm going back over there and you're staying here. Deal?" he queried, prepared to leave her as she lay, to tie her to the bed if necessary.

At the reluctant nod of her head, he laid beside her, pulling her against his side, her head resting on his chest. Cupping her face, he lifted it so that she looked up at him. With tender, gentle strokes, he brushed the hair off her cheeks. His lips traveled across her forehead to close her eyes then on to caress her cheeks and lips.

"I love you," he whispered, smiling at her sleepy reply.

Stan closed his eyes, savoring the moment. The woman he loved was in his arms. Thunder rumbled and lightning flashed as the storm howled, at odds with the soft, sweet, kittenish sounds she emitted as sleep claimed her. The fire crackled and hissed, reaching out to bathe the entire cabin with its warm, amber glow. If he died in that moment, he would die content.

True he'd never gorged on the fruits her flesh could offer, but he'd feasted his eyes on her beauty and tasted the sweet nectar of her love. He'd wallowed in her desire, felt the pain and pleasure of its burn, sampled and savored her sweetness. He'd held innocence and fire and was content with that.

He awoke some time later. Careful not to disturb Amber, he moved her out of his arms. The rain continued, softer now, gentle. Putting on his socks and boots, he wiped down the saddles and cleaned up the mud off the floor. Going out, he rubbed down the horses with handfuls of hay he found stashed in the corner of the lean-to. Saddling them up, he went back inside to wake Amber.

Chapter Seventeen

Craig paced the porch while the storm unleashed its fury on the earth and watched with concern when it continued into its third hour, alternately praying and cursing, frustrated at his own helplessness. His daughter was somewhere out in that. Taking advantage of a lull in the rain, he went out and saddled his horse.

Tamera heard his frustrated oath when Mother Nature renewed her assault with a fresh outpouring of pelting drops. He ran through the rain back onto the porch. Handing him a towel and a steaming cup of coffee, she sat on the swing, fighting her own rising fears. At the next break in the weather she begged him to wait while she saddled her horse also.

"Someone needs to stay here in case they get back," he argued.

"Sam is here. He can use the flare gun if they get back. I'm going with you."

They rode out in a northerly direction, not sure which way the kids went. Reining his horse to a sliding halt, Craig muttered an oath. "Where are they?"

"Calm down, Craig. Think. Where would they go? They're not stupid. They probably sought shelter." Her eyes widened when they met his.

"The cabin," they realized in unison.

Craig's fear escalated, not so much for their safety now. His recent fight with Amber weighed on his mind. As they neared the cabin his fear grew then turned to anger, until it crowded out everything in his mind except pain and betrayal and disillusionment.

Reining to a halt outside the door, he didn't notice the horses were dry and saddled, nor see the thin wisps of smoke from the chimney indicating merely embers smoldered in the fireplace. He didn't notice because he was off his horse and through the door in one fluid motion with Tamera on his heels.

What he did notice was Amber stretched out on the bed, Stanley though dressed leaned over her, holding her clothes in his hand. With a low, ominous growl, Craig grabbed him by the shirt, jerked him away from her, and hauled him out of the cabin. "You little bastard," he hissed, flinging him out the door. "I trusted you!"

"Craig, wait." Stan's appeal was cut off when Craig's fist connected with his jaw then cheek. Pain erupted in his head. He tasted blood. Once down, he stayed down, shaking his head to clear it.

Craig stood over him fighting the urge to kill.

Amber sat immobilized for one stunned second as the scene unfolded around her like something out of a bad movie, or a nightmare. Struggling out of the blanket, she screamed for her mother to stop them. Raking her hands through her hair, she fought to get her still-damp jeans on. Flinging her arms into her shirt, she grabbed her mother's hands. "Oh, God, you've got to stop him, Mama!"

Tamera sank onto the bed realizing how angry her husband was and what he was thinking. "Oh, Amber," she groaned, hoping they were wrong.

"Mama, nothing happened!" Amber insisted, tugging at her mother's hands.

Searching her daughter's wide, terrified eyes, Tamera knew Amber was telling the truth. Realizing that, she was out the door on Amber's heels when, skipping her boots, she raced after them barefoot.

"Stop it!" Amber screamed, flinging herself between her father and fiancé while Tamera went to Stan.

Craig looked stunned when she flung herself at him. This was no little girl, but a woman, a full-grown she-cat fighting to protect what's hers.

"How dare you! Leave him alone!" she insisted, pushing at him. Kicking and screaming, she fought with her father until he was away from Stanley.

Craig grabbed her by the shoulders, giving her a furious shake. "I ought to beat you, Amber Nichole."

"Then do it," she insisted, nearly hysterical, fighting him with every ounce of strength she possessed. "Beat me all you want, but leave him alone," she cried.

Craig caught her flailing fists in his hands and pulled her firmly against him.

"No!"

They turned in unison at Stan's strangled cry. Craig's eyes narrowed when Tamera stopped Stanley from interfering between him and his daughter. "You want a piece of me, Boy?"

Raising his hands in defeat, Stan shook his head. It was obvious Craig far outweighed him. Not so much in size, but in age, and experience. Besides, fighting would solve nothing.

Glaring down at his daughter's bare feet and messily snapped shirt, Craig flung her away from him with a look of disgust. His furious gray gaze sought Tamera's.

"If I catch him on this property before she turns eighteen, before they're properly wed, I'll kill him," he ground out between his teeth. Unable to trust himself to face them another moment, he mounted his horse, leaving his wife to pick up the pieces of broken hearts and shattered dreams. Pain and anger were like twin knives speared deep into his soul.

They watched in pained silence as Craig rode away, kicking his horse into a dead run. Tears streamed down Amber's cheeks and she began to tremble in the aftermath of emotions. Stanley went to retrieve her boots and close up the cabin while Tamera enfolded her daughter in her embrace.

Setting her boots down, Stanley brushed the hair off Amber's cheeks. His eyes sought Tamera's. "Nothing happened, Tam," he assured, using the pet name he'd devised for her. "I swear."

Tamera nodded. "I know," she replied, urging Amber to put on her boots.

Amber looked up at Stan's busted lip and rapidly swelling eye and burst into fresh tears. "Oh, God!" she cried, cupping his face in her hands. "Look what he did! I hate him!" she raged.

"Don't say that, Amber," Stanley chided. "He's your father. He was only acting out of love."

"If he loved me, he'd trust me," she muttered, tugging on damp socks and boots.

Feeling the same, Stan swallowed his own disappointment and pain but refrained from comment. The three of them rode back to the house in silence, relieved yet concerned, that Craig wasn't there yet. After tending to the horses, Tamera urged Amber into a hot bath, insisting Stanley do the same the minute he got home. "And put some ice on that eye and lip," she added, wincing at his bruised and battered face.

Hours after dark Craig got home. Rubbing his horse down, he gave him an extra helping of oats before making his way up the stairs into his bedroom. Once there, the war within him continued. He paced the floor.

Tamera sat unmoving and silent in the bed, waiting for him to calm down before speaking. They answered in unison the soft knock on the door.

Craig's heart clenched at the sight of his daughter's face, which was flushed from hours of crying, her eyes red and swollen. He waited in silence while she walked over to him, unafraid of his boiling wrath. With a slight, defiant lift to her chin, she met his gaze, hers unwavering.

Her trembling lip threatened to give her away.

Amber's eyes searched her father's, hurt by what she found there. Taking a deep breath, she apologized. "I'm sorry Daddy, for what you saw. What you thought you saw." Turning, she walked to the door then looked back over her shoulder.

"I asked Stanley to stay home. He wanted to come over and try and talk to you but I figured it would be better if he waited for you to have a chance to cool off."

Craig's eyes narrowed. "You think it's that easy, I'll just cool off and welcome him back?" He snorted, shook his head. "What, exactly, makes you think that?" he demanded through clenched teeth, his hands curled into fists by his side.

"Because you're wrong, Daddy. Nothing happened. Once you calm down and think things through, you'll realize I'm telling you the truth." Amber saw the pain and doubt in his eyes. Hers filled, but she blinked back the tears. "I've never lied to you, Daddy," she said, her tone soft, lip trembling. "I have no reason to start now," she insisted, closing the door behind her.

Craig collapsed into a chair with a groan. "Oh, God, she's not lying," he moaned, burying his head in his hands.

Tamera waited until he raised devastated gray eyes to search her face before going to him. "Think about it Craig. Think about how you found them. Stanley was fully dressed..."

"He was holding her clothes," Craig interrupted

Tamera shook her head. "He was holding her jeans and shirt. She was wrapped up so tightly in the quilt it took two-minutes for her to struggle out of it. She was wearing a robe and her underclothes." She took his hands in hers. "No, Craig, she's not lying, nothing happened between them." Her voice was soft, not accusing.

Craig felt the accusation anyway, deep down in his soul. He was wrong. He'd accused them without preamble, acted out of emotion and judged them through pain and anger. "I hit him, Tamera. I hit a kid. I hurt him. And I hurt my daughter."

Tamera fought down her own anger and pain and wrangled with the need, the desire, to reach out and soothe his hurt pride and bruised ego.

"That's it, Craig. This is exactly where you mess up," she insisted, urging him to look at her, praying for the words to make him understand.

"He is *not* a kid. He's a grown man. And he loves her. Not as you love her or I love her, but as we love each other. Until you realize that, until you face it, you're going to keep hurting them. You're going to keep hurting yourself. And you're going to risk losing her, or pushing her away. Don't force her to make a choice between you, Craig. You may be surprised and disappointed at the choice she makes."

Craig felt the truth like a shaft of hot iron in his heart.

Tamera saw the pain of realization shining in his eyes. Then and only then, when he finally realized the truth and couldn't hide from it, did she pull him into her arms. Rocking him, she stroked his back in a soothing caress while he faced the fact that he couldn't stop his daughter from growing up and falling in love.

Craig realized that, no matter how much he wanted otherwise, he couldn't protect Amber from heartache or pain, or from making mistakes. Those were all part of becoming a woman. What he could do was stand by her and be there for her if everything fell apart around her heart.

He couldn't be the only man in her life forever. But he could, and always would, be the father she needed. And though it hurt, he realized, the hardest part of being a good father was learning when and how to let go. To let go and let God make of his children what He wanted them to be. They were, after all, only a gift; entrusted to him for as long as God chose. And He'd chosen Amber to be entrusted to Stanley as a wife. For the rest of her life Stanley would be there to love, honor and cherish her, in a way Craig never could. As only a husband could.

Peace came with understanding. Letting it soothe his bruised feelings Craig stayed in his wife's embrace until he faced not only the truth, but also what he had to do. Swallowing his pain, shame and pride, he went to his daughter. Without waiting for a reply to his knock, he entered her room to find Amber crying into her pillow. He spoke her name, his voice soft.

"You didn't have to hit him," she insisted, turning away, sobs tearing through her in painful torrents.

Craig fought not to touch her, to pull her in his arms and beg her forgiveness. They had to talk this through. "I know that, now, and I'm sorry."

Amber struggled with the impulse to throw herself in his arms. She scrambled into a sitting position drawing her knees up against her chest. "It's not me you should apologize to, it's Stanley."

"I'm apologizing to you first."

Pain darkened his eyes to gunmetal gray. Again Amber fought the urge to simply curl up against his chest and sob her heart out. "I can't believe you think we would be so irresponsible."

"I was worried and afraid, especially after the other night. I acted out of emotion and without thinking," Craig admitted, reaching out to stroke her hair. She jerked away and it was like a knife in his heart.

"For your information he is the one who always says no." Amber heard her father's sharp intake of breath, saw him tense, and knew her words had struck straight and true.

There was no joy in the victory.

"Is that supposed to make me feel better?" Craig asked, teeth clenched, jaw muscle twitching.

"It's supposed to make you understand!" Amber exclaimed, ignoring the narrow, steely eyes and throbbing muscle in his jaw which indicated her father was quickly reaching the edge of his control. She shook her head and held up a hand, denying him the right to say another word. She had to make him understand!

"I am *not* a baby anymore, Daddy. I love him! I have feelings you know, I have needs and desires just like Mama. Just like you!" she declared, poking a finger in his chest for emphasis.

"That's enough, young lady." Tamera's sharp voice shot through the room. They turned to see her standing in the doorway.

"He had no right!" Amber insisted.

"He had every right, he's your father." She held up a hand to silence her daughter's protests. "All these years, I've stood by and let you and your father settle your differences without my interference. But I will *not* stand by and watch you disrespect him in such a manner." Tamera walked to the other side of Amber's bed and sat beside her daughter.

"Your father came in here to apologize for misreading the situation. The least you can do is be woman enough to accept his apology," she chided, her voice gentle despite the severity of the words.

"But I thought he trusted us."

"Trust has absolutely nothing to do with what happened, Amber. God has entrusted your safety and well-being into your father's hands. You can't punish him for doing his job. You can't punish him for his feelings. You're asking him to understand how you feel?" Tamera continued at her daughter's nod.

"Well, you need to put yourself in his shoes. How would you feel if the situation were reversed? Better yet, how would you feel if he didn't even care whether or not you and Stanley were having sex?"

Burying her face on her knees, Amber began to cry, deep, heart-wrenching sobs which shook her slender frame.

Without hesitation Craig pulled her into his arms. "Oh, Amber," he groaned, swallowing the hard lump of tears in his throat. "I'm so sorry, Sweetheart," he whispered, holding her firmly against his chest. The breath he hadn't realized he was holding escaped in a sigh when she slid her arms around his waist and buried her face into his shoulder.

No other words were spoken. None were needed. Forgiveness came as natural as the apology. Craig held her until the sobs subsided and she fell into an exhausted slumber. Brushing the silky strands of hair off her face, he tucked the covers around her, and then kissing her cheek, he left. The next apology would be a little more difficult, but just as necessary. Craig prayed for God's help to get him through it.

* * * * *

Stanley heard the knock and opened his door, surprised to find Craig standing there.

Craig's eyes narrowed when he took in the boy's cut lip, noting also he had one heck of a shiner. Grinding his teeth in mortification, he attempted a grin. "Not as bad as I thought," he said, cupping Stan's chin with his hand.

Stan jerked away. "I'll live," he muttered.

Justly chastised, Craig tucked his hands in his pockets. "I came to apologize, Stanley."

Gray eyes pleaded. They eyed each other for a long, tense moment. Stepping back, Stan opened the door, allowing his entrance. Seated across from each other in the living room, he waited in silence for Craig to continue.

Taking a deep breath, Craig opened his palms in a gesture of supplication. "Every reason I can name is no excuse for what happened, Stanley," he began in a quiet voice. "All I can do is apologize, and try to explain."

"I don't know what I have to do to get you to trust me," Stan commented, his voice raw with bitterness and hurt.

Craig took another deep breath. "I do. I know that may be difficult to believe right now." He shrugged at a loss for words. Reaching out, he put a hand on Stan's shoulder and explained the best way he knew how.

"Listen to me, Stanley, and please, try to understand. One day you'll hold a tiny, living, breathing, miracle in your arms and you'll vow to protect her at all costs. If you're smart, you'll accept her growing up with each step she takes toward womanhood." Craig sighed and shook his head, wondering if words could ever truly explain how he felt, what he was going through. His eyes searched Stanley's for some indication the boy understood. Seeing hurt and pain there but no condemnation, he continued.

"If you're overprotective, blindly, stupidly, fiercely overprotective, you'll fight it. And you'll screw up, just as I have. If I had to handpick a husband for Amber, he would be someone just like you. I'm not going to lie to you. It worries me that you two want to get married so young. Amber's never really dated much before you. But she knows her own mind."

Though he knew what Stanley's answer would be, Craig asked anyway, "are you sure you're ready for such a commitment?"

"Have I ever given you a reason to think otherwise?" Stan demanded, his gaze unwavering.

Craig shook his head and sighed.

Stanley nodded. "Then I'll tell you like I've told Amber. I'd marry her tomorrow if you'd let me. Just name the time and place and I'll be there." He tried to grin but winced instead. "Just give me enough time to let my face heal."

Craig grinned, relieved Stanley could joke. "Maybe I should blacken your other eye and buy myself some more time."

Stan shook his head. "No need for that. You'll have to settle the issue of time with Amber."

"Thanks, Son. Thanks a lot," Craig groaned in mock horror. "I just love arguing with my daughter." He sighed. "She's as stubborn and hardheaded as her mother."

"And whose fault is that?" Stan wondered, a hint of sarcasm in his tone.

"Guilty," Craig admitted. "I should have beaten her when she was little then maybe she wouldn't be so hard headed now. Take that as advice, beat them regularly and keep them in line."

Stanley heard the mockery, and the warning, in Craig's tone and shook his head. He would never raise a hand to Amber, or a child of his.

Craig read the truth in Stanley's eyes and nodded his approval. "Never, Stanley or you'll answer to me," he promised in a soft voice. "Though God knows you'll be tempted."

Stan grinned as much as his busted lip would allow. "Amber is the physical manifestation of the word in its every form," he assured her father.

Craig's laugh was rich and quick. Standing, he offered Stanley his hand.

Stan accepted the handshake without hesitation and willingly received the embrace when Craig pulled him into his arms like he would a son.

Chapter Eighteen

Gazing at his daughter, ever the blushing bride, Craig nearly choked on the emotions flooding his senses. Her cheeks flushed, her eyes sparkling, she was just as beautiful as Tamera had been in the wedding dress which had been saved and preserved throughout the years for just this occasion. Though reluctant, he'd agreed to the marriage taking place in the time span between Amber's birthday and graduation.

Amber smiled up at her father. "What do you think?" she queried. Tears welled up in his expressive gray eyes. "Don't, Daddy," she pleaded, wrapping her arms around him.

"I don't want to let you go," he mumbled, pulling her against his chest and stroking her hair, his voice raw and fierce.

"You're not letting me go, Daddy, just sharing me. Not that much will change. I promise," Amber insisted. "I'll come by every day. I'll pick Ace up after school and bring him home, just like always. Stanley understands and doesn't mind. We've already talked about it. And since we're not taking a long trip for our honeymoon not that much will change, you'll see." Her voice broke with excitement and nerves, tears of the same rolled down her cheeks.

Craig knew everything would change. It already had. "Oh, Baby," he cupped her cheeks in his hands, brushing the tears away with his thumbs. "You are so beautiful. Are you sure this is what you want, Amber? It's not too late to change your mind. The wedding isn't until tomorrow."

She flushed. "I'm sure. I want to spend the rest of my life with Stanley. I love him. And I want to give you and Mama a whole slew of grandchildren to make up for the babies you lost."

Craig felt the pieces lock together, her desire to wed so young, and her insistence that she loved Stanley. His fear grew. "Amber, as much as I love you for it, that is no reason to rush into marriage. Your mother and I have accepted the loss of those children and rejoiced in the two God gave us. Please, please, don't mistake the desire to fulfill our dreams, to make up for our loss, as love for Stanley."

"Oh, Daddy, I'm not. I do love Stanley. So much. I want to be with him always and to have his children. He wants them too, as many as God blesses us with. We are not going into this blind. We know it won't be easy. Nothing worthwhile ever is. But with God all things are possible. Right? I love Stan. And I love you. And Mama," she assured him, her tone rich with emotion. "And I *am* sure."

Craig nodded. "Okay," he said. "Promise me, if you have any doubts, any whatsoever, you will not go through with this wedding. It's never too late to back out. There's no shame in waiting until you're sure. Promise me, Amber," he urged, unable, unwilling, to accept she was doubt free. "We don't want that kind of sacrifice from you."

"I promise, Daddy. But I won't change my mind. I love him. Isn't that the kind of love Jesus taught us, sacrificial love, to put others before yourself? He loved us enough to die for us. I love you and Mama enough to give you the children you so desperately wanted. And I want to do so with Stanley. I do love him, Daddy. I'm not stupid. Nor blind. I know the real meaning of love and commitment."

She smiled tenderly, rubbing his knuckles against her cheek. "I had real good teachers. I want to make that commitment with him. Only him. He's what I've been waiting for my whole life."

Searching the sapphire eyes he loved so much, Craig saw no signs of doubt. Only love. Deep, abiding love that he'd encouraged her to wait for since she was a little girl. Pulling her against his chest he held her, knowing it would be the last time he held her as his little girl. After tomorrow she would belong to someone else as well. Choking back tears he left her alone to examine her looks and her heart.

When he left, Amber turned back toward the mirror, pleased at what she saw. Closing her eyes, she got on her knees. In the wedding dress her mother wore, with tears of joy on her face, she thanked God, praying her marriage would be as strong and beautiful as that of her parents.

Beginning at noon the next day, time slowed down to a crawl and Amber found herself with a bad case of butterflies. The closer the hands approached two o'clock, the more butterflies gathered in her stomach. The wedding had been planned down to the minute and so far, every single detail had fallen into place. Scott and Trina, who'd been married less than six months, had arrived late last night, but not too late for Scott to accompany Craig and Stanley out for his bachelor party. She smiled remembering their teasing about the girl in the cake and how she'd threatened them with castration should that occur. Turning at the sound of someone entering her room, she welcomed her mother and Trina who came up for last minute preparations and advice.

Tamera swallowed hard the lump of tears in her throat at the sight of her baby standing before her wearing the same wedding dress she'd worn almost twenty years ago, with minor alterations, of course.

Where Tamera had worn white lace-up boots, Amber, due to her height, donned satin slippers. The dress served as something old and borrowed. The slippers and tip veil added to the white velvet hat were something new. The sapphires in her engagement ring and a lacy blue garter, not to mention the bluest eyes in Texas, completed her ensemble.

They greeted the knock on the door, shielding Amber from the visitor's view until assured it wasn't Stanley.

Scott opened the door and whistled, winking at Trina. "Wow! Had I known how beautiful you'd turn out from the gangly little girl I once knew, I'd have waited for you myself!" he teased, lying to her for the first time in his life. She'd never been gangly and she'd always been beautiful.

Amber laughed with the other women. She shrugged. "Missed your chance," she chided, laughing at his response that he'd been afraid of her father. "Right, besides, I'm glad you didn't. I'd have broken your heart when I met Stanley. And I'd never want to do that," she admitted, wrapping her arms around his waist and lifting her cheek for his kiss.

Scott chuckled. "Speaking of Stanley, isn't he the guy with the reddish-brown hair and blue eyes? The same guy who's downstairs, pacing, snapping and growling at every one, just about ready to pass out?"

Amber grinned at the picture he painted with words. "He's nervous?"

Again, he chuckled. "Only since your father told him you'd disappeared this morning on horseback with your saddlebags full. And of course Craig's playing it to the hilt; pacing the floor, looking worried, muttering to himself. The fact that Stan hasn't seen or heard from you since last night isn't helping. I had to get out of there while I could. One of them is bound to crack soon."

Amber rolled her eyes. "Mama," she pleaded.

Tamera laughed. "I'll go reassure him, Sweetheart," she promised, glancing at her watch. "And I'll send your father up. It's almost time."

When she got downstairs Craig was standing at the window blocking Stanley from looking out.

"Oh, no," Craig said. "Can't risk you seeing her, if she gets back," he added in an under-breath, his tone thick with worry, and a hint of laughter Stanley missed.

Tamera walked over to him. "That's enough," she chided. "It's time to walk the bride down the stairs. Go," she ordered.

Craig chuckled.

Stan glared at him. "If you weren't the father of the bride, I'd shoot you."

Craig's laugh escaped, rich and hearty. His gray eyes sparkled mischievously.

"Wait, what if I just refuse to walk her down?" He grabbed Stanley when he headed toward the door.

Tamera smiled. "Knowing Amber, she'll start without you."

"Welcome to the family," Craig teased, holding Stan in something between a bear hug and a headlock. Releasing him, he swung Tamera in his arms, pulling her firmly against him. "You know, it's not polite to outshine the bride on her special day," he chided in a soft, husky voice, causing a flush to rush to her cheeks.

Stan grinned. If Tamera was even a slight indication of how beautiful Amber looked, his bride was stunning. He closed his eyes for a minute trying to envision her. He knew she was wearing her mother's wedding dress and tried to picture her in it. The vision his mind created wreaked havoc on his senses. His body tightened with need.

Tamera patted his cheek. "She is beautiful," she confirmed as though reading his thoughts.

"So are you," he said, kissing her cheek.

"You sure you want to go through with this now that you see what kind of father-in-law you're getting?"

Her eyes brimmed with mirth. Stan grinned. "Just get Amber down here and this show on the road. I'll have the rest of my life to figure him out."

Tamera eyed him, her eyes laughing into his, her smile sugary. "I've known him almost twenty years and still haven't figured him out."

Stan rolled his eyes. "Thanks for the encouragement, Tam. Thanks a lot," He muttered, but he was smiling. "May I?" he queried, offering her his arm.

She hugged him then let him escort her to her seat. "Welcome to the family, Stanley."

* * * * *

Amber smiled accepting hugs, kisses and best wishes from Scott and Trina before they went downstairs. Within moments her father stood beside her, ready, if not overly enthusiastic, to walk her down the stairs.

"I hear you've been tormenting my fiancé?"

He chortled. "Just funning him a little."

She rolled her eyes, chiding him with a firm look and took his arm. Standing in the doorway as rehearsed, they waited until Stanley started singing a John Denver classic.

Eyes trained on the staircase, in a voice thick with emotion, he sang...

"You fill up my senses like a night in a forest..."

Tears dripped down her cheeks when Amber heard the range of emotions in the breathless, husky voice she loved so much. Rounding the curve in the staircase, they stopped for a full minute.

Stanley's eyes widened and voice faltered when he gazed upon the beauty that would soon become his wife. With hands trembling as violently as his voice, he finished the song and put down the guitar.

Amber smiled when he rubbed obviously damp palms over his thighs. His gaze swept over her in a look so incredibly masculine, so boldly appraising and brazenly triumphant that she trembled, color rushing to her cheeks.

Craig's eyes narrowed but he smothered the reaction. It still unnerved him someone would look at his daughter that way. Male pride made him admit he couldn't blame the boy. He understood. His gaze swept over Tamera, just as appraising and a lot more knowing.

Standing, Stanley waited for Craig to escort Amber to his side. Dragging his gaze from her long enough, he ignored the urge to punch her father, shook hands with him instead, and then pulled Amber against his side.

The vows were blessedly short and sweet. Turning, Stanley pulled her in his arms before the preacher had the chance to give him permission. His hands shook when he cupped her face in them, brushing the tears off her cheeks. "I love you," he whispered in a thick, thick voice, his eyes swimming with emotion. "I love you so much." His lips covered hers in a tender caress.

"I love you too," she whispered, when he drug his lips from hers. Turning as the preacher pronounced them 'husband and wife,' she let him lead her through the crowd of guests and out to the patio where the reception would be held.

Though the ceremony was short and sweet, the reception seemed to drag on forever. They went through the traditional cutting of the cake and toasting the bride and groom. Stanley watched with increasing restlessness while

Amber danced with her father yet again. Between Craig and Scott, he'd hardly danced with his bride at all. Tamera walked over to him.

"He's still finding it a little difficult to let her go," she remarked, her tone soft.

Sapphire eyes pleaded with him for understanding. Putting himself in his father-in-law's position for a moment, Stanley nodded. "Can't say as I blame him, I imagine it's hard sharing her after all these years."

Tamera laughed. "It is. But, you can leave anytime, you know. She *is* your wife now."

Grinning, he whispered his thanks and kissed Tamera's cheek before cutting in on Amber and her father. "Hey, Sweetheart, don't want you getting too tired," he said in a husky, suggestive tone.

His eyes sparkled with love and laughter. Amber blushed. Laying her head against his chest, she felt the first flutters of fear of the night ahead. Though her mother had assured her she probably wouldn't really notice, talk of the pain that accompanied lovemaking the first time circled in her head.

Sensing her unease, Stanley tightened his embrace. "I love you, Amber," he whispered, rubbing her back in a soothing caress.

She returned the endearment, her smile tremulous. Finishing the dance, she allowed him to lead her toward the door. Pausing long enough to kiss and hug her parents and brother, as well as Scott and Trina, they rushed through the mob of rice-throwing guests to climb into her gaily-decorated car.

Pulling her against him, Stanley kissed her before starting the car and then drove away with one arm holding her against his side. After they'd pulled out of the ranch drive, he let her go so they could buckle up. He occupied her thoughts, encouraging her to relax with tender, intimate conversation all the way to San Antonio. They would spend the next two nights as a short honeymoon made possible by Mr. Strickland's gift of a paid day off on Monday.

Arriving at the honeymoon suite reserved for them, he swung her up into his arms and carried her over the threshold. Putting her down, he pulled her close, his lips covering hers in a thorough kiss. "Oh, God, Amber," he whispered on a moan. "I can't believe this is real. Pinch me," he teased, then winced, laughing when she obliged.

"Well," she blushed. "What now?"

She gazed up at him her eyes burning with love and excitement. Stan cupped her cheeks in his hands. "Right now, I just want to look at you," he stated, his lips brushing over hers in a tender caress. Stepping back, he removed her hat, careful not to tear the veil. Pushing his hands into her hair, he shook the pins loose, reveling in the silky mass. "Oh, look at you," he whispered, his voice thick with adoration. "You are so beautiful.

Amber's hands trembled when she ran them up his arms and into his hair. "You don't look so bad yourself," she mumbled, her lips brushing across his. "I want to look at you, too," she whispered, pushing the jacket off his shoulders. Tugging the bowtie at his throat off, she loosened the top buttons on his shirt, and rested her cheek against his chest. "I'm so nervous," she admitted, a flush stinging her cheeks.

Stan chuckled. "Me too," he confessed, running his hands over her shoulders and back in a soothing gesture. "I love you so much and want you so desperately, I can hardly think straight. And the last thing I want is to rush or hurt you."

Tears filled to her eyes at his declaration, a smile trembled to life on her lips. "Well, maybe we should try and think of this logically," she suggested, a tender, teasing note in her voice.

Stan grinned and brushed his lips across her cheek. "There's no logic when it comes to love, My Sweet. If there were, you'd have nothing to do with me."

"Nor you, me," she answered.

"Oh, no," he argued. "You're a treasure any man would be honored to find and foolish to lose."

"Please don't put me up on a pedestal, Stanley. I'm sure to fall."

"Never," he whispered, his lips caressing her ear, arms drawing her close. "Not in my sight."

Cupping his face in her hands, she looked into his shining eyes. "Then don't stand there and tell me I can't feel the same way about you," she commanded. Rising up on tiptoe, she pressed her lips to his, putting an end to further conversation. Wrapping her arms around his neck, she pressed herself against him. "Kiss me like you really mean it," she urged, her lips parting beneath his.

His mouth covered hers in a scorching embrace, hands shook when he undid the tiny buttons along her back. "I love you so much," he whispered, the words punctuated with feathery kisses across her cheeks, eyes and mouth.

"I love you, too," Amber assured, swallowing the lump of emotion clogging her throat. "Hold me, Stanley, make me your wife," she invited.

In answer Stanley swung her up into his arms and laid her on the bed. His hands trembled as he undressed her, covering inch by inch of precious skin with kisses. With the tenderness born of love and control he didn't know he possessed, he kissed and caressed her, mumbling soft, sweet words of love and longing. He nearly lost control when, with trembling hands, she finished unbuttoning his shirt and began placing whisper-soft kisses on his skin; nipping gently at the tender flesh of his broad chest and circling patterns of fire over his skin with her touch.

Amber forgot everything she'd ever heard when he took sweet possession of her body, and felt nothing but the incredible heat, the glorious ache, and the delirious need building to a shattering crescendo within her. The heat of his touch circled through her leaving scorching brands on her flesh wherever he stroked her with gentle hands and followed with hot, possessive kisses. Their vows were consummated in a tender celebration of love.

Afterward, Stanley lay in her arms, shuddering in the aftermath of glory until she relaxed her hold on him. Her hands caressed his back in soothing strokes while their thudding hearts got back to normal. Ignoring her soft murmur of protest, he rolled away, keeping her in his arms and pulled the bedcovers up over them.

He awoke sometime later, reached for his wife and found her gone. He sat up, surprised to see her standing at the window brushing her hair, gazing in the direction where she grew up, a solemn expression on her face. Deep down he knew she was thinking of home.

Much to his surprise, the thought didn't bother him but filled him with a renewed sense of awe and gratitude that she was his now, finally and truly his. The satin negligee she wore clung to flesh, revealing curves he doubted he'd ever get his fill of, crowding his mind and body with need. Grabbing the phone he walked to her and wrapped one arm around her waist.

"Know what I'm thinking?"

Amber leaned back against his broad chest with a smile. "What?"

"I'm thinking it's a shame this pretty gown is gonna spend the rest of the night piled up in a heap on the floor."

She shivered at the huskiness of his voice but refrained from comment. In a single move he wrapped his other arm around her offering her the phone. She looked at him, her eyes wide and pleading. He simply grinned and nodded. Without hesitation she picked up the receiver and dialed the familiar number.

* * * * *

Craig answered before the phone rang a second time. "Hello," he said, his voice raw from the sleep he alternately sought and fought.

"Goodnight, Daddy," Amber said, her tone husky with emotion.

"Hey, Sweetheart, make it all right?"

"We made it just fine, Daddy. I love you."

226

"Goodnight, Sweetheart," Craig murmured, his tone thick. *Thank you, Stanley*, he added silently placing the receiver in its cradle. Tamera stirred beside him.

"Who was it?"

Pulling her in his arms, his lips covered hers in a tender caress. "Amber called to say goodnight."

She smiled, pulling his lips toward hers for another kiss, aching as much as he with the emptiness which comes naturally when a child leaves home.

Craig accepted the invitation of her body, taking advantage of the opportunity to think of something besides the hole in his heart and the ache in his soul.

* * * *

Amber stretched, a long, luxurious movement of flesh and muscle. Her body ached from the night of loving. She opened her eyes, surprised to find Stanley watching her. His gaze kindled.

"Good morning, My Sweet," he murmured against her lips.

She smiled. A shy flush rushed to her cheeks. "Good morning."

Holding out her arm, she watched sunlight glint off the diamond in her engagement ring and bounce off the gold in her wedding band and heaved a lusty sigh. "Mrs. Stanley Morrison, Mrs. Amber Nichole Harris Morrison, Mr. and Mrs. Arthur Stanley Morrison the Second, sounds good, doesn't it?"

He chuckled running a hand down her body from shoulder to hip, stroking a firm thigh. "Feels good, too." She flushed again, her eyes sparkling.

"What do you want to do today?" she asked, watching the kindle in his eyes turn to flame.

"Well, I thought we'd make love, and then call room service for breakfast. Make love. Take a shower." His voice lowered a husky notch. "Make love. Have lunch..." he chuckled when, getting the gist of his intentions, the first giggle escaped her. By the time he outlined his plans for the rest of the day, she was sprawled across his chest shaking with laughter.

He eyed her, his face set, trying hard not to grin. "What, you don't like my plans? Got any better ideas?" he challenged, tugging at the sheet that had somehow gotten between them. The grin escaped.

"Do you think we could squeeze in some sight seeing amongst all that?" she asked, between giggles.

He rolled his eyes. "'*All that*' she calls it. You're the only sight I wish to see," he murmured, kissing her palm, pleased at the quick flare of passion in her eyes. Pulling her atop his long frame, he watched desire turn her eyes from brilliant indigo to smoky midnight blue.

"I love you, My Sweet," he whispered, before indulging in the luxurious taste of her lips and reveling in the sweetness of her embrace.

Chapter Nineteen

Craig wiped the sweat off his brow with a sigh. Lord, but it was hot! Grabbing the water jug out of the fridge he took a long, soothing drink, and swallowed a guilty grin when Tamera glared at him.

"I don't know what it'll take to get you and Ace to use a glass. That's disgusting."

He chuckled, dumped the jug, rinsed it with hot water and refilled it.

"Thank you," she muttered. "I'm thinking I'll put a pretty, pink pitcher of water in there for me. Then you and your son can share all the germs you want."

"Are you through fussing at me?" he queried, his eyes a soft hazy gray.

Tamera nodded.

"Can I have a kiss now?" he asked, pulling her in his arms. Releasing her after a long, thorough kiss, he grinned against her lips. "There's more than one way to share germs," he teased, a husky chuckle escaping when she blushed.

"Jerk," she muttered.

He laughed. "Heard from Amber?"

She shook her head. "Not yet. I'm sure she'll call or come by."

He sighed. In the weeks since his daughter's marriage, he'd yet to get used to her not being home at night. The house seemed large, too large. And empty. Funny how one person could make such a difference in life. But he had to admit he was proud of the kids.

As soon as they returned from their honeymoon, Amber showed up on the doorstep with Ace. She'd picked him up after school as promised, and did so every day the rest of his school year. Graduation went without a hitch. Voted Valedictorian of her class, Amber graduated with honors and a paid scholarship to the college of her choice. She immediately registered at the nearest university and started classes right away. After much discussion, she decided on a degree in Elementary Education. With that, she could work with children from any age between preschool to junior high and could always go back for a Master's degree later.

Craig accepted Tamera's offer of a glass of tea with a nod. Hanging his hat on the rack by the door, he answered the phone on its first ring. "Hello?"

"Mr. Harris, Craig?"

"Yes."

"This is Bubba Clark, Bandera County Sheriff's Office."

Craig frowned. "Yes?"

"I hate to be the one to tell you this, but your daughter's been in an accident."

Heaving a sigh, Craig collapsed into the nearest chair. "When, where, what happened?" Swallowing hard, he held up a hand to ward off Tamera's worried questions while the officer answered his.

Tamera stood frozen to the spot. She could tell by her husband's expression and tone of voice, something was wrong, terribly wrong. Impatience simmered while she waited for him to get off the line. When he did, his eyes were haunted, his face pale.

"Where's Ace?"

"Out back. Why?"

"Thank God," he groaned. "Amber's been in a wreck."

"Oh, my God! How is she?"

"I don't know," He swallowed the hard lump of panic rising in his throat.

Slamming his tea down in front of him, Tamera raced to put on her boots. Running a comb through her hair, she grabbed her keys, frowning when Craig caught her arm.

"Wait," He held her firm, fighting his own fear and panic while she struggled against hers. "Calm down, Temper, just a minute." When she was calmer, waiting for him to explain, he continued.

"I'll go. You go get, Stanley," he said, his tone firm. "Meet me there. I don't know anything more than I've told you. He needs to be told. You may have to drive him, Tamera. You understand?"

She nodded.

"Tell Sam to keep an eye on Ace," he reminded, giving her directions to the accident before he walked out the door.

Tamera sat a full minute in the car praying before heading to her daughter's house to fetch her son-in-law. Finding him out back with the horses, she picked up his shirt off the fence and walked toward him. He turned, his smile welcoming.

"Hey, Tam." His eyes narrowed seeing the signs of panic in hers. Something was wrong. He stiffened. "What?"

Her voice was soft, thick with worry. "Amber's been in an accident."

Stan paled.

"Come on, I'll take you."

"Oh, God!" He jerked the shirt on. "Where? What happened?"

"I don't know." She grabbed his hand when he reached for his keys. "I'll drive you," she said.

"Hurry, Tam," he urged when they buckled up. "God, please hurry."

Tamera drove as fast as she dared; following the directions Craig had given her. Fear filled her when she pulled up to the sight of the accident. There were ambulances, firemen and cops everywhere. Identifying herself to the officer directing traffic, she parked where she was told. Throwing the car in park, she flung the door open as Stan bolted out of the car toward the crowd. "Stop him!" she yelled, knowing without a doubt he would rush right in without waiting for permission, not knowing or caring if he was allowed, or if it was safe.

Craig, who was pacing on the outskirts of the crowd of rescuers, heard Tamera's cry, saw Stanley's face, and grabbed him as he ran toward them.

"Amber!" Stan yelled. "Let me go, damn it!" he insisted, fighting the hold Craig had on him. Fighting panic.

"You can't stop me! She's my wife!" he jerked away, swinging wildly. "Let me go!"

His fist caught Craig on the jaw. Totally unprepared, they glared at each other a full moment.

Craig saw the fear in his son-in-law's face and the panic in his eyes. All he could think was Stanley needed to calm down. Before Stan could blink, Craig whirled him around pulling him firmly in an embrace, his arms like steel manacles around Stan's chest.

"You're not going to be much use to her dead," he said in a quiet, lethal voice. Stan stopped struggling and went limp in his arms, his breathing harsh and uneven.

"Listen to me," Craig said, his tone urgent but gentle. His hand stroked his son-in-law's arm and brushed through his hair, soothing as he would a frightened colt. "Are you listening?"

Stan nodded.

"Okay. She's alive. She's trapped in the car but from what they can tell, she's not hurt too badly. Her legs are caught up against the dash and they're going to have to cut her out of the vehicle. She has a bad gash on her forehead and she's slipping in and out of consciousness. That's all we know. They keep her talking as much as possible, but we won't know more until they get her out of the car. It's important she not panic. If she sees you like this, it'll only scare her. Do you understand?"

He held him until Stan nodded. Turning him around, Craig looked into the worried face of his son-in-law. "You have to calm down, Stanley," he ordered, fighting his own rising fear. They had to get her out of the car, and soon. Whispers of conversation hinted the firemen and police were worried something might catch fire or blow up.

Keeping a firm grip on his arm, he led Stan closer to the scene then stopped, concerned when Stanley froze, his eyes trained on the smashed car housing his wife. His breathing sharpened, face paled even more. His panicked gaze sought Craig's. He swallowed hard.

Craig pulled him close for another minute. "Easy now," he soothed. "Calm down. Tamera's with her. I'm not letting you near until you calm down."

Stan fought against the panic threatening to devour him. Clenching his jaw and fists, he squeezed his eyes shut, fighting tears and praying silently until his breath resembled something close to normal. Moving a little closer, he could hear Tamera and the fireman nearest her, talking to Amber.

Amber's frightened eyes met her mother's worried ones. "Is it bad, Mama? My car? Is it?"

Tamera smiled. "Oh, not too bad. How are you?"

She shrugged and winced. "I hurt all over."

"Be still, Sweetheart. You'll be out in a minute. Stan's here."

Amber's eyes searched the crowd. "Where?"

"He's with Daddy."

"I don't want him to see me like this, Mama," she begged, turning wide, pleading eyes to her mother.

"Why? You look beautiful," the fireman interrupted, in an attempt to make them smile.

"Sure. My hair's a mess, there's blood all over me. I'm sure he'll find me irresistible."

The fireman chuckled. "Who is Stan?"

For a moment she forgot her pain and glowed up at him. "My husband."

"Figures," he muttered with a grin. Moving back and bringing Tamera with him, he made room for the paramedic to check Amber's blood pressure then resumed his conversation, hoping to keep her calm. Within moments, she drifted out again despite his efforts. The paramedic took over as Tamera walked away. Checking her pupils he urged Amber to open her eyes.

Tamera trembled, tears dripping down her cheeks. Craig pulled her against him while keeping one hand firmly on Stanley's arm.

Within minutes the firemen had the door off the car and the paramedics moved in to remove Amber. Careful of her trapped legs, keeping her head and neck braced, they eased her from the seat and onto a stretcher.

Stan pulled against Craig's restraining hand. When Craig released him, he walked to Amber on trembling legs. Without asking permission, he took her hand in his. She moaned, opening her eyes. "Hey, Sweetheart," he said, attempting a smile.

Brushing the hair off her face with sweaty hands, he talked softly urging her attention away from her injuries. Walking with her to the ambulance, he let the paramedic take over, listening to her answers when she was questioned as to the extent and area of pain.

Ready and waiting, the emergency room hopped in anticipation of their arrival. They wheeled Amber away immediately for x-rays and cat scans. Craig and Stan paced the waiting area like two huge cats behind cage bars.

Tamera looked up from the magazine she'd thumbed through without reading a word. Tears blurred her eyes. She blinked them back, determined in the face of their worry, to be optimistic, hopeful at least. "Will you two sit down? Or at least take turns. You're wearing out the floor."

Stanley turned in an angry huff. "How can you be so calm?"

Tamera's face paled, and eyes widened.

Stan raised a hand in defeat when Craig glared at him, a low growl sounding in his throat. "I'm sorry," he whispered, collapsing into a chair and burying his face in his hands.

Craig watched her through narrowed eyes and could tell by the slight tremble of her hand and lip, Tamera was barely hanging on to her emotions. Kneeling at her feet, he took her cold hands in his. "Darling?"

She began to cry when he pulled her in his arms. "Shh," he soothed. "She's gonna be fine."

Tamera fought for control while he soothed her. Pulling herself together, they stood with Stanley and faced the doctor when he walked in asking for them.

"It's a miracle," the doctor observed. "She has a broken leg—the knee will need surgery, and a couple of fractured ribs. Her head is banged up but there's no sign of swelling around the brain and she's bruised horribly everywhere. Other than that, she's okay. We need permission to operate on the leg," he addressed Stanley. A nurse handed him the necessary papers.

"When can I see her?"

"You can see her for a minute before we take her into surgery. All of you can go in, but only for a minute."

Taking the papers from Stanley, the nurse led them into Amber's room.

Amber looked at her husband with wide-eyed horror. "They're going to operate on my leg," she whimpered in a frightened, little-girl voice.

"It's okay, Sweetheart," Stan soothed, brushing her hair back. "I promise it'll be fine." Her eyes wide and frightened, fuzzy from the anesthetic, searched the room, and found her mother.

"Where's Daddy?"

Craig moved closer so she could see him clearly. "I'm right here, Sweetheart."

Her lip trembled, tears rolled down her cheeks. "I'm sorry about the car, Daddy."

He smiled and bent down to kiss her cheek. "No problem, Darling. We'll have you a new one tomorrow."

Stanley snorted. "Make it a truck, a one-ton flatbed."

Craig grinned. "Okay by you, Am?"

They heard her sleepy giggle as the medicine took affect and she nodded.

Stan, Craig and Tamera murmured their encouragement, hugging and kissing Amber while the orderlies wheeled her out of the room and into surgery. They returned to the waiting room.

Relief overwhelmed, making him giddy. Stan looked at his father-in-law. "Hey, I'm sorry for losing it out there."

Craig grunted rubbing his jaw. "I guess I've had it coming." His grin took the sting out of the words.

Stan chuckled. "For quite some time now," he agreed with a cocky grin.

Tamera giggled.

Craig smiled a soft, dangerous, smile. "Just don't let it happen again. I may not be so generous next time."

Seeing the teasing light reflected in his eyes, Stan smiled. "Yes, Sir."

Craig glanced over at Tamera. "How about something to eat or drink? We're going to be a while." In mutual consent, they went down to the cafeteria.

An hour after they returned, the doctor came out of surgery, his face grim. Stanley stood, fists clenched, waiting.

"Well," the doctor sighed, rubbing his eyes. "The surgery went fine." He hesitated. "But..."

"What?" Stan demanded, fear clawing through him.

"She miscarried," he told him, his tone gentle.

Stanley collapsed and Tamera began to cry, clinging to Craig who buried his face in her hair with a groan.

"Oh, no, we had no idea she was pregnant," Stan moaned.

The doctor sat beside him hoping to soothe. "I know. She wasn't very far along. It's probably for the best. She'll be on a lot of medication for pain." As noble an effort he made, it was to no avail, they were devastated.

Harsh sobs shook Stanley's frame. Tamera knelt in front of him, pulling him against her in a soothing hug. Craig joined them.

Stan looked up, his haunted eyes searching the doctors. "Does she know?"

He shook his head.

"When can I see her?"

"We'll let you know when she's in recovery. If there's anything you need..." He trailed off when Stan shook his head.

"I'll tell her. Don't let anyone do it," he insisted.

The doctor nodded. "I'll make sure there's a notation in her chart." After he left them, Tamera hugged her son-in-law again. "I'll go get her some things. Ace and I will be back in a while. Can I get you anything?"

Stanley looked at her, his eyes devastated and shrugged. "A change of clothes, I guess. I'm staying with her."

Tamera nodded reaching for her husband. "Okay," she said.

Craig walked with her to the door then returned to wait with Stanley. When Amber was in recovery, they sat on each side of the bed urging her to talk to them.

Amber swam up through the drug-induced fog to awareness. She smiled squeezing her father's hand as he held hers, brushing the hair off her face.

"Hey, Baby," Craig's voice was harsh with relief and pain.

"Hi, Daddy. Where's Stan?"

"He went to get some coffee and talk with the doctor, Baby, he'll be right in," he assured his voice gentle, smile tender.

As if on cue, Stanley walked through the door. "She awake?"

Amber opened her eyes again. "Yes, she's awake," she teased in a thick voice. "What did the doctor say? Can I go home?" Stan's smile was strained. So were his eyes. Troubled. Sad.

Pulling himself together, Stan kissed her hand. "Not yet, Sweetheart, they're going to keep you a day or so. Don't worry though; I'm not leaving your side."

She frowned, dozed, struggled awake. "Did you bring me some coffee?"

"No. But I brought you some juice. Want it?"

She nodded. Craig poured the juice in a cup of ice. Holding the straw to her lips, he encouraged her to drink.

Later that evening, after her parents and brother had left Amber smiled, running her fingers through his hair when her husband folded his arms and rested his head on the bed beside her. "Sing for me, Stanley," she pleaded.

Stan struggled out of his depression unable to resist those wide, pleading eyes. He felt like singing about as much as he felt like jumping off a bridge. "What do you want to hear?" he queried, his smile tight.

She shrugged. "Your voice."

Taking a deep breath he closed his eyes and sang the words which burned in his heart. *"Amazing Grace...."*

"Not that," she whimpered, pulling him toward her. "Anything but that." She began to cry as waves of aftershock shook her and the fears she'd held at bay for so long threatened to overwhelm.

Shuddering, Stan buried his head on his arms again, afraid to hold her for the bruises and cracked ribs. "I was so worried Amber. So scared. God!" His voice trailed off knowing no words to express the horror he'd felt at seeing her trapped in that tiny piece of scrap metal called a car.

"I'm sorry," she sniffled. "I guess everything's catching up on me."

Unable to resist any longer, Stanley climbed up beside her and held her close running his hands over her in a soothing caress. "It's okay, My Sweet. It'll be all right," he soothed. "I promise."

He sighed, relieved when she dozed off, spared for the moment from telling her about the baby. He knew not telling her was cowardly. It was wrong. But he hadn't been able to bring himself to tell her just yet. Tomorrow, he thought closing his eyes and mind to the pain.

Amber spent a restless night, whimpering in pain and being awakened every few hours for vital signs. His night just as raw, Stanley paced her room while the nurses checked in on her once again. It was nearly dawn and he expected Craig and Tamera would be up at any moment. When they arrived, he walked down the corridor with them.

"How about some breakfast, Stan?" Tamera queried.

"No thanks. I'll get a tray when Amber gets hers."

Craig put his hand on Stan's shoulder. "You okay?"

He shrugged, shook his head. "It's been a long night." His voice broke. "She had a miserable one."

"Did you tell her about the baby?"

He shook his head again. "No. I..." his voice trailed off, he struggled with his emotions. "I thought I'd wait until she got home. She's been through so much."

"You have to tell her, Stanley," Tamera interrupted. "You want me to do it?"

"Or me?" Craig offered.

"No! No. I'll tell her. I just," he choked back a sob. "I just need to deal with it myself first. I...," his voice quivered.

Craig pulled him against his side. "I know how you feel, Stanley. You need to deal with it together. It'll be easier if you deal with it together. The longer you wait, the harder it'll get. She has the right to know."

Stan sighed, nodded. "I know. I know. And I will take care of it."

Craig sighed. "All right. When does she get to go home?"

He shrugged. "I'm going to ask the doctor today. I'm sure she'll rest better without being woke up every few hours for a pain pill or sleeping pill," he muttered with disgust. "Why can't they just leave her alone if she's sleeping?"

Craig grinned. "It's their job to make her as comfortable as possible while she's in here."

Stanley snorted. "She'd be more comfortable at home," he grumbled.

Tamera grinned.

Craig laughed. "When she gets out, you need to bring her to the house." He cut off Stan's protests with a pleading look. "I'm asking, Stanley, not ordering. She'll need someone to look after her. You can't do it all by yourself. You have a job to do and horses to take care of."

Stan sighed and nodded. "You're right. Okay."

Craig hugged him once more. "Thank you." He winked at Tamera. "I hope she's a better patient than you," he teased, laughing when she rolled her eyes.

"I hope Stanley's not as domineering as you."

The man in question looked puzzled. "Did I miss something here?"

Craig chuckled. "Inside joke."

Turning, they headed back to her room to check on Amber and wait for the doctor.

Chapter Twenty

Craig walked down the stairs surprised to see a dim light coming from the den. He stood in the doorway as Stanley walked around the room smiling at the many pictures of Amber there. He watched with concern when Stan picked one up and stroked it with a trembling hand. As though sensing his presence, Stan lifted haunted eyes to search his. His eyes were devastated, his face ravished with pain.

"I always loved this one the most," he whispered in a hoarse voice. "Was she always like this?"

Craig nodded his smile tender. He knew the picture intimately, Amber at about three years old sitting on her rocking horse and laughing. Her eyes sparkled and a flush covered her cheeks. You could almost see the black silk curls bouncing on her shoulders. There was a smug, defiant tilt to her little chin as she ignored her mother's warning to slow down. Her blue velvet dress was flung high by her wild riding, showing layers of lace petticoats and a shocking amount of lace underpants. The memory sent an ache right to the core. Craig waited in expectation for Stanley to voice his next thought aloud.

A soft sob escaped Stanley, his eyes searched Craig's. "I wonder what our child would have looked like."

Having been there, he understood all too well. Without hesitation Craig walked over and pulled Stan against his chest, swallowing hard the lump of tears in his throat. That's something they wouldn't know, until there was another child.

Fighting down emotions, he bit back his questions, somehow knowing what the answers were. It was obvious by the depth of turmoil the boy was expressing, Stanley still hadn't told Amber about the baby they'd lost. Though Craig disagreed wholeheartedly, he'd promised Tamera he wouldn't interfere. He went back to bed with an aching mind and heavy heart.

Stanley walked up the stairs alternately praying Amber was awake and hoping she wasn't. He knew it was cowardly to not tell her about the baby. It was wrong. He just hadn't been able to bring himself to do so. Oh, God, he thought. What am I supposed to do?

"You know what to do."

I can't, he argued, suppressing a sob. I just can't. Stopping outside the door of Amber's bedroom, he leaned his head on the door and prayed. God, help me.

"The truth will set you free."

The truth will destroy her!

"My Spirit will comfort you both."

I don't want comfort I want my child!

God remained silent at his blatant disobedience.

Opening the door, Stanley walked quietly into the room and stood by the bed, staring down at his wife. I love you, he thought. I love you so much! He watched with concern when she began to murmur and whimper in her sleep.

Amber struggled to wake up as the dark shadow approached her window. She watched in horror when he leapt through the air latching onto the screen with his claws. No! She heard his wolf-like growls and he struggled, trying to tear the screen. Unable to wrench her gaze away she watched, horrified, while he continued to try and rip the screen off her window. Something dangled from his mouth. With an angry snarl he shook his head and jumped away. She awoke with a muffled scream of terror.

"Amber?" Stanley touched her cheek. "Are you all right?"

A sob shuddered through her. "Oh, God, Stanley, it was so real."

"What, Sweet?" She looked up at him when he turned on the bedside lamp. The terror in her eyes tore at his heart.

"The nightmare, the monster, he was back Stanley, trying to get in. I don't understand," she shook her head. "It's not raining or anything." She thought a minute. "He had something in his mouth." She frowned. "It looked like...."

Her eyes widened in horror. "Oh, God, Stan, it looked like an unborn baby." She began to sob

Stan felt the blood drain from his face. He took her in his arms, rocking her against him. "Shh, it was just a dream, My Sweet."

"I don't understand," she sobbed.

"You've been through a traumatic experience, Amber. It'll be all right," he soothed. "I'm here now. He won't bother you again," he promised, wishing he hadn't been so adamant about being the one to tell Amber about the baby and cursing his cowardice in not doing so now.

* * * * *

Stan glared down at his wife who glared right back, the nightmare of last night forgotten in the bright light of day. "No, Amber, and I'm not saying it again!"

She growled, pounding her fist on the bed. "Why not?"

He sighed heavily. They were arguing again, over the same thing. She'd been home barely more than a week and had been after him to get her a pair of crutches. "The doctor said for you to take it easy and that's exactly what you're going to do."

"The doctor said I could get them as soon as I felt strong enough. I had a few fractured ribs, not broken. At least I'd be able to go to the bathroom by myself!" she hissed.

Her eyes sparkled with fury. Stanley shook his head. "I've got to get to work." Leaning over, he kissed her chin then the throbbing pulse in her cheek. "Behave now, and don't give your parents a hard time. I'll see you this afternoon."

"If you don't bring the crutches, don't bother to come home," she ground out between clenched teeth, jerking away from his lips.

Pulling away, he stomped to the door. "Craig! Come in here and talk some sense into this daughter of yours before I beat it into her!"

Craig chuckled from the bottom step. He'd heard the same arguments for days as Amber tried to get them on her side. "No way, I promised I wouldn't interfere."

Stan rolled his eyes with a grunt. "Great," he muttered. "When I need him the most, he decides not to interfere," he complained. "Interfere! Please!"

Craig merely laughed and shook his head. "I put up with Tamera. Now you put up with Amber. She's your wife."

Since Amber's release from the hospital, Stanley had heard the tale of Tamera's accident before her marriage to Craig and how stubborn she'd been during her recovery. He shook his head. His father-in-law had tried to warn him, he admitted silently, and sighed. Turning back to the door, he opened it a crack.

"Have a good day, My Sweet, and get some rest," he ordered, closing the door quickly when she threw a book at him with a muttered curse. It hit with a resounding thud. "Stubborn wench," he mumbled, heading down the stairs.

That afternoon he arrived with a six pack of beer, of the root variation, and a pair of crutches. Craig eyed him and the half-empty six-pack with a knowing grin. "Three already?" he taunted. If every man had to have his vice, root beer was Stanley's. He simply loved the rich, sugary drink.

Stan snorted. "Yeah, one for courage, one for strength and one for patience." Craig laughed and Stan reached for a bottle. "Maybe I'll take another for patience. Help yourself," he offered, nodding toward the remaining two.

Craig grinned, opened one and eyed the crutches. "You shouldn't give in to her so easily. You'll spoil her."

Stan grunted, rolling his eyes. "You're a fine one to talk. You've spoiled her beyond repair and I'm not supposed to give in to her? Exactly how do you suggest I manage that and stay sane?" he asked his eyes wide with mock horror.

Craig grinned and shrugged.

Stanley shook his head. "Oh please, not even one word of advice or encouragement?" he muttered.

Craig chuckled and shook his head.

Making a show of squaring his shoulders Stan picked up the crutches. "Here goes nothing," he mumbled, leaving his father-in-law in guffaws behind as he climbed the stairs to Amber's room. Opening the door, he watched Amber stiffen, refusing to turn over and greet him. He rolled his eyes, grinning to himself. Closing the door behind him, he tossed the crutches where she could see them. Her eyes widened in surprised pleasure.

"Just one blasted minute," he warned, when she reached for them. She hesitated, lifting wide, innocent eyes to his.

"If I even hear of you attempting anything but the bathroom, I'll break them in half and hog-tie you to this frigging bed. Do you understand me?"

She smiled and tilted her face for a kiss. "Yes, Sir," she complied in a silky voice.

"And don't pull that innocent act on me. It won't work."

She giggled and pulled him toward her for another kiss and a hug. Accepting his assistance, she stood for the first time in what seemed like an eternity. She sighed, promising to never again take walking for granted.

* * * * *

Scott and Trina arrived for the weekend. Amber was a wreck. Scott held her while Trina tried to soothe. "It'll get easier, Amber. I promise," she whispered, in a hoarse voice.

"I know. I'm just so tired of being cooped up," she sniffled.

A warning look from Scott stopped Trina's next words: *you're young; you'll have other children.* They were useless words anyway. She knew. She'd heard them all before herself. Out of respect for their grief, Scott and Trina kept her newly confirmed pregnancy a secret.

Physician's intuition told Scott, Amber still did not know about the baby she'd lost. Holding her, he held back his frustrated anger until she calmed down. Kissing her on the forehead he laid her back against the pillows and signaled to Trina. "She doesn't know," he hissed. "Be careful what you say."

Trina nodded and went in search of Tamera. Scott stormed down the stairs with someone else in mind. He cornered Stanley in the den. "Why haven't you told her?" he demanded.

Stan paled at the anger in Scott's eyes but stood to face it. Between Amber, his job, his horses and home, and the weight of grief and guilt he carried, he fought to keep from crumbling. His wife was hurt, his faith had been tested to the limit, and, after too many days of feeling so low he'd have to reach up to touch bottom, he was mad as hell for miserably failing the test. His patience snapped.

"I don't think that's any of your business."

"Wrong answer, Pal," Scott muttered, hauling him up by the shirtfront until they were eye to eye. "Everything about her is my business. I've known her; I've *loved* her since the day she was born. She's up there going through an emotional hurricane and she doesn't even know why! I've been her doctor, her friend for years. How dare you say it's none of my business?" he demanded, giving Stanley a slight shake.

"Enough," Craig said from the doorway. "He's right Stanley. He's as much family as you are," he said, sighing with relief when Scott released his son-in-law. He shook his head and walked into the room. "She has the right to know Stanley. You've known all along."

"Know what?"

The men turned in unison to find Amber standing in the doorway.

Stanley chose anger and worry instead of truth. "What are you doing down here? You promised not to try too much too soon!"

Amber ignored him. "She has the right to know what?" she asked again, her eyes moving from one man to the other. "Stanley?" she queried in a soft, pleading voice when fear began to gnaw at her. "Daddy?"

Blood pounded in her ears when she saw the pain and guilt on their faces. Things suddenly began to make sense: The emotional roller coaster she'd been on, the depression, the period from hell with its vice-like cramps and excessive bleeding which she never thought would end and had attributed to the accident. Stanley's pensiveness, the absence of music from him, and his insistence that he was just too tired.

The nightmare.

She paled, turning away with a sob.

"Amber, wait!" Stan moved toward her.

"Don't touch me!" she cried, jerking away when he reached for her. "Don't you dare touch me!"

Reminded again of Craig's warning about jeweled daggers of ice, Stan recoiled from the anger and the pain in her eyes. He'd never seen her so coldly furious. "Please, Amber, we need to talk," he pleaded.

"I don't want to hear one word you have to say! You lied to me!" Her angry gaze turned to encompass all of them. "You've all lied to me!"

Sobbing she turned toward the stairs, wanting nothing more than to get away, to escape from the pain and guilt on their faces. And the sorrow. To get away from her own anguish.

Fighting to control her sobs and blinking back tears, she stumbled, spurring Stanley into action. Ignoring her biting remarks, he picked her up. "Stop it, Amber. You've a right to your anger, but I won't let you hurt yourself!"

She held herself rigid until he laid her on the bed then unleashed all of her fury in a single slap. His head jerked with the impact.

Amber struggled with the impulse to hit him again, wanting nothing more than to hurt him as much as she was hurting.

Though he'd warned her before to never slap him, Stan clenched his fists but made no move to retaliate. He deserved this one. He'd punished her enough already.

"Get out," she ordered in a calm, deadly voice.

He nodded. "I will, but only after you hear me out." Though she turned away he continued. "I'm sorry, Amber. I know it was wrong, knew it all along. I just couldn't handle it. You'd been hurt so much and...." his voice trailed off and he struggled with his emotions. "I just couldn't bear to see you hurting as much as I was. I thought, I'd hoped, to spare you that, to protect you from it."

"You lied to me," she accused bitterly, glaring at him. "Even after that nightmare the other night, you didn't say anything. *How could you?*" She shook her head, holding up a hand to ward off any more words from him. "Just get out. I don't want to hear your excuses," she muttered, turning away from him once more.

Clenching his fists, Stan fought the urge to touch her. Tears filled his eyes. Tears she didn't see. "I'm sorry," he whispered, swallowing hard the panic and fear bubbling in his throat, fear that he'd lose her too. "I love you, Amber, and I'm sorry," he whispered. Turning, he did as she asked. He left.

When the door closed behind him, Amber gave into the overwhelming need to cry. Pain and anger battered away at her until there was nothing but a huge, gaping hole where her heart had been. She ignored the knock on the door. She heard it open but refused to turn over. She just wanted to be left alone.

Tamera walked toward the bed, praying for the words to comfort and guide her daughter. The pain she knew all too well threatened to steal her voice. Wrapping Amber in her arms, she held on tight rocking, soothing, when fresh sobs shook Amber's slender frame, tears pouring out of her in painful torrents.

"I'm so sorry, Baby," she soothed.

"He lied to me, Mama. Everyone lied to me."

"Oh, Darling. We didn't mean to lie to you. It was not our place to say anything. It was Stanley's."

"Stanley wasn't doing his job!" she insisted hysterically, wanting desperately to pull away and refuse her mother's comforting arms, needing just as desperately to cling to them.

"I know," Tamera soothed, tears streaming down her cheeks to mingle with Amber's. "I know. I'm sorry." She held her until Amber calmed somewhat. Brushing the hair off her face she cupped Amber's cheeks in her hands, urging her daughter to look at her.

"You know Stanley loves you," Tamera insisted, watching the tears fill her baby's eyes again as Amber agreed with a reluctant nod. Her smile tender, she sought words of guidance.

"I don't know why men have this inherent need to protect the women they love, even if it means protecting them from the truth. It's just one of those mysteries women may never understand. I'm not saying it's right. I'm just telling you what's in my heart. And, having been there, that I know how you feel. I know how Stanley feels too. This has been a terrible strain on him, Amber. Whether you believe it or not, whether you want to hear it or not, it's true. I know you're angry with him right now. And I understand. But you will have to forgive him, Honey. Try and put yourself in his place, for just a moment. And try, pray, to understand, and to forgive. Your marriage will not make it otherwise," she said, her voice thick with warning.

"My marriage won't make it if he insists on keeping the truth from me either."

"I know that, Darling. Stanley knows it too. If I may offer one other piece of advice?" she asked then continued at Amber's nod.

"The family who prays together stays together. Never lose your faith, Amber. It's vital to every part of your life, even your marriage, *especially* your marriage. I know Stanley is a spiritual man, and you've been raised in faith. Hang on to it, even during the rough times. It'll pay off. God rewards those who diligently seek Him and He will always be there for you even when you don't understand."

They turned in unison to answer the knock on the door. Craig walked in looking haggard and guilty. Tears filled his eyes when he reached for his daughter, holding her against his chest. "I'm so sorry, Sweetheart," he rasped.

Amber clung to her father. After years of living with him, of understanding his need, his desire to protect her, and fighting against the rigidity of it, she found it easy to forgive him. Silently she prayed for the strength and the grace to forgive her husband also.

Dinner was subdued when Stanley didn't come back and Amber refused to eat. Afterward, Trina went to see Amber and to offer comfort. They'd all been there. She held her while she cried then handed her an envelope. "Not long ago I lost someone I loved very much and a very beautiful, very special, young woman gave me this letter. It was such a comfort I decided to pass it on to you."

Looking at the envelope in her hand, Amber gasped in surprise to recognize the letter filled with Scriptures she'd sent to Trina after the death of her mother nearly a year ago. "I can't believe you still have this after all this time."

Trina smiled and brushed the hair off Amber's cheeks. "It's been a great comfort to me, especially on those days when I miss her, and the child I lost, the most. I'm sorry for your loss, Sweetheart. My heart aches for you and for Stanley."

Amber's lip trembled. "Thank you, Trina. I don't think it would be so bad if I hadn't found out like I did. I just can't believe he kept something like this from me. How can I ever trust him not to do it again?"

Trina pulled her close once more. "I think you can, Darling. I think Stanley has learned his lesson. He's hurting too, Amber. Remember that," she urged. "It was his child too."

"I know," she sobbed. "I know. Mama said the same thing. I know I'll have to forgive him, I'm just so angry and so hurt."

"I'm sure you are. Just remember how very much he loves you, Amber. Trust in it, and in your love for each other. Sometimes that's the best, the *only*, thing we can do.

"I will," Amber promised, welcoming Trina's embrace once more.

Though Craig had stopped him from beating the hell out of the boy earlier, Scott went in search of Stanley. He found him at his and Amber's home, out in the back with the horses. Walking up beside him, he placed a hand on Stan's shoulder.

Stan remained still, too tired, and too emotionally spent to shrug it off.

"I'm sorry if I was out of line, Stanley."

"Me too. I guess we all get out of line when it comes to Amber."

Scott chuckled. "I don't think Amber holds the corner on that market. We men tend to get out of line about any number of things when it comes to protecting the women we love. But we can't always protect them from the truth, Son. It tends to come out one way or another."

Stan nodded burying his head on his arm. "I know," he admitted.

"We've all been there, Stan. We may be upset, even angry, but no one is judging you. From the looks of it, you've judged yourself pretty well as it is."

Grinding his teeth, Stanley fought the tears, and lost. Scott embraced him when his shoulders shook with huge, heaving sobs.

"I messed up, big time. Craig warned me, but I did it anyway. I tried to protect her when I should have been honest."

Scott nodded in agreement and understanding. "We've all done that, Stanley. That's why we can warn you. But you have to make your own mistakes, live with them, and hopefully, learn from them."

Stan nodded into the generous brown eyes. "Thanks," he said.

Scott smiled. "You ready to come back? I'm sure she'll see you now."

Stan shrugged, not so sure of that himself. "I'll be there in a while. I need to finish up here."

"Okay."

Returning to the Rockin' H, Scott took a turn at comforting Amber. Taking her in his arms, he rocked her while she cried. Swallowing hard the lump in his throat, he cupped her cheeks in his hands, brushed the hair off her face and kissed her forehead. "Do you remember the fight Trina and I had while on vacation with you and your family last summer?"

She nodded.

"Remember what you and I talked about?"

Amber gazed into the tender brown eyes of the man she'd known and loved all of her life and repeated the words she'd spoken a year ago. "Love's not always easy, is it?"

"That's right, Sweetheart. It's not. Remember what I said when you asked me that question back then?"

She nodded. "But when it's right, it's worth the fight and every moment of pain."

He nodded and hugged her again. "You and Stanley will get through this, Amber. It won't be easy, but if the love you share is right, and I believe it is, you will get through this. On those days when you can't remember why you love each other, remember that the Bible says *Many are the trials and tribulations of a righteous man but God delivers him out of them all.*' Cling to God and cling to your love and your marriage will weather the storms of life," he promised. "Remember what I told you about being patient?"

Amber smiled, his words floating through her mind as though he'd spoken them yesterday instead of a year ago... "Be patient with the men you love, we're a bunch of hot heads when it comes to the women in our lives."

Scott smiled and hugged her again. "That goes for Stanley more than anyone else, Sweetie. He may have learned a lesson in all this, but it won't be easy for him to avoid making the same mistake again," he warned.

"I'll try to remember that," she promised.

They were still talking when they heard the sound of Stan tuning his guitar. His voice, though thick and hoarse, rang out clear and true. The words didn't matter. All that mattered was, he was singing.

"Help me, Scott," Amber pleaded, reaching for her robe while he got her crutches. Settling herself beside him, she reached for her husband.

Stan went willingly in his wife's arms. He'd been held by his mother-in-law, embraced by his father-in-law and friends, but in her arms he found the most comfort. "I'm sorry," he whispered, his voice hoarse, tears running down his cheeks to join hers. "I'm so sorry. Please forgive me. I couldn't bear it if I lost you too."

Amber held him, rocking, soothing until his quiet sobs subsided. "You know what hurts the most?" she queried, continuing at the shake of his head. "While you were hurting, I was arguing and fighting with you about crutches, acting like a spoiled brat. I wasn't there for you. Not knowing, I couldn't be there for you." Her voice trembled.

In that moment Stanley understood the heart of their vows. Though he'd heard them clearly during the ceremony, now they echoed in his soul and he listened with his heart. Especially the words *and he shall cleave only unto her and the two together shall become one.* He eyed her in quiet solemnity. "It'll never happen again."

Knowing that would be a difficult promise for him to keep, a tiny smile tugged at the corner of Amber's mouth. She leaned her forehead against his. "I'll forgive you when it does."

The guitar slid from his hands, Stanley wrapped his arms around his wife, pulling her gently but firmly against him. His lips covered hers, soft at first, then hungry, until their breaths were coming in short gasps. "I need you," he whispered for her ears only, his eyes searching hers.

The quiet invitation in those beautiful eyes answered his question. Only the fact that they weren't alone, had an audience in fact, and she was injured, stopped him from loving her there. The guitar lay forgotten, as did the crutches, when he swung her up in his arms and carried her to the bed.

Craig moved to pick up the forgotten objects, frowning down at Tamera's restraining hand. "They'll be fine now," she assured him, her eyebrow arched meaningfully.

His eyes cut to the closed door of Amber's bedroom with dawning clarity. His daughter. His house.

Her husband, he realized with a dark flush.

"I get the point," he muttered, turning on his heel and following them into the kitchen.

Tamera giggled. "Sometimes it takes a while, but he always manages to get the point."

Scott and Trina joined her in teasing Craig.

Stan clasped Amber to him, careful of her bruised and battered body. Desire roared through him, tempered by the need to be gentle. His hands roamed over her flesh while his mouth devoured hers then moved to kiss the bruises which still marred her beautiful skin.

"Be still," he murmured, when she clung to him sweetly, lost in the passion of his hands and lips. "I don't want to hurt you. Don't want you to hurt yourself," he added, mumbling soft, sweet words of love and desire. When he finally loved her, he loved her with every ounce of tenderness he possessed, his body and soul seeking tangible evidence of her forgiveness, physical proof of being alive.

Fighting the demands of his flesh, Stan urged her up and over the crest time and again. When he could stand trembling on the edge no longer, he succumbed, falling into bliss with her. Ecstasy settled around them like a soft sunset, all warm and glowing. He lay in her arms as long as his trembling body would allow. Afraid of resting his weight on her, he rolled away, holding her snugly against his chest.

"Wow," he teased, kissing her. "It's pretty potent, My Sweet, being in total control and having you at my mercy." His chuckle died in his throat when her hand played across his chest, moving lower still. His stomach muscles jumped reflexively, breath stuck in his throat with an audible hiss.

Amber's eyes searched his, the tempered fire of desire illuminated by the bright light of love.

"Complete control?" she taunted, her eyebrow arched in teasing.

He grinned. "Guess not," he conceded. "I guess it was kind of rude of us to leave them all out there standing around like that."

She giggled, a hot flush stinging her cheeks. "Probably, but I think they understand."

He kissed her again. "I love you, Amber. And I'm truly sorry."

"I know. Listen to me, Stanley," she urged, capturing his gaze with hers. "If I wanted to be protected from life's little ups and downs and tragedies, I would have stayed daddy's little girl forever. I love you and I'm trying to understand your reasons for not telling me. Even if I never understand, I forgive you. But you don't have to protect me. I married you to share my life with you. Good and bad. Do you understand what I'm saying?"

He nodded pulling her in his arms again. "I never wanted to hurt you, My Sweet," he assured his voice deep with regret.

Lying together, sated in the aftermath of love, they talked and cried, mourning the loss of their child. Somewhere deep in the night understanding came. Healing began.

* * ** *

The next morning after breakfast, Tamera cornered Scott and Trina in the den. "All right, you two, is there something you wish to share with us?"

They looked at each other in surprise. "Like what?" he asked.

"Don't be coy with me, Scott Hensley. I know you too well," Tamera chided.

He grinned. "How did you know?"

"Know what?" Craig asked, clearly confused.

Scott laughed, pulling Trina close. "We're going to have a baby. We weren't going to say anything just yet, out of respect for your grief."

"Out of respect... What? You should know we'd be thrilled for you," Craig insisted hugging Trina and shaking Scott's hand. "Congratulations! When?"

"In about seven months," Trina admitted. "We just found out for sure a couple of days ago."

Scott turned to Tamera. "I still want to know how you knew."

Tamera smiled and hugged them. "Little things, like Trina turning pale and not eating like she usually does, crackers and 7up by the bed, and that special glow in her eyes and on her cheeks."

Scott pulled Trina in his arms once more. "She is incredibly beautiful, isn't she?" His lips covered hers in a tender caress.

Craig and Tamera murmured in agreement.

"I think you should tell the kids," Tamera said, thinking it may give them a sense of hope.

"Tell the kids what?" Stanley asked while helping Amber into the room.

Scott stuttered.

Trina flushed.

Amber gasped with sudden insight. "You're going to have a baby, aren't you?"

Trina nodded.

"Oh, Trina, that's wonderful!"

Stanley kissed Trina's cheek and shook Scott's hand. "Congratulations."

Kneeling at her feet, Scott took Amber's hands in his. "Are you two okay, really? We'd never want to hurt you and were afraid our news would only add to your grief."

She leaned her forehead against his. "You, of all people should know me better than that," she chided in gentle admonishment. "We're fine. A mite jealous, but just fine," she assured, when her husband picked up his guitar and began to sing.

Epilogue

Amber watched in silence while the waiter lit the candles on the table. Tonight they were celebrating Stanley's birthday and, unbeknownst to the others, something more. A secret smile tugged at her lips when her parents and Ace joined them.

They'd been married nearly five years and it had been perfect. Nearly perfect. The only bone of contention between she and Stanley was when he refused to use the rest of her college fund for their horse ranch. With her college tuition and fees paid by scholarship, her father had given the money to them.

Stanley insisted they put it up for the future, determined to make a go of his dream. And he had. In just under five years, he was already becoming well known for the quality of stock he carried and the exquisite care and training which went into every foal he birthed and sold.

As for her, she'd finished college. A degree which usually took most people four years, she earned in three. She'd done her stint as a student teacher and now worked fairly regular as a substitute in every level from preschool to eighth grade. The situation was perfect, allowing her plenty of time to write as well as use the skills she'd worked so hard to learn and excel at, in the field she loved.

They'd taken her mother's advice to heart in keeping God first in their life. By keeping her tradition of giving to the underprivileged, they always managed to give back into His kingdom. And the blessings kept coming. She listened with half an ear at the conversation flowing around them. Signaling the waiter, she ordered.

"Three glasses of champagne please. And two milks. Put the milk in champagne glasses though, we're celebrating."

Stanley eyed her. "Amber, why are you ordering champagne and milk?"

She smiled. "It's a celebration, Darling. We need champagne," she answered, evading a direct answer.

"Yeah, but why are you ordering milk?"

Craig watched the exchange with a grin. Gut instinct told him what was going on. Amber looked especially beautiful tonight, all soft and glowing. He'd seen that look before, on Tamera, and recognized it immediately.

"Well, Stanley, how does it feel to be twenty-six and already a small success in your chosen profession?" He asked, managing to slip Amber a wink while Stanley answered the question. The conversation which ensued kept Stan's mind occupied for a few minutes, but his eyes kept straying to Amber, who glowed.

A soft flush covered her cheeks. Her eyes were bright with an inner fire. Kind of like the proverbial cat that ate the canary. She'd never seemed more beautiful. The waiter arrived carrying the tray of drinks. When he left, she raised her glass in a toast.

"Happy birthday, Darling," she murmured, touching her glass to Stan's.

Stan kissed her. "Thank you," he replied, knowing it would do him absolutely no good to demand an answer to his previously asked question. Whatever she had to say, she'd say in her own sweet time. He could only bite back the questions for so long.

"Okay Amber, what gives? Why did you order champagne for us and milk for yourself? I know why Ace is drinking milk; he's too young for champagne. But you're not..." his voice trailed off, a thought occurred to him. He eyed her. "Amber?"

Her smile was as brilliant as the light in her eyes. "My doctor told me just this morning, not to drink alcohol."

"What did you see a doctor for?"

"Oh," she hesitated, sipping her milk.

Stan groaned, rolling his eyes in frustration. "Amber, what did you see a doctor for?" His heart thudded in his chest, waiting for her reply.

"To confirm a test I took yesterday."

He ground his teeth. "What kind of test?" She smiled an impish light in her eyes.

Amber shrugged as if it weren't important. In truth, the excitement was eating her alive. "A pregnancy test," she said in a stage whisper.

Stan put down his glass. "Excuse me?"

She tossed her head back with a laugh. "I didn't stutter. Did I, Daddy?" she queried innocently of her father who was grinning like a donkey. Her mother looked pretty smug too.

The smile started in his eyes and spread to cover Stanley's entire face.

"Pregnant? You're pregnant?"

At her nod he whooped. Lunging from his chair, he pulled her in his arms twirling her around. "Oh, wow! What a birthday present. When, how?"

She laughed. "Well, the doctor's not too sure. He said, by my examination, I seem further along than I figured. But," her voice softened in teasing. "I'm sure you know how."

Craig chuckled. "Well Stanley, looks like you'd better sell a couple more horses."

"Maybe not," she informed them, after Stanley returned her to her chair. "I received a letter from a publisher today. They're interested."

"That's wonderful!" everyone chorused, taking turns at hugging and congratulating her and Stanley.

* * * * *

Craig and Ace took turns pacing the floor of the waiting room while Tamera sat quietly, praying the delivery of her daughter's child would be a safe one, and that both mother and child would be healthy. The months had passed so quickly, or so it seemed. The baby had developed normally but she had a feeling he or she was early. Or, the kids weren't telling them something.

Having been a veterinarian for many years and a mother herself, Tamera had the feeling she knew what they

259

weren't telling, but hadn't asked, allowing the kids their sense of surprise. She looked up when Craig stopped pacing and Stanley walked through the door, grinning from ear to ear.

"Twins," he informed them. "Both girls, and they look exactly like their mother." He walked up to Craig. "I guess God decided since I took your daughter to wife, He'd replace her by giving you two granddaughters." He shrugged.

"One for me and one for you. Take your pick: Kaitlyn or Ashlyn," he offered generously, then grinned and withdrew a quarter from his pocket. "Flip you for her. Heads I win, tails you lose."

Stanley's eyes shone like a cool summer sky reflected off the clearest of lakes. Craig grunted, catching the coin in midair. "Not only is that *not* a fair bet, but this is probably a two headed coin," he muttered, slipping it into his pocket. "Besides, as their grandfather, I get to spoil them both."

He grinned and hugged his son-in-law. "Know what it really means?" he asked, pulling Tamera against his side. "It means I only have *one* female to put up with. You have three. And I hope they both inherit those sassy sapphire eyes and drive you to the brink of insanity."

Stanley roared, picking up his mother-in-law and twirling her around. "I'll gladly take a dozen, even if they all have those sassy sapphire eyes!"

He put Tamera down and embraced Ace in a headlock. "Well, Ace, are you old enough for a cigar yet?" he queried, knowing his young brother-in-law would try one out of typical teenage rebellion whether he was old enough or not, and despite his father's wrath.

They all gathered around the bed when Amber, holding two squirming, tightly wrapped bundles, was wheeled out of delivery.

"They're beautiful, Sweetheart," Craig crooned. "How will you ever tell them apart?" he teased, eyeing his identical twin granddaughters.

Amber smiled, a tender light in her eyes. "I guess I'll just have to adjust their armbands while I can. Then I'll have to write their names on their foreheads or embroider them on their dresses until we figure out some other way," she teased. "What do you think, Mama?"

Tears of joy and thanksgiving rolled down her cheeks. Tamera hugged her daughter. "That's right, Sweetheart," she agreed, silently thanking God because both of her prayers had been answered.

Dear Readers,

I hope you've enjoyed Amber's story as much as I have. Though the message is no less important, writing it was certainly a welcome relief after the roller coaster ride of emotions experienced in *Tempered Dreams.*

As Christians we are called to train up our children in the way they should go...to do our best then trust God to do the rest.

I know, I know, easier said than done.

As the parent of four grown children (two by blood and two by marriage), I could identify with Craig one hundred percent, though Amber's frustrations were every bit as real to me.

As mentioned in my dedication, I hope you were blessed with the reading and God glorified in the writing. Once again, it is my sincere hope that if you don't know Him, you will seek Jesus as your Lord and Savior and if you do, you'll endeavor to know Him on a deeper, more personal level. And as always, may God bless and keep each and every one of you—and yours- in the palm of His loving hand!

Sincerely,
Pamela S Thibodeaux
"Inspirational with an Edge!" ™
http://pamelathibodeaux.com

Now a sneak peek into Book 4, *Tempered Joy!*

Based on Psalms 126:5: "They that sow in tears will reap in joy."

All around rodeo cowboy and heir to the Rockin' H Ranch, Ace Harris is determined not to fall in love. He's only loved one woman in his life, his mother, and no one can even come close to filling her boots. Her death has left a hole in his heart and emptiness in his soul.

Lexie Morgan thinks rodeo cowboys have rocks for brains and a death wish for a soul. A broken childhood and the death of her father and best friend leave her doubting and questioning God (despite her years of religious upbringing) and afraid of love.

Can two young people who clash from the onset learn to trust in the healing power of God and find love and happiness amidst tragedy and grief?

Chapter One

Alexis Jayne Morgan, better known as Lexie, frowned over at Ace Harris while her foster-father Scott Hensley, marveled on and on about Ace's accomplishments. Ace had competed in rodeos since before his freshman year, and won in every event from roping to bull riding. Now, as a junior, he held more titles than any other boy his age. Lexie grunted in a very unladylike manner. "A true cowboy."

"Lexie." Scott's voice held warning.

She ignored his tone and turned to him, eyes wide. "Well everyone knows, rodeo cowboys have rocks for brains and a death wish for a soul," she remarked, her tone a tad too innocent.

"Enough, Lex," Scott insisted.

"It's okay, Scott," Ace interrupted. "It's obvious she doesn't know what she's talking about." All afternoon he'd listened with his father while Scott talked of the return of their most recent foster child. He'd spoken fondly of the girl who had been in and out of their home for the past two years. *'She's bright and intelligent, smart as a whip. And, sadly, wise beyond her years.'*

Now all Ace could think was how moody she was. Within the span of an hour she'd gone from shy to happy to grouchy. Her opinion of rodeo cowboys grated on his nerves worse than the sound of a gate that needed oiling and challenged the very core of his identity. He met sarcasm with arrogance. "I'll have you know, *Miss Ma'am*, I've won enough money in prizes and scholarships to pay my entire college education. And all the while I've maintained a four-point-o average."

"Well, what do you know, a cowboy with a brain." She pushed her plate away and turned an imploring gaze on her foster-mother. "May I be excused?"

A twinge of guilt twisted her heart when Katrina nodded. A frown tugged at her mouth. The day had been a terrible one for her foster-mother. Despite Trina's best efforts, the boys Robert and Richard, ages four and seven, argued and whined and downright rebelled over the clothes she bought, and now here she was antagonizing Trina's guests. Lexie rose from her chair and paused to give Trina a hug and whisper an apology in her ear.

Trina turned to Craig after Lexie left the room. "I have no idea what has gotten into her. Lexie is never like this."

Craig chuckled. "It's okay. She's probably just feeling left out or outnumbered."

Ace snorted. "TFF." He referred to his favorite phrase: Typical Friggin' Female.

"Ace," his father warned in a tone similar to the one Scott had used with Lexie.

"Well, it's true. Women!" He rolled his eyes. "God, generous as He is, had wonderful, loving intentions when He created them. But somewhere along the line something went wrong. They've turned into moody, unpredictable creatures."

"And it's all man's fault." Katrina defended herself, her foster-daughter and her species with flashing eyes and a challenging smile.

Ace grinned and rose from his seat. "Present company excluded of course," he retracted with a gallant bow and lifted Trina's hand to his mouth.

"Hey boy, are you flirting with my girl?"

Ace's grin spread to encompass Scott's barb. "Don't have to. She's loved me since the day we met. Huh, Trina?" he taunted with an impish smile.

His gray eyes shone like sunlight dancing off of sheet metal. Trina's heart melted. "Go on, Ace Harris." She shooed him. "Get out of here, with your devil-may-care grin and cocky attitude."

Ace chuckled and kissed her cheek then glanced at his father. "You coming with me or riding with them?" he asked then held his hand in a gesture of supplication for his father to toss him the truck keys.

Craig hesitated only a moment before he threw the keys to his son. He had no qualms about Ace going to the arena early since it was his habit to spend some quiet time with his horse, and in prayer, before a rodeo. "See you later. Be careful, Ace."

Ace grinned. "That's my name," he assured, as he headed for the door. "Careful Ace Harris."

Scott shook his head. "He's as bad as you were at that age. I bet Tamera has her hands full with the two of you. How is she anyway?"

Craig tossed his head with a laugh. Having his only son compared to him was the ultimate compliment. Or insult. Depending on who uttered the comment and the tone they used.

"Tamera's fine. She flew to Mississippi to close the sale of her house. We don't go there much anymore so she decided to sell it. Besides, she can't stand to watch her baby ride bulls," he remarked explaining the rare instance that his wife wasn't with them. "She goes to every rodeo and buries her head in her lap until it's over. She's always so proud, and relieved, but she can't stand to watch," he admitted with a chuckle.

* * * * *

Lexie watched Ace leave from her bedroom window. Embarrassment at her behavior washed over her in angry waves. She had absolutely no idea why Ace Harris affected her so except she couldn't stand arrogance and *that* he had in abundance. Still, his family and Scott went way back. More family than she was at the moment, although she loved Scott, Trina and the boys as the family she never had. She was thirteen the first time they met.

She had come home from a friend's house to find her father passed out. Unable to rouse him, she called 9-1-1. The ambulance took him to the hospital where Scott worked in the emergency room. That incident marked her father's first bout with a near overdose of alcohol. He'd been warned then to stop drinking, that his liver suffered and would continue to deteriorate if he didn't. He hadn't listened.

Scott and Trina took her home with them that night and she had been in and out of their home for over two years since. Lexie hoped if her father didn't live she would be able to stay, at least until she finished school and turned eighteen. She leaned her forehead against the windowpane and absorbed the warmth from the setting sun, then closed her eyes, and took a deep breath. The scent of beeswax and lemon filled her nostrils. She smiled to herself and let the love she felt for her foster-family fill her heart and mind. She knew what she had to do. She rubbed the glass to rid the window of the oil from her forehead and tried to pray.

"Father in Heaven, help me," she muttered, though in all seriousness she doubted God heard, or cared, despite her years of religious upbringing.

She went downstairs, swallowed the lump of nerves in her throat and apologized. "I'm sorry, Scott," she said, and then turned to Craig. "My apologies to you also, Mr. Harris, and to your son."

Craig chuckled. His gray eyes danced with mirth. "It's okay Sweetheart. Every now and then Ace needs to take a tumble off the pedestal his mother put him on the day he was born."

"Craig," Scott warned. "How on earth can we teach the child manners if you so blatantly disregard her rudeness?"

"You're right," Craig agreed, then winked at Lexie, and continued. "I'll accept your apology on behalf of myself and my son. We'll keep it our little secret, though. Don't need him thinking he's won any more points, he's arrogant enough."

Her lightning-quick smile took his breath away and Craig couldn't blame Scott for being enamored with her, especially after hearing of the life she'd led.

Lexie turned back to Scott. "Can, *may*, I go to the hospital tonight?" She could tell by his quick frown Scott wanted her with them tonight and she anticipated his argument. "He's my father Scott, as long as he's still alive, I need to be there."

Scott sighed. She was right. A brilliant, self-made man described Lexie's father to a T. A computer genius, a modern-day gypsy who traveled with his company to set up businesses, train employees, and make a fortune. As with most human beings though, he had vulnerability, a downfall. Steven Morgan's downfall was alcohol and Lexie. Oh, he loved his daughter beyond reason, was often over indulgent with her. The one thing he couldn't handle was the responsibility of parenting. He never made time, the quality time, she needed to feel loved and secure. He provided for her well enough, sometimes too well. She was spoiled and selfish and often undisciplined.

Scott watched her while she waited for him to give permission to spend the night at the hospital. Those expressive green eyes were clouded with emotion. "Okay

Lexie, we'll drop you off on our way to the rodeo. And," he added at her relieved expression, "we'll pick you up afterward. You don't need to spend another night there."

In an elaborate gesture, Lexie rolled her eyes but bit back her arguments. She understood Scott only wanted to protect her from the reality that her father may not wake up from this coma. She kissed his cheek. "Thank you."

He caught her hand when she turned away. "It'll cost you though."

She turned back, laughed at the glint of humor in his eyes. "What?"

He shrugged. "Oh, I don't know. What do you think Craig? We'll have to leave early and go out of our way to drop her off, and then pick her up."

Craig chuckled. He remembered the same game he'd played with his daughter years ago, and felt a tug at his heart. Though she'd given him two beautiful granddaughters, he still missed his little girl. "At the very least, a hug, and a kiss, oh, and, definitely a smile." He gave her one of his own. "That should just about cover it."

"Think you can handle all that, Lex?" Scott teased.

She tossed her head with a snort. "That's an awful lot for just a few minutes out of your evening," she drawled in her rich, south Louisiana accent.

He grinned. "Your dialect is charming."

"That so boy-O?" she queried in an intriguing combination of Cajun heritage and Irish ancestry which was more evident in her flaming auburn hair and green eyes than her forced accent.

Scott chuckled. "You've listened to too many wannabe Irishmen in your drama class," he drawled and pulled her on his lap.

Despite years of living in Louisiana, he still sounded like a Texan. Lexie giggled. "At least I don't talk like this," she taunted. Her nasally attempt at a Texas drawl made them laugh.

"Oh no, that does it." Scott tossed her onto the floor and followed to attack her with a barrage of fingers, tickling until she shrieked with laughter and begged for him to stop. He pulled her against his chest and accepted the hug and the kiss before he let her go. He rose to his feet then helped Lexie to hers.

Lexie smiled at him then at Craig. "Guess I'll go help Miss Kitty with the dishes."

Craig arched his brow in a curious gesture. "Miss Kitty?"

Scott laughed. "She heard me call Trina "kitten" one day. It's been Miss Kitty ever since. Sure you don't want to go to the rodeo, Lex?"

"Oh, please," she begged. "Spare me from any more cowboys."

Scott laughed. "There are cowgirls too."

She turned, grinned. "Do they compete against the boys?"

"No. The girls compete in a class of their own."

"She snorted. "Proves chauvinism still exists. I'll pass, thank you."

* * * * *

Ace won "All-Around Cowboy" for the third year in a row and considered the rodeo a smashing success. Another clash between him and Lexie occurred after they got home.

Scott's oldest son Richard, who had a bad case of hero-worship toward Ace, rode home with he and Craig. Lexie and Robert rode with Scott and Trina. Ace grinned at Scott with a teasing wink. A look Lexie missed. Then he turned to Richard.

"Race you to bed, Ritchie," he offered, as they walked through the door and toward the stairs.

Richard, who hated to be called Ritchie by anyone *except* Ace, frowned. Though he feigned irritation, the ritual occurred every time the two met.

"Don't call me Ritchie," he insisted. "My name is Richard, or Rick."

Ace bit back a grin. "Ricky, Ritchie, what's the difference?"

Lexie got in on the tail end of the conversation and flew to Richard's defense. Before anyone could stop her she was between them, shoving at Ace. "Don't pick on him you big bully. Pick on somebody your own size."

Ace hissed in frustration. "I wasn't picking on him, you little idiot. It's an old joke, one that's been around longer than you've known him," he bit out, and then regretted the words the minute they left his mouth, especially when tears filled her eyes.

Lexie blinked, fought tears with fury, and pushed him away. "Maybe so, but I love him more than you can imagine and I'm telling you to leave him alone!"

Ace grabbed her by the arms while Richard called for his father.

Craig and Scott hurried in just in time to see the two square off and glare at each other, both faces taut with fury. Green eyes and gray clashed and each waited for the other to back down. A gentle hand on his arm stopped Scott from rushing in to rescue Lexie from Ace's fury. Fury evident by the throbbing muscle in his jaw. *Ace had to learn to handle his temper.*

"Ace."

Subtle warning edged his father's voice and forced Ace to swallow the bitter bile of anger in his throat. He choked it down, but it left a sour taste in his mouth. With a snort, he shoved her away. He turned on his heel and stomped out of the room.

Lexie was left to explain, which she did in very eloquent terms, leaving no doubt as to her fury, and embarrassment.

The next morning when they prepared to head home, though Lexie was nowhere in sight, Ace apologized to Scott. "I'm sorry, Scott, if I've been out of line."

Scott accepted the apology with a chuckle, and grabbed Ace in something between a bear hug and headlock.

"It's okay Ace. I know you well enough to understand. Lex can be trying sometimes, but she's going through a lot," he remarked, defending the girl he already thought of as a daughter. Deep down he wanted to adopt her. He and Trina had talked often but hadn't discussed adoption with Lexie yet. It was too soon. So much still hung in the balance.

The Harrises said their goodbyes and headed home to Bandera, Texas. Ace rode high going into his senior year. About midway through, his whole world crashed.

Don't Forget Books 1 & 2!

Tempered Hearts

Rancher Craig Harris and veterinarian Tamera Collins clash from the moment they meet. Innocence is pitted against arrogance as tempers rise and passions ignite to form a love as pure as the finest gold, fresh from the crucible and as strong as steel. Thrown together amid tragedy and unsated passion, Tamera and Craig share a strong attraction that neither accepts as the first stages of love. Torn between desire and dislike, they must make peace with their pasts and God in order to open up to the love blossoming between them. It is a love that nothing can destroy when they come to understand that only when hearts are tempered, minds are opened and wills are softened can man discern the will of God for his life.

Tempered Dreams

Dr. Scott Hensley (introduced in Tempered Hearts) has built a wall around his heart since the death of his wife and parents. Katrina Simmons is recovering from scars inflicted on her as a battered wife. Can dreams be renewed and faith strengthened? Can they find joy and peace in God's love and in love for one another?

About the Author

Pamela S. Thibodeaux grew up in the town of Iowa, Louisiana. She is a mother, grandmother and deeply committed Christian who firmly believes in God and His promises.

"God is very real to me and I feel that people today need and want to hear more of His truths wherever they can glean them. People are hungry for practical (and real) Christian values, not some 'holier-than-thou' beliefs that are impossible to believe and impossible to live up to," Pamela says.

"I do my best to encourage readers to develop a personal relationship with God. The deepest desire of my heart is to glorify God and to get His message of faith, trust and forgiveness to a hurting world."

Other Titles by Pamela S Thibodeaux

Love is a Rose

Music is the magical entry into the spirit world; the golden gate into the Kingdom of God. But we mustn't be of the mindset that God only uses Christian music to reach out and touch our mind, heart and spirit. God uses any and every means available to speak to His children.

Our job is to be open and receptive.

In this devotional, Pamela S Thibodeaux shares how God opened her spirit to a deeper understanding of the abundance of His grace and mercy through the words of the song, The Rose sung by Country & Western artist Conway Twitty.

Pamela offers Seeds to Ponder and a prayer as she parallels the love of God and the Christian life to each verse of the song.

Lori Strickland (introduced in Tempered Fire) has always been known as her father's "wild child" with no desire to change until she meets ex-bull-rider-turned-preacher Rafe Judson. Her attempts to change her wanton ways come to naught until she realizes redemption only comes with true repentance. Can she find redemption and win the heart of the cowboy preacher? Find out in ***Lori's Redemption***

A visionary is someone who sees into the future Taylor Forrestier sees into the past but only as it pertains to her work. Hailed by her peers as "a visionary with an instinct for beauty and an eye for the unique" Taylor is undoubtedly a brilliant architect and gifted designer. But she and twin brother Trevor, share more than a successful business. The two share a childhood wrought with lies and deceit and the kind of abuse that's disgustingly prevalent in today's society. Can the love of God and the awesome healing power of His grace and mercy free the twins from their past and open their hearts to the good plan and the future He has for their lives? Find out in ***The Visionary*** ~ Where the awesome power of God's love heals the most wounded of souls.

The Inheritance is about the chance we all long for...the chance to start over. Widowed at age thirty-nine and suffering from empty nest syndrome, Rebecca Sinclair is overshadowed by grief and loneliness. Her husband has been deceased for a year, her oldest child has moved to New York in pursuit of an acting career and her youngest child is attending college in France. Having spent over half of her life as a wife and mother, she has no idea what God has in store for her now. Will an unexpected inheritance in the wine country of New York bring meaning and purpose to her life and give her the courage to love again?

US Postal worker Raymond Jacobey has been in love with the little widow since he first set eyes on her. A wanderer searching for the ever-illusive soul mate, Ray has never stayed in one place too long. Raised by self-centered, high-power executives, he's longed for the idyllic life of residing in a cozy house in a small town with the love of his life. Will he gain the heart of the lovely widow or will he lose her to the wine country of New York? Find out in ***The Inheritance***

Single mom Cathy Johnson is tired of running her life alone...what she needs is a well-trained angel to help out. Jared Savoy gave up the dream of having a family when he discovered he is sterile. Can a confirmed bachelor and the mother of four find love amid normal daily chaos? Find out in ***Cathy's Angel***

Best-selling novelist and songwriter, Camie Rogers has penned numerous accounts of the secret love she holds in her heart. Country-Music Superstar Kip Allen has changed from the shy, humble boy, to the epitome of "star." Can the two rediscover each other after one night of his Home is Where the Heart is Tour? Find out in **Choices**

Anthony Paul Seville is known as the 'most eligible bachelor' in New Orleans, possibly even the entire state of Louisiana, but finds himself alone—completely and explicitly alone. Jessica Aucoin is a writer on her way to fame and fortune, but is haunted by a man from her past. Will the "champion" lawyer and the author of romantic suspense find love written in their future? Find out in ***A Hero for Jessica***

Sienna has survived what most succumb to - the death of a spouse and child and has maintained her faith despite her troubles. William has never met anyone who actually lived out what they say they believe. Is it true love between the faithful optimist and broody pessimist or simply ***Winter Madness?***

Grade school teacher Carson Alexander has a gift—a gift that has driven a wedge between him and his family. Worse, it's put him at odds with God. Feeling alone and misunderstood, Carson views God's gift of prophecy as the worst kind of curse...that is until he meets Lorelei Conner, landscape artist extraordinaire, and perhaps the one person who may need Carson and his gift more than anyone ever has. Lorelei Connor is a mother on the run. Her abusive ex-husband has followed her all over the country trying to steal their daughter. Distrusting of men and needing to keep on the move, she's surprised by her desire to remain close to Carson Alexander. Through her fear and hesitation, she must learn to rely on God to guide her—not an easy task when He's prompting her to trust a man. Can their relationship withstand the tragedy lurking on the horizon? Find out in ***In His Sight***.

Jason Stockwell has been commissioned to interview Kylie Erickson and to review her books. Only problem is, she won't give the time of day much less an interview to someone whose type of writing she deems not worthy of respect. Can they suspend their judgmental attitudes and find true love? Find out in **_Review of Love_** (A FREE read from White Rose Publishing!)

**Temperance
Publishing**